CHAGOS ARCHIPELAGO

Chagos Archipelago

a novel

TOM LUTZ

Red Hen Press | *Pasadena, CA*

Book layout by Ava Morgan

Library of Congress Cataloging-in-Publication Data

Names: Lutz, Tom author
Title: Chagos Archipelago: a novel / Tom Lutz.
Description: First edition. | Pasadena, CA: Red Hen Press, 2025.
Identifiers: LCCN 2025021069 (print) | LCCN 2025021070 (ebook) | ISBN 9781636284279 paperback | ISBN 9781636284293 library binding | ISBN 9781636284286 ebook
Subjects: LCGFT: Thrillers (Fiction) | Novels
Classification: LCC PS3612.U9 C47 2025 (print) | LCC PS3612.U9 (ebook) | DDC 813/.6—dc23/eng/20250502
LC record available at https://lccn.loc.gov/2025021069
LC ebook record available at https://lccn.loc.gov/2025021070

The National Endowment for the Arts, the Los Angeles County Arts Commission, the Ahmanson Foundation, the Dwight Stuart Youth Fund, the Max Factor Family Foundation, the Pasadena Tournament of Roses Foundation, the Pasadena Arts & Culture Commission and the City of Pasadena Cultural Affairs Division, the City of Los Angeles Department of Cultural Affairs, the Audrey & Sydney Irmas Charitable Foundation, the Meta & George Rosenberg Foundation, the Albert and Elaine Borchard Foundation, the Adams Family Foundation, Amazon Literary Partnership, the Sam Francis Foundation, and the Mara W. Breech Foundation partially support Red Hen Press.

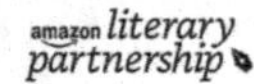

First Edition
Published by Red Hen Press
www.redhen.org

CHAGOS ARCHIPELAGO

I
Mónica

SHE WAS HIT with some of the same exhilaration she had felt the first time, as her blade punched through the heart wall and into the softer tissue. The man's last three heartbeats reverberated through the handle of her knife, the final one fainter than the others. *¡Qué delicioso!* she started to think, as she had other times, but then realized that it wasn't exactly delicious anymore; that, thrilling as it might have been, maybe she was getting tired of all this. The dead man's eyes had already gone blank, though still wide with horror, and she found herself, not for the first time, surprised by how fast it was over.

Minutes earlier, as the sun had set without clouds, only the slightest orange tint remained along the horizon under the darkening blue of the sky. The slight offshore breeze blew as she had watched the soon-to-be dead man's bodyguard build up the fire, and then watched the man sit by himself and poke it, sending sparks upwards, the baobab trees darkly outlining themselves against the Madagascar dusk. She walked out of the bush and sat down next to him, asking, *Is this seat taken?*

He was, of course, shocked. He would have assumed that, since the last of the tourists and locals had all left and gone to their homes and hotels, the only person he would meet that night would be the person that had blackmailed him into this bizarre and improbable meeting. He would have spent some time thinking about who that person was likely to be, but he would never have guessed anyone like her. She always had that advantage—nobody expects a woman, and nobody ever expects her kind of woman—young, sexy, pretty, relaxed. Women were less surprising now as race car drivers, army generals, governors, or CEOs, but in her line of work they were still unicorns, despite showing up in films and TV shows. And on top of that, she was reliably surprising because she was, well, who she was. No one ever expected her level of star quality. One of her favorite workdays was the guy who said, in a loud, astonished voice, *¡Guapa!* just as she stabbed him. This latest guy, sitting at his fire, was shaken, too, because he had been feeling weirdly safe. He had two beefy, well-armed bodyguards, and he'd counted on them to keep anyone from sneaking up on him like this. When the blackmailers arrived, the bodyguards would, he assumed, neutralize them as physical threats, take their guns, and make them have to talk it out. The man tried to act cool when she showed up, but he couldn't stop his head from jerking this way and that, looking for the burly guy, bodyguard number one, now laying a couple meters away with his throat slit, or the wide guy, out by the road, bodyguard number two, with his throat slit as well. And so yes, our man was staggered. Maybe he'd read a scene like this in a novel, or seen it on screen, but when it happened to him, he couldn't process it. His attempt to stay nonchalant fell completely apart as soon as he looked down to see her hands and saw they were in blue nitrile gloves, covered in blood, holding a large hunter's knife.

"Oh, this?" she said to him, when his eyes glued to the knife. "This is not going to kill you." She lifted it up with her right hand, and his eyes followed it. With her left hand she plunged a smaller knife through his ribs.

She couldn't have asked for a better crime scene. She slit his throat with the larger knife—police loved patterns, so she always slit their throats, usually when they were already dead—and then threw that knife on the fire. She stabbed the dead man a couple more times with the smaller knife, using her left hand to match the cuts on the other two vics, which made the kills look less expert, as if the heart shot was one of a half-dozen wild cuts. She threw that knife on the fire, too, and hoped the rural police would follow her clues and conclude there were two killers, one the stabbing flailer, the other the stronger neck slasher. She grabbed the man's wallet, pulled out his cash and cards, and did the same for the bodyguards and their considerably thinner ones. She pocketed the cash, threw the credit cards in the fire, and dropped the wallets on the bodies. The bodyguards had company IDs from Darkwater, the big military contractor, so the company must have known he was there. This guy was the CFO—you'd think he would have better security, and more muscle—so probably the company didn't know why he was there. She put on a men's size 10 pair of Nikes from her backpack and walked around the crime site in them, carrying the biggest log she could find. She dug the sneakers into the dirt in front of each of the dead guys to simulate a little struggle, then out to the closest tire tracks, and then did the same with a pair of men's size 9 Adidas. Then she threw both pairs in the fire and put on the throwaway beach sandals she'd been wearing. She peeled off her nitrile gloves and dropped them to curl and melt in the flames. She tossed the coverall she'd worn and a second coverall she pulled from her backpack on the fire, too, in support of the two-killer theory. She didn't have to worry about heavy forensics on the footprints, tire tracks, or ashes—the local police wouldn't have the chops to chase the shoes down beyond size and manufacturers, and she'd leave the jeep and the clothes she had on to be scavenged in Antananarivo as she flew out of the country. The cops would say that there were two male killers wearing sneakers and coveralls, and that the right-handed one had slit the throats with a large knife, and the left-handed one used a smaller blade to stab them around the heart. *All three of the victims had the contents of their wallets pilfered, in an apparent murder/ robbery,* the report would say.

An easy job. Not stunning, but excellent, and it should have been more satisfying. Leaving traces of two killers had become her trademark, and when she started doing it, she got a kick out of building her rep, at least with Eamon and his employer, but beyond them, too—word got around. Twenty hours of driving, a couple hours waiting at the airport, and she'd be in the air and gone. Eamon would be very pleased with this one, the twisty *bolsa.* But she kept thinking that each time now, she was feeling less—less what? Less happy? The thrill was starting to feel puerile, trifling, maybe even a little filthy.

There was enough light from a toenail moon to outline the baobabs—cartoonish trees big and fat as a house at the bottom, a hundred feet tall, with a tiny fan of branches at the top, like hands with no arms. She wondered how they could get so large, such a minute number of leaves photosynthesizing for such a massive body, like a tank trying to run on a penlight battery. They thrust up from barren, bone-dry sandy soil that otherwise only kept a few tufts and desert shrubs alive. No leaves, no water, gargantuan trunks. Spooky.

She also wondered, as she was doing a lot these days, what her end game was going to be. This was an athlete's job—she would age out of it soon enough, even if she wasn't disenchanted. She had to make the fact of her leaving appealing to them, she knew—she had to make it seem like a good idea to let her disappear, and that meant making it much less appealing to try and hunt her down and kill her. She needed, more than anything, to make her exit while she was still at peak dangerousness. She imagined herself, if she waited too long, old and washed up at forty, a sitting duck for whatever sociopath they'd replace her with. She wasn't, she knew, skilled at combat. She wasn't a fighter, and if they sent a fighter after her she was doomed. She was just good at putting people off their guard, confusing them, not giving them the time or inclination to attack her. She was, she liked to think to herself, *disarming.* That was all. When she tried to fight off her stepfather, she lost, and got hurt. When she stopped fighting, and just let him in for two minutes, he was dead by minute three.

Her only ace in the hole, her only hope of getting out, was that, yes, although Eamon and his bosses didn't like loose ends, they liked messy ends even less. She needed to get out while she could still guarantee them a lot of messiness if they tried to fuck with her. She had come out alive of every scrape she'd been in, which made her look formidable, scary. That was also, in its way, disarming. She knew her limitations, despite having had all the martial arts and weapons training. But her adversaries and targets didn't know it, and it didn't matter—she had stayed alive so far because she always had the jump.

After the first few times she cut people, she thought about going into medicine, becoming a surgeon. But she was too old for that, twenty-eight, and after three years doing this kind of work, she'd seen enough blood and guts. Maybe, she thought, the next step was money. "Make a killing," as they say. People talk about it as a similar high, taking somebody's millions—high-stakes poker, roller coaster thrills. It couldn't be as exciting as what she'd been doing, but who knows? As she got older? Maybe taking people's money instead of taking their lives would be fun enough. People got boring as they got older—everyone knew that. So she would, in all probability, get boring, too. Why should she be any different?

This thinking about the future made her grumpy, and she felt like a child stomping her foot. She was supposed to call in and get her next assignment, but why did she have to do every little thing Eamon wanted? Jump when he said jump? Life is short. She should live it on her own terms. *Jajaja,* she knew what Eamon would say, that if she had been living life on her own terms, she would still be in prison in Valladolid—*that's* why she lived on his terms. True, maybe. But *¡bastante!* Enough! She had earned a little vacation, at least. *Mañana por mí,* she thought. Eamon would be pissed, but she suspected that he got off a little whenever she refused to follow protocol, that he still enjoyed what a rebel she was. Just like on the stupid TV show he loved, with the woman he really loved. So playing hooky wouldn't just be for her. It would be a bit of a buzz for him, too, a little excitation. He was a pervy guy, but she knew him, knew him better than he thought. He walked around thinking he was some kind of mystery man, never telling her anything about himself. But she knew. He was a man, old style. She understood how he ticked and how he tocked. As much as he hated her breaking his rules, he loved her for it, too.

She opened a new phone, checked a couple lists of "best resorts in Madagascar," pulled the SIM card out, broke it, threw the phone on the fire, and headed to the most expensive resort she could find.

II
Alain

ALAIN WOKE TO the seagull shrieking overhead, the same bird that he had heard every morning for the last six months. Maybe it was the same gull, maybe another, but who cared? It made exactly the same sound of panicked agony, the same noxious blare of pain that it had been screaming, or its brother or cousin had had been screaming, every morning since he got dropped on this woebegone rock. He debated whether he should open his eyes. He decided not. No need to. He knew what he'd see. The same scene as the last 236 days.

Alain had hated almost every minute of his time in the Foreign Legion. He had hoped, when he joined, that it would be a way out of Antananarivo, out of Madagascar, really, since the only place he would want to be in Madagascar was the capital. Tana was the best his country had to offer, his home, boring home, and he had wanted to go to Europe, to France. The French in the ex-colonies, people told him, were different than the French in France, where Africans, Arabs, Americans, Indians, Vietnamese, and yes, even Malagasy, mixed with each other and the Parisians, and racism was uncool and outlawed by the Parliament. The French in the colonies were behind the times, people said, weeping in their imported wine about their lost privilege. The French in France were cosmopolitans, post-colonial.

But, no. He signed up for the Legion and was shipped for basic training to France, where he got a constant pelting rain of racist bullshit, which put a solid end to that fantasy. It wasn't that he was a stranger to racism. He and everyone he knew hated the French—and white people in general, on the assumption they were French or worse—but he had never tasted it up close and personal the way he did at The Farm, the *Légion étrangère*'s basic training base in Castelnaudary, a boring town in the wet and boring and 100 percent white French Dordogne. The officers of course were assholes—maybe because it is their job to break you, maybe because they were bigoted dickheads—but it wasn't until he went into the small villages off the base that he was exposed to pure, white-hot, white hate from the French, and even worse, from the British expats. They called him an African—they had no idea what the Indian Ocean was, much less the Indian Ocean islands, much less the difference between the Africans and the Malagasy. They looked at him and they saw *nègre, noire, sub-saharienne, kebla,* or *Africaine,* like he was from the jungles or somewhere else on the continent. He was obviously Merina, like the rest of the people in Tana, not like the African-looking people on the west coast, the Sakalava and the Bara, but these French couldn't tell the difference between him and people from Côte d'Ivoire, Kenya, or Zimbabwe. That was some racist goggles right there. Not a single person in Madagascar or Côte d'Ivoire would mistake him for an African.

The other grunts were great, the guys just like him from French Guiana, Morocco, and Congo. But the French? They were only good for a thousand small deaths and a paycheck. It made his first shit-duty postings in Chad and Djibouti feel like relief.

Donc, this island post was terrible, but at least it was a respite from the constant bigotry. They had plopped him down on this desolate rock with a tent, six months' rations, and a satellite phone, only to be used once a month to report in—*not* to call home. Why not? Because they want your life to suck. They knew you wouldn't risk court-martial since they told you over and over that every call on their goddamn phone was logged without fail. Still, even this enforced loneliness was preferable, utterly, to the aggressive faux camaraderie and subtle digs by the officers and French civilians in Chad and Djibouti. He'd rather be here than there. Also, here he could take a swim every day. Djibouti is on the water, but you need a special pass to get off the base, and guess who could never seem to get a pass approved? That's right. And in that sun, the water was boiling anyway. In Chad, they don't even remember what water is.

They had sentenced him to solitary, pure and simple, ocean or no ocean—he was a young man, dammit, not meant for this Robinson Crusoe bullshit. And Crusoe at least had Friday, a solid, non-European friend. In fact, *he* was Friday. There was no Robinson Crusoe. *Je m'en fous.*

Maybe, just maybe, if there was any point to this mission, it would help. If he had been sent to protect people from some dictator or warlord, stop an army from raping and pillaging their way through a jungle, stop the Americans, Russians, or Chinese from invading, he wouldn't feel so useless. He was charged with "holding" the island, protecting it from enemies, keeping it from being seized, but by whom? Like the Americans, Russians, or Chinese would want it. It was a pile of rocks barely sticking out of the ocean, with a small clump of shrubs in the middle, and global warming would sink it in a few years anyway. Nobody in their right mind would want anything to do with it—proof of which was that in 236 days, not a single person had come within twenty miles of it, not counting his monthly supply boat. And if someone did want it, all they would need to do was send any kind of ship and it was theirs. He had a rifle. What was he supposed to do with that if someone sent the army, navy, marines, or a gunship his way? He'd surrender in a flash.

Even—he had decided right away—even if some crazy old guy showed up with a rusty old gun from yesteryear, he'd lay down his rifle, put his hands up, and give it away. Why should he or the other guy die for this pile of rocks? The nearest inhabited island, Diego Garcia, was home to an American naval base, top secret, nobody allowed onshore without security clearance, colonialist *putains.* He could see, sometimes, with his binoculars, massive warships heading toward it, far, far away, and fighter jets would sometimes tear across the sky in that direction. The most likely military encounter he might have would be one of those young American fighter pilots deciding, on a lark, to use him for target practice. Then he could shoot his rifle at it—why not?—for all the good it would do.

He thought of his wife and kids at home and hated the French even more. Then he thought of how angry his wife was at him, and he was swamped in shame. She had agreed that it was a good idea when he told her he had enlisted, but of course she had, because she was furious at him. She had a right to be pissed, he knew. He couldn't really blame her for being glad to see him shipped off, couldn't blame her for wanting to make a point of saying good riddance. He had cheated on her, and he deserved it all.

So he hated the French, but he knew, of course, that he couldn't really blame them for his banishment. He'd done it to himself.

He dropped his shorts and walked out to the water, waded in, turned around, pushed off backwards, and let himself glide, the water rustling past his head. The breeze was soft and cool enough once he was wet, the sun, as always, the sun. A few clouds gave the sky some depth, the birds were taking a break from complaining, and for a minute, he was at peace. But just for a moment: like clockwork, he started to feel his grudge again. What bugged him was that he was, like all the brown and black people in the Legion, lured into it because the French had impoverished them and their countries. The British ex-colonies were booming. Look at Singapore, Malaysia, and, for Christ's sake, look at America—they had thrown off the colonial past and were all getting rich. The

French colonies—Congo, Algeria, Djibouti, Haiti, Niger, Côte d'Ivoire—they were all a mess, all dirt, dirt poor. All a swamp of corruption and decay. What can we young men in these places do? Offering us a job in the Foreign Legion was a kind of entrapment. It was extortion, basically—do what we want or starve.

Still, still, still, yes, he had chosen it with his own free will. He was in for three years, like an indentured servant, but he had signed the contract, it was his idea. Neocolonialist, neoimperialist fuckers. They knew he was out of real choices. He hated them.

III
Skye

"NO," HE SAID to Skye, to her first question.

He was a Frenchman of around forty, already craggy from a lot of time under tropic suns and from too many cigarettes, sporting a movie-star flounce of black hair with a white streak in the front, like Susan Sontag. He had a Gallic world-weariness that meant he let out an excessive gravelly sigh with every exhale of smoke, and he was always smoking—what is it with these old guys and their cigarettes? If you're going to have a disgusting habit, at least vape. He stood there judging, and Skye knew, as well as she knew anything, that nothing he saw ever met his standards, even his minimal standards. He found an excuse every minute or two to run his hand through his impressive mane in exasperation. If, Skye thought, he cared about anything worthwhile, maybe she wouldn't find him so pitiable. But he was just a bureaucrat, really, with the soul of a bureaucrat, and way too old for this adolescent pose.

Maybe, of course, she was being too harsh. It wasn't his fault Sontag was a heroine of hers, that she saw his hairdo as an affront. And not his fault that she was allergic to male vanity. She watched him shaking his head in performative exasperation as he inspected the packing job his subordinates were doing, and concluded no, she wasn't being too harsh. He had tried out this petulant, superior act as a young man, she guessed, trying to assert an authority he didn't yet feel, and got stuck with it. But no matter.

If you pretend to be a dick long enough, you're just a dick. People complain about the boomers destroying the planet, and yes, they did, but it is really these geriatric millennials that are the worst. They should at least know better.

Around him, twenty young people laid out gig bags of equipment—the top zippers all open for a last check—and boxes of supplies. Skye scanned the stacks and piles for things that might be useful down the road. One section held surveyor's tripods, telescopes, microscopes, anemometers, bathythermographs, current meters, cytometers, transmissometers, pyrometers, Doppler profilers, barometers, hydrometers, and radiation sensors. Another area had collecting nets, surface drifters, rosettes of sampling bottles, dredges, coring tubes, sediment traps, and a few things she couldn't identify. One corner had large racks of wetsuits and scuba tanks, another had solar panels and batteries, tents, sleeping bags and pads, and kitchen gear. A big reinforced case, open like a steamer trunk, was full of radios, satellite phones, and all manner of cameras, computers, hard drives, diagnostic machines, and wires. In the far back were copious cartons of freeze-dried rations, water, supplements, and medical supplies. Finally, what looked like individual people's personal packs and duffels were lined up against the far wall.

The crew was excited, most of them from France, happy to be in the Indian Ocean even if it wasn't their first time. They were off on a big job, nervous and expectant. She followed Forelock—his name was Devry, the expedition leader—until he turned and saw her still there. She looked him in the eyes with a pleasant smile and let his rudeness linger. After a minute, he couldn't take it—which gave her some satisfaction despite knowing it would happen—and spoke to her.

"We most definitely *do not* need an ethnographer, Madame—?" he said, pretending to forget her name, a petty power move—a man that wedded to his clipboards doesn't forget names.

"Peterson," she said. "But call me Skye."

"Ninety percent of the places we go have no ethnos because they have no people, nobody but the soldiers holding a tiny island—or the scientists we have dropped there. An absolute lack of local culture. Isn't that what you ethnographers study, local culture? You would be better off to stay here in La Réunion. We can't afford to have useless disciplines on our expedition."

What an asshole! You call anyone's field a useless discipline to their face and you're an asshole. "Yes, we study culture," she said instead of any of that. "But I'm sorry, Monsieur Devry, I didn't explain myself very well. I have been made a guest of the expedition, not a member of it."

She had been dropped in Saint Denis not an hour before, after a short flight from Mauritius. She felt silly about that, going to Mauritius—she hadn't had any reason for it, but in her line of work, the worst thing that can happen is that somebody says, *yes, I was working in Mauritius—do you know it?* and you have to say no. Deeply embarrassing, and in her male-dominated business they all loved to pull rank on the short girl with the curly red hair. It was a bro-bro-bro-bro world, and the fact she was young, and could turn on the vivaciousness at will, made it easier to get things done day to day, but still, she knew, it also made their desire to undermine her that much stronger. They wanted so bad to put her in her place, to prove that she didn't have what it took to be in their league, and at the same time they knew, deep down—it made her smile—that the opposite was true, that they weren't in *her* league. They took one look at her and knew not only that she would pass them by professionally, but also that they would never, ever get a second look. Hence the vindictive upmanship. In any case, she had added a stop in Mauritius. It was an island with few surprises. Nice enough people, except for the old colonials still shuffling around. White beaches. Sugar cane. Dead volcanoes. She didn't like that she was getting jaded, but it was an occupational hazard.

"I am on a tight budget here, Madame, with no provisions for guests."

"Tomorrow morning provisions for me will arrive, with extras for your crew, including additional medical supplies, everything sent from my university. And yesterday you should have received a note from your governor here in La Réunion."

"It is not a governeur, it is the president of the region—"

It was almost too easy. She knew giving him the wrong title would allow the prick to feel superior again.

"My mistake."

"And medical supplies? We are not going to war, Madame."

"No," she said.

He paused, as if trying to figure out what was sinister about her tone. One of the women performing inventory asked, in French, if she should do anything else. Skye watched him come up with something, since, she knew, he wouldn't be able to resist giving her some kind of order. He told her to check and make sure that none of the crew were exceeding their baggage allowance, then turned back to Skye.

"Perhaps I am being naïve," he said, trying to look clever and not naïve. "But there is already a Chinese 'guest' along, and you Americans and Chinese always seem to be up to no good—it is bad when you two are at odds, but even worse when you agree. Are you hijacking my scientific expedition for a cold war?"

The Chinese guy *was* rather worrisome. And although Devry hadn't said it, the guy did look too built to be a scientist, so maybe, probably, yes, a spy. Chances were he was going to be a problem.

"I'm afraid you've read too many novels. I am nothing but a boring academic, and I'm sure he is, too. Isn't he from a school in the provinces?"

"You see, you are a spy—how could you possibly know that?"

"My job, Monsieur, is to ask questions—it is what we ethnographers do, as you said. I have gotten good at it. I'm a champeen, blue-ribbon question-asker."

"'Champy. Blue ribbon.' I don't understand the idioms sometimes, but okay."

She watched him floundering, becoming that sad beast, a man unsure of how he had misplaced his power. Ha! She remembered seeing a young male elephant, in Zimbabwe, jumping around wildly, and since it weighed tons, it was frightening—it could do real damage if it wanted to. But it had no real power—the big male elephants in the herd would run it out of town any day, and it would spend its days skulking off with a bachelor herd, permanently unhappy. It wasn't dangerous, it just wanted a little admiration, or, if not that, at least an acknowledgment that it *could* do damage if it wanted to. The other people on her safari backed up and cowered, petrified, and that was enough for the elephant. He gave a couple last kicks in the air and then walked away in a huff. She decided to do something so this Frenchman with the white streak in his hair wouldn't have to jump around too much.

"If you have a few minutes, I would love to ask you some questions, too."

"No, no, no, no. You see all this equipment? We are doing last-minute inventory. We will have many days at sea for you to ask questions. And even, perhaps, for spy novels. Madame," he said, bowed and walked away, even more full of himself than when they met. Perfect, she thought. He gets to say no—the big thrill for people with puny authority—which is why she asked him. Again, almost too easy. She was quite confident she'd never have to ask Monsieur Devry another question about anything.

Skye had her mother to thank for her sense of how people work. She loved her father, and he had been a flawlessly benign parent, but he was squashed under her mother's thumb, as manipulable as Play-Doh, and Skye learned at the feet of a master, her mother, how easy it was to pretend to be helpful while inserting a ring in someone's nose. Her mother could turn a concern about her father's blood pressure into having him get the car washed. Whenever she wanted, she could use an expression of undying affection to cancel any of his drinking and fishing excursions, or send him on one if she wanted him out of the way. She could have him picking up the dry cleaning before he knew he'd been told to do it. The fundamental lesson Skye took from her home life in Mamaroneck, New York, was that the world was yours to control. You have to be smart, and keep the endgame in mind, not the passing show. But it's doable. Just don't be a chump. You watch why people get happy and unhappy, why they burn with shame or with pride, why they obey and disobey, and then you make them do what you want.

In college all her classmates were feminists out to smash the patriarchy, and she was just a little embarrassed—although she never admitted it to anyone—that part of her felt that the patriarchy was much easier to manipulate than an equitable system would be. Men's presumptions of power always worked to her benefit. Men's underestimation of her gave her vast arenas of maneuverability. Men's assumption that she didn't know what she was doing allowed her to do exactly what she wanted. Patriarchy, and the ideological blinders of patriarchy, were the foundation on which she built her power. Her classmates only read female authors. She read the males, the dead, white males. Conrad, Machiavelli, Greene, and Amis were her guides to power, not Virginia Woolf. She didn't want to smash the patriarchy, she wanted to outpace it. If that meant she smashed a couple of patriarchs along the way, all the better.

The rest of the French crew were good-natured, going about their business, readying the gear for transport, and they didn't suffer from any superiority complex. For the most part, she could see, they recognized her strength and capability. The more power people had, the less they could see hers, and the better she could operate. She told the rest of the crew how attractive and impressive she thought them, and they, unsurprisingly, found her to be a very nice person. The Chinese guy might be a problem, and Devry would be a problem, but always a manageable and usable one. Otherwise: all systems go.

IV
Frank

THE WATER WAS placid, the air light, the sun peeking up, and for a moment Frank Baltimore felt—well, he wasn't sure what. Weightless? Buoyant? He had moored his 72-foot ketch in Antongil Bay, the largest and quietest along the northeast coast of Madagascar. He dropped an anchor a few hundred yards off the beach. A village poked out of the palm and mangrove along the low-lying shore here and there, but long stretches of coastline were empty. He loved waking up like that, offshore in a sheltered bay—rather than in a slip or at a dock—with nobody else around, no eyes, no voices, just the breeze, sand, birds, and whatever calm water he could call home for a night or two. He had a thousand classics of world literature on his tablet and a perfect hammock to read them in.

He was lucky, he knew, profoundly fortunate in most things, but that morning he had a heightened sense of wellbeing. Something felt new, different—what? It was like realizing that the seasons had changed, or that a storm or illness had passed. He looked out at the unspoiled, spectacular bay, at his mast gleaming in the new sun, and stretched his neck. Maybe it was nothing. Down in the galley, he put on the kettle and a pot of congee. He peeled a dragon fruit and sprinkled peanuts, seaweed, dried shrimp, and mustard pickles on the congee, and was suffused with that particular gratitude that a good breakfast can bestow, especially on a beautiful day. He took stock as he sat under his canvas shade and realized what he was feeling. A spell had been lifted. He was free from longing.

The last two years he had spent sailing away from Dmitry, Yuli, and all that mess, leaving the scene of the crimes, leaving the Gulf of Thailand and the Andaman Sea behind. He had hugged the coast of the Bay of Bengal but otherwise sailed resolutely west, stopping to wait out the cyclone season the first year in Myanmar, the second in crazy Dhaka, but otherwise running into the wind like there was a bloodhound on his tail. He sailed down the east coast of India, with a few days' detour to circle Sri Lanka. Coming up the west coast of the subcontinent, he spent time in Kerala, skipped touristy Goa, stopped in Mumbai, Karachi, and Muscat before staying put for a number of weeks on Socotra, off the coast of war-torn Yemen, a few hundred miles out to sea from the violence. Through all of it, all those days at sea and in port, he had never, he realized, not for one moment, felt at peace, even on Socotra, a magical island, a piece of the Sahara dropped in blue water. Socotra was sublime, but he couldn't completely relax there—he had stalled because he was afraid of sailing past the Somali pirates, perhaps reasonably afraid, perhaps made paranoid by too many Tom Hanks movies. When he finally got up the nerve to leave, he swerved away from Mogadishu, farther out to sea than usual, and kept going all night. He crossed the equator with no speck of land in sight, making landfall here, at the top of Madagascar, ten days and 1,500 miles later. Africa, although not quite Africa.

He'd had plenty of time to reflect, in other words, on what had gone wrong, what he had done wrong, what he had misunderstood. Which was approximately everything. He had fallen heedlessly in love with his friend's wife—a woman who, however convincing an actor in their sordid drama, was far from reciprocating that love, and who was not at all the person he thought she was. He had fallen in love with an illusion, a cliché of the exotic woman. He had been pursuing not her, but some obscure need of his own. He knew that now, too late, but as they say, better too late than never. He was Don Quixote, and Yuli had been his Dulcinea: "A world of disorderly Notions, pick'd out of his Books, crowded into his Imagination." Or, worse—he was Madame Bovary. Like her, addled by the novels he had read, he encouraged the worst indulgences he was capable of, giving literary pedigree to witless extravagances of feeling and desire. He was deluded, besotted, self-bamboozled.

He had thought, at the time, that Dmitry, his erstwhile friend, was dead, and that Yuli, Dmitry's wife, was Jacqueline Kennedy, a heroic, stoic, grieving widow. He was just there to help. But maybe he had known all along that none of that was true. Dmitry had been hiding from people who had good reason to want to kill him, which, he understood later, turned him, Frank, into a buzzard, circling the not-quite-dead. If he had really known, deep down, that Dmitry was still alive, it made him worse than a predator. As he offered his self-serving empathy, his vampiric embrace, he had been nothing but a scheming scavenger, hoping and praying for his friend to get caught and killed.

But at the time, he had seen himself as a savior, not a predator or a vulture. Dmitry—who he had known for over a decade, who he had known well—*he* was the abuser, the user, the predator, the criminal, and Frank was the man who respected women, who put their needs above his own, who served them, who was a force for good. Dmitry didn't just abuse women, he abused everyone, as much a misanthropist as a misogynist, and he abused the planet too. He spent his life in investment banking, helping dictators and drug lords and oligarchs maximize the returns on their ill-gotten gains. He was the money launderer of money launderers. He also spent his life, as it turned out, skimming from their accounts. When his embezzling of their funds was about to come to light, he destroyed the evidence in a blast that killed many people, including many of his own coworkers at the Crédit Lyonnais office in Taipei, people he had worked with for years, burying them, alive or dead, in the rubble. He was a megalomaniacal, sociopathic monster. Dmitry was a much worse person than him in every way, but Frank had come to realize, over the last year or two, that it was like being at a party with a lot of very drunk people—you can become very drunk yourself, but their slurring, stumbling, and breaking things makes you feel stone sober by contrast. It is only when you try to walk away that you realize you, too, passed your limit a few pops earlier, and were much more inebriated than you thought. Dmitry's misogyny had made Frank feel like a saint. He knew now he was anything but.

When it was over, he had ended up with nothing of any real value, nothing he really wanted, nothing he had been longing for. Unlike in the Henry James novels he loved, where renunciation, the hero ending up with nothing, was noble and inspiring, his desserts in the Dmitry story were blah, blech. He beat up on himself for years, day in and day out, and at the end of this period of rigorous self-flagellation was left so distrustful of his sense of himself, and so distrustful of the strangers he met, that he avoided people whenever he could.

And that was why, while spending so much time alone on the open sea, he had become not just inured to being solitary, but comforted by it. He had come to relish it, to feel secure in it, so much so that he worried he had become unfit for company. He had made a few friends in Myanmar, that one cyclone season, and a few in Colombo when he put in to replace his sails, but he had been otherwise solo now for years. Dhaka and Chennai had been so inanely crowded he could stay in those places, splendidly alone, without even trying, and he did.

And so, on this particular morning, breakfasting on his boat, he was surprised to find himself afloat on a new sense of freedom, to find himself finally ready once again for company, for people. He looked around his pristine bay and pulled up his charts. Time to find a real port. Time to come in out of the cold.

V
Mónica

EAMON DID NOT sound like he was enjoying the little entertainment she had lined up for him.

"Stop acting the maggot!" he said. "Yuv got me right pissed off!" As if she should care. She had spent an hour meditating before their call and that always helped her stay even-keeled, made her feel everything was cool, *guay*. Eamon wasn't keeping his cool at all—he only devolved into Irish slang when he was upset. The rest of the time he spent trying to sound, unsuccessfully, like he went to Eaton.

"Not my intention," she said. She had strolled out of her villa and onto the dock. The water, she saw, was only a foot deep, and way too shallow to have any boat pull up. It was a decorative touch, the dock, she guessed, made for sauntering on like she was doing. Or, more likely, built to look good in the resort's brochures.

"Ay! Your intention! Which was?"

She was reminded that he was a little man, very short, and had a little man's problems, including that he couldn't stand anyone trying to bully him. Well, too bad. She wasn't going to humor him this time.

"A holiday, a vacation—staycation, I guess, because I stayed a couple extra days."

"Since when do you take vacations?"

"Exactly. But now, my darling Eamon—"

"I am not your feckin' darling Eamon! I'm your bloody boss!"

"Well, technically you are simply customer. You contract with me. I am freelancer, *caro*. I no have boss." Sometimes, leaving out her articles and messing with her syntax helped men find her *different*, as the ones from the American Midwest put it, and thus attractive. Besides, people are always suckers for wonky grammar. Look at Borat. Or Penélope Cruz.

"Cute," he said. "And now I know you are nervous—you always drop your articles when you're nervous. Are you doing the next job or not? Should I get a new *freelancer*?"

"Yes, get someone else." She hung up.

He could be such a schmuck, she thought, so huffy, making fun of her English—even though she was screwing it up on purpose—and then throwing around threats. Someone else! *¡Callate!* Like there was someone else like her! Go ahead, try to find them!

She pulled out the SIM card, broke it, and threw it and the phone off the end of the pier. She could still see them in the shallow water. Oh, well. The sun was setting and the water was blue and the air was perfect, warm, slightly cooler in the breeze. She was relaxed, and she didn't hate that, she realized. She had always found the idea of relaxation confusing—you mean you want to do nothing? You want nothing exciting to happen? You *want* nothing interesting to happen? Why not? Tiny waves lapped at the shore.

But now that she had tried it, relaxation, okay, it's not so bad. She had started meditating a year earlier, in preparation to kill a man. He was a cult leader in upstate New York who had been a Transcendental Meditation instructor before deciding to go into competition with the Maharishi, and to prepare for the job she took a TM course. The man had been improbably successful, as a cult leader, and had beguiled the two daughters of a very rich man. Their money helped him expand and buy a big spread in Vermont, and that brought in even more devotees, including rich friends of the rich sisters. The rich father, though, asked Eamon's boss for help in getting his daughters out and deprogrammed. She, Mónica, was the help. Once the cult leader was dead, the deprogramming kind of took care of itself.

She'd been meditating ever since. She liked it. Twenty minutes a day or so. The stillness was very good for her, left all her senses sharpened and her mind at rest. It was like cleaning a gun, a pleasure in itself, with everything well-oiled and smoothly operating after. It had also, she recognized, prepared her for this next step—taking a vacation like a normal person. She had always been half embarrassed by her work ethic—the Spanish had invented the *siesta,* were famous for strolling around the *paseo* and taking hours and hours for lunch and dinner. She was the opposite. Driven. Always working. Almost American. Now, finally, she could do Valladolid proud, and be a real Spaniard once again. Look at me, ma! *¡Me gusta rejalarme!*

Eamon was a lout, and twisty as all fuck, but he was straitlaced when it came to business. Everything by the book, everything on time, everything reconsidered a million times, no loose ends. He would do well to learn from her example and be more spontaneous, be a situationist, create the future in the act, not as a five-year plan. But she knew that that was impossible for him. Strung too tight.

That aside, he had been very good to her. It was Eamon who found her in jail eight years after the murder of her stepfather, Eamon who had pulled her out of that hellscape, that chaos, Eamon who had set her up with a new name, a new apartment in a new city, a new country, a new life, and, in the end, a new appreciation of her own peculiar skillset. He came and sat with her in the prison visiting room and told her about a movie, called *La Femme Nikita,* in which a young woman, in prison for murder, is freed in order to be an assassin. He arranged with the warden to have her see it, and then asked if she would be interested in something like that herself. She didn't see any connection—the girl in *Nikita* was a psycho, a nihilist, a punk drug addict. She was none of those things. But she gave him a simple yes. She would have agreed to anything to get out. He had her released on some legal technicality and put her through boot camp. He hired a tutor to teach her English, a martial arts instructor to give her the basics of force and balance and physiology, and a theater director to hone her every trick in the seductress's handbook. And now, in her working life, Eamon made whatever arrangements she asked for, got her whatever weapons or potions she needed, paid for everything, and never pushed back on even her most outrageous requests. She made sure that the setups were what she needed, and that she would never actually have to fight anyone. Eamon had things arranged so she could just walk up to the targets, and while they tried to figure out who the hell she was, while they had little fleeting thoughts of getting in her pants, she had all the time she needed to slip in the blade. The idea for each setup was hers, but she made him manage it, made him do all the logistics and all the arrangements and all the finetuning. She knew very well she wouldn't be who she was today without him.

On the other hand, she knew *she* had made *his* life what it was, too—the fact that he ran the world's most proficient and creative assassin turned him into an asset worth ten times what he had been worth to his bosses before, when he was a run-of-the-mill goon and fixer. He denied it the few times she had mentioned this, but he was unconvincing—he got huffy, which is how she knew when he was lying. He was untouchable because he ran her, and she was the best. Besides, in the meantime she had seen the various *Nikita* movies and shows like *Killing Eve*. She knew that she was in the power position, knew exactly how to work it. Nikita had a handsome glamorous handler she was crushing on, which was not her problem—Eamon was among the least crushable people on the planet. Villanelle had a handler that was a perfect screen for projecting daddy issues. Eamon was vicious, blotchy little thug. No daddy of any kind—*Dios no lo quiero!* And unlike Villanelle's runner, Eamon never showed up unbidden in her apartment. It helped she didn't really have an apartment, at least never had one for longer than a week or two. Airbnb and an endless supply of IDs, only half of them supplied by Eamon, had helped make her untraceable.

She would call him again tomorrow. Meanwhile, time for a dip in the pool, a lobster on the beach, and a bottle of Dom. It was late in life—she was already almost thirty—but hey, better late than never. She was learning to breathe, learning to vacate, learning to be chill, to unwind, just like a real person.

VI
Alain

ALAIN'S CRAB TRAP was full, for a change, and he'd eat well. Days like this he'd feel a quick high. Butter was the main thing missing from his life, he thought. Well, butter and beer. And love, sex, friendship, music. And newspapers, television, clean clothes that didn't smell like low tide, love, sex, four walls and a roof that was more than a few millimeters thick, ice cream, love, sex—good fucking god, he thought, how did I end up here?

But all that aside, crab today and tonight, plenty of crab. He had caught a couple fish in his net, too, added them to the trap, and lowered it into the corral he had built in the rocks. He threw in his scraps from the day before so they wouldn't eat each other. These small acts of self-sufficiency—he'd feel the contentment again as he built up the fire and roasted his bounty on it—punctuated his self-pity, and helped make the other dozen hours a day feel less forlorn.

His wife, he knew, thought it was a raw deal, too. Yes, Angela liked the money, the Legion paid well. She was in a better apartment in Tana, and she didn't have to be in a panic at the end of every month. She got through the scandal of his infidelity by bragging to her girlfriends about how she had sent him packing. But she was stuck with the two kids all day, without him to spell her, and, of course, however well she played it, the scandal was still a great cloud of venomous nastiness hanging over everything. The scene that played over and over in his mind was her shrieking at him, calling him a scumbagging, Tiger Woods, double-dipping, *Maury* show fuckface. The kids, he was hoping, were too young to remember any of the words, but they weren't too young to know that he had screwed up bigtime. He wondered how much easier it would be to be sitting like a dumbbell on this bullshit island if he wasn't wallowing in constant shame.

And add to all that the fact that his sideshow, Raissa, was pregnant. My god. She was Luc's teacher, too, which complicated things to no end, and thinking of his wife dropping the boy off at school every day made him glad he was this far away. By the time he was back, Luc would be in a different grade, at least, and of course Raissa would be home with her new brat. My god. He had really fucked up. Another mouth—another two mouths—to feed. He needed to stay in the Legion even longer. God damn, but he'd fucked up.

In his own defense, Raissa initiated everything, and, objectively speaking, she was hot as molten aluminum. He had just been being nice—everyone agreed that he was a nice guy, that he was charming, that he was open and friendly, everyone agreed—and Raissa, too, was someone everybody loved, so young and so pretty, eyes afire and aware, friendly, non-confrontational, innocent, almost, and when she touched him he didn't take it personally, because he could see she did it to everyone, touched their arms, touched hands lightly, nothing sexual, she did it to Angela, too, and she was very loving, huggy, and touchy with the kids, too. Just who she was. The day he understood that it was something else in his case, it was his wife's fault—after Raissa laughed and touched him lightly on the chest, Angela shot her a death star look, and then shot him one, too. *What?* he shrugged at his wife, *what?* He was married, after all, already twenty-six, two kids, and this young teacher girl couldn't possibly be serious. To her he must seem like just another old washed-up father, not a boy she would hook up with. She was barely twenty, on her first teaching job, not looking for some old married has-been father of one of her tiny students. She would be looking at all the boys that, like her, were just getting out of school. He'd been out for ten years already.

But after that look from Angela, all of a sudden he could see it, could see that Raissa was paying him a little more attention than usual, smiling at him more than at the other fathers, that she was, he supposed, even being flirty. His wife thought so, anyway, and so for days he had had to act aloof when Angela was around. Raissa accepted that as a kind of tribute.

Whenever Angela wasn't around, he enjoyed this pretty young thing's attentions, started to notice her brighten up when he was around, more than with the other dads. She was into him. He didn't do anything, didn't act any different, he just appreciated it more and let it soak in. She had the face of a movie star, the body of a swimsuit model, and she was so cheery, and light, and happy—ah, he thought, how could he help it? He had been a rugby star in school, and then on the national team, heading for the Olympics until he blew out his knee. He thought of all the attention he got then as the natural benefits of being eighteen years old. Everybody had their glory days. He had accepted that at twenty-six, those days were all over. He didn't feel cheated or resentful, it was just the way of the world. There was a new batch of hot-shot eighteen-year-olds every single year to take their turn being the players, in the beds and on the fields.

And so part of him assumed all along she wasn't being entirely serious. Maybe it was all a game to her, and when he thought that, he thought good, we are both playing a game, a skit, cosplay, romcom nonsense that had nothing to do with our real lives. He wasn't going to leave his wife and kids. She wasn't going to settle for an old man. A spot of fun wouldn't kill anyone, and it was all in our heads. *Nothing happened.* That was the important thing. She wasn't serious, and although he sometimes found that fact a bit deflating, it was better for everyone. He wasn't serious, either.

But day followed day, pretending along, making believe, and in the end, who cared what he had been thinking, or what she had been thinking? Nobody. The outcome of it all was serious enough. Fuck.

Meanwhile, after they got physical, even if nobody was still serious, he spent his weeks in heaven. Raissa was passionate. She threw herself into his arms with the warmest, sometimes even tearful, most enveloping sex of his life. He loved Angela, he did, and they had a great sex life, too, but this was something, as the kids say, extra. Now it was all over, all of it dead and gone, stranded on his solitary island, but whenever he wasn't awash in shame, he was floating on the glorious memories of their time in bed, on the floor, on a desk, in the shower, everywhere.

His friend Pascal had got caught cheating the year before. He and Pascal played in a band together when they got the chance, along with the only other two people in the whole country that were into heavy metal. Without telling anyone, Pascal joined the French Foreign Legion and was gone. Alain didn't get it at the time and was pissed, because where was he going to find another heavy metal drummer? But when his life fell apart and his wife kicked him out of the house, he remembered Pascal and went straight to the recruiter to sign up. It was much better money than he was making, so there was that. He wanted Angela to feel bad, and thought that if he was whisked away to a foreign land and out of their life together, leaving her on her own, she would snap her out of her anger and want him back, and so there was that.

He didn't have time to find out, though, because they don't fuck around, the Legion, and a week after the blow-up, he was on a plane to France for basic.

He called Angela from his base in Castelnaudary, and she didn't say a word, silently handing the phone to Luc. Luc, of course, wanted to know when he was coming home.

"When does your Mama say I'm coming home?"

"Mama?"

He heard her say, *No, I don't want to talk to him!* in the background.

"Yes, when does she say I'm coming home?"

"She don't talk to you."

"Ok, sweet Luc, you don't worry, I'll come home as soon as I can."

"Are you married to Miss Raissa now?"

"No! Who told you that?"

Luc didn't say anything.

"Daddy's a soldier now," he told his son. "You know, with a gun?"

"A gun?" All he had done was confuse the poor boy more.

It was like that, all the time. Brutal. Brutal.

"I love you, son."

"When do you come home?"

"Soon."

"Now?"

"Soon."

What did Angela tell Luc? Maybe she was already suing for divorce. It would serve him right. How would he even know, now that he was on this rock? Could he even go home, then? Maybe, once he finished his tour of duty, he should stay away. Maybe he would become a soldier of fortune. Work for Darkwater, Wagner, or another big outfit like that. A gun for hire. If he was going to go down as a lousy philanderer, shunned by all and sundry, why not go down with some glory, and some money? Lots of guys left the Legion for the private security sector and ended up doing well. And maybe, even if he didn't get rich, he could go down in a blaze of gunfire. Not die of a scorpion bite on a stupid pile of rocks in the middle of the fucking nowhere ocean. Go down in an online game-style blaze of ordnance and explosions, all with a classic Rage Against the Machine soundtrack.

One thing he was not going to do was go home and be the has-been divorced dad living in a basement while Angela and her new rich husband took Luc and the baby to Disney World.

Fuck that.

It wasn't just Pascal that had landed him here. When he was a kid, an older cousin had joined the *Légion étrangère,* and he saw how the girls looked at him in his uniform, the kind of status it gave him with everyone. He was somebody, all of a sudden, like the heroes of all those Foreign Legion movies. Even Pascal, when he joined, stopped being yet another young tool who had screwed up his marriage and his life—he became an adventurer, a romantic figure in a fresh, starched uniform. Sitting in the middle of the ocean, Alain felt duped, felt like he's bought cut glass at diamond prices, like Pascal, his cousin, and those inane movies he watched as a kid had sold him a bill of goods, a mess of potage.

Maybe, though, he could fix it. Maybe he could go into private security, like the rumors in Castelnaudary had suggested, maybe that was what the doctor ordered. He'd make good. He'd buy a Mercedes Benz, show them all.

VII
Skye

Sometimes work and inclination merge in perfect, synchronized moments, and for Skye, being on the bridge that afternoon, sitting with her new best friend, Jean Claude, the navigator, was one of them. Jean Claude was a tall, thin man in his early sixties, with abundant gray eyebrows, welcoming light blue eyes, and a quiet intelligence about him. She found him relaxing, in part because her usual tricks didn't work on him particularly well—she tried small flatteries and he shook them off like a talk show guest acknowledging the audience's applause, someone inured to compliments, pleased enough, but unmoved. Still, he seemed to like her company and seemed to be her friend, which was what the flattery was designed to accomplish, anyway, and she looked forward to seeing him each day.

Jean Claude had spent the first part of his life doing sound for big prestige films, working for a famous French director, feted at the Cannes, Tribeca, and Toronto film festivals. But he had always been, in his heart, he told her, not a soundman but a sailor, and he had used every spare moment when he wasn't working on a film to cruise the Mediterranean, or, when he was lucky and on location, to take brief cracks at other seas. He quit the movie business when his director died and found work on tramp ships like this one, making his way, rustbucket by rustbucket, around the world. He had learned navigation before it was all done on the computer, which made him valuable in the older ships, when you never knew if the electronics would last through the voyage. He could get you home with nothing but a compass, a sextant, and his charts.

"No," he said, in response to Skye's question about whether he had children. "No, never. I'm now an orphan in both directions, with no family left anywhere. *C'est parfait* for my life as a sailor." He said the last with a twinkle in his eye. He was a charming, old-world gentleman, with the emphasis on gentle—not fatherly, exactly, because he asked for nothing, insisted on nothing, suggested nothing. He just remained, in his quiet, unassertive way, ready for any conversation, and ready to receive anyone with equanimity. Skye knew people found her pushy and selfish, and she knew that with people like Jean Claude, she needed to be her most relaxed version of herself. That was fine, she could do relaxed. She *loved* relaxed, whenever she had a chance to try it.

The bridge was where she always wanted to be on a ship—yes, she was bossy, the men would say, although never the women; the women might say she was a pain in the ass, but they would never accuse her of being bossy. Either way, she would have volunteered to be captain of any ship at any time. She always wanted to be in the mix for any decisions being made, always ready to take control if called upon, or frankly even if not called upon, always ready to suggest she should, in fact, be the one called upon. Why wouldn't she? Any objective observer would conclude that she was more fit to lead than, say, Clipboard Devry. And one reason was gender: she didn't need to strut around acting like she was in charge. It was always much more efficient to just *be* in charge.

With Jean Claude, though, she could stay easy and receptive, not directive. The glass of the ship's massive windshield had been replaced years ago with plastic, and it was discolored, scratched, and cracked. Rust bubbled up under and through the grey paint here and there on the metal walls and floors, and none of the original instruments still worked. Jean Claude worked from a desktop computer, the instruments and weather all coming through different programs—not state of the art by any stretch, and he needed to change apps regularly—radar, depth finder, chart, weather, wind, comms; in a newer ship each would have its own screen. And he wouldn't have to step outside to get a clear view of what was in front of him. But it was comfortable, she decided, in the way beat-up furniture can be more comfortable than new. Except for the stink of diesel that waxed and waned but never went away, it was very pleasant.

"Everyone supposed Emmeline and I—Emmeline Grangé, the film editor I mentioned—were a couple, which was a natural conclusion, I must concede, since we lived together, and we did everything together. We went to dinner together, we went home together, we went to the cinema together, we went to our country house together. But no, we were friends without benefits!" He was telling her, she assumed, that he was gay, but she wasn't ready to have a conversation with someone his age about sexuality—she knew people that old just didn't have the vocabulary. He was a goldmine of information about the boat, the sea, the islands, and the mission, and an enormously pleasant companion for the long, long stretches of open sea, but she wasn't sure how well he knew himself. Eventually he said yes, he supposed Emmeline and he were both gay, but, he corrected himself, they were actually asexual—whether through laziness or, in his case, maybe, low testosterone, he was never sure.

"Did you ever have it tested?" Skye asked.

"Nooooo," he said. "I didn't even have enough interest to do that. I assume this is what it is like to be a monk. To not think about it very much."

"I always assumed monks thought about it all the time and had sex with each other all the time," Skye said.

"*Oui, oui, oui, oui,*" he said, "but you are a cynic. And cynical about love, I'm guessing, too."

"Not really, I just don't get why people find it so imperative. You know, like the Boomers and Gen Xers who were all-sex-all-the-time. I'm bored by hookups. They're just a waste of time." She didn't usually talk like this, but she hadn't talked to a non-hetero cis male in so long she found it liberating. "I mean, I'm completely sex-positive, politically."

"Hm," he said.

"Did you ever read Jules Verne?" She had never read him, maybe because he was too male.

"Of course, he is French curriculum, we all read him as boys."

"Should I read him?"

"My dear, is that a real question? Read him if you start one and find you like it. If you want sea stories, Melville or Conrad are better. But of course, this is now psychology—I don't do psychology."

"Show me where we are on the big chart," she said. She could see the ship's position on his computer screen, but there it was a dot in the middle of endless water, no land in sight.

"*Bien sur,*" he said, laying out a paper chart on the table. "You see, we are on a straight course from Réunion to our first stop, this southern dot of the Chagos Archipelago, northeast, a heading of 41 degrees, to be precise." He had used a pencil and ruler to lay out their course. "We are here."

"I always wanted to go to the Chagos."

"Did you? That sentence is not said very often. Most people have never heard of them."

"Ah, but Jean Claude, I am not most people!"

"No, Madame, you are certainly not most people!"

"And the dot where we are headed?"

"This place is hardly an island, an islet, but the French Foreign Legion is there, keeping it safe from the marauding British!"

She spent time looking at the waters surrounding it, and there were no underwater surprises, no hidden rocks or wrecks, nothing to worry about.

"And then?"

"We can't go to the one place everyone would like to see, Diego Garcia, of course, and the expedition is not surveying any of the Chagos Archipelago proper. Just a few of these little outliers." He pointed them out.

"Why are we even going?" she asked.

"Yes. Well. A number of the islands are disputed, but held by us, the French. They are *all* disputed, I should say, including Diego Garcia, in that Mauritius has never given up its claims to the Chagos, but nobody cares about that. The Americans own Diego Garcia, at least for the next fifty years—that is, they lease it—and the international courts and the UN can say whatever they want, and in fact they ruled again last month that the British have no right to the archipelago. But the British aren't about to stop collecting the money the Americans pay them to lease the base, and the Americans are not about to give it up."

"And if they did give it up, China would take it," Skye said. She'd heard him make an anti-Chinese remark earlier. "It's so strange, isn't it? The British leasing it without owning it—and it's supposed to be the most gorgeous of the islands. Why don't they make it another tourist destination, another Seychelles?"

"My dear, you are acting like you don't know, and I don't know why you would do that!" He twinkled at her again—he really was a delightful man. She was, of course, pretending to not know, but she thought Jean Claude would enjoy telling her—it was an anti-British and an anti-American story, something no Frenchman could resist. He was on to her, though, and so she smiled and said he was right.

"Yes," she said. "I know. America. But I don't know the whole history."

He looked at her sideways, to see if she was kidding, and couldn't quite decide. He chose to tell the story anyway.

"The archipelago was uninhabited," he said, "until the eighteenth century, when my French forefathers tried to build plantations there, and they brought Africans and Indians from all over the empire to do the work. And you know ethnogenesis, yes?"

"Yes, when an ethnic group develops over time from a mix of peoples."

"You see? I like it better when you don't play dumb!" Twinkle.

Such a shame, she thought in passing, that when he was in his youth no one understood sexual fluidity; maybe he would have been happier. Chagossians, he went on, they came to be called, and they spoke their own pidgin—a mix of French, several African, and a couple of Indian languages. And they became a people, most of them living on Diego Garcia, the largest of the islands, but some on other islands. Under the French Empire, the archipelago was considered part of Mauritius, administered by Mauritius so many hundreds of kilometers away. Then, when Napoleon lost at Waterloo, he also lost Mauritius to the British, and with it these little scattered islands. The plantations never worked out very well for the French, and so they were already neglected when the British tried to make them profitable. Changing owners a few times didn't help. Sometimes they even brought the French back, sometimes new British owners, but always absentee landlords. They all failed to make decent businesses. The Chagossians worked the land as best they could, and fished, and got by with help from the British government. "And then you know the rest," he said.

Yes, she knew, the British kicked the Chagossians all out and leased Diego Garcia to the US as their Indian Ocean base.

"In the sixties," he said to her nod, "when all the colonies were declaring independence, a few days, really, before Mauritius declared independence from Britain, the British made the Chagos a separate dependency—it covers a lot of ocean territory, but altogether there aren't enough people to cause the Brits any trouble, and not enough resources to make Mauritius fight for it immediately. And since they rented Diego Garcia to the US straight away, it meant Mauritius would have to go up against both the UK and the US to get the islands back. The world courts have all ruled that the UK has no rights to the place and that the US lease is invalid, but who will enforce this? My guess is that the British will do as they did with Hong Kong, and say okay, on such and such a day—which will happen to be the day the current lease runs out—the islands will revert to Mauritius. In the meantime, it is not like Mauritius will go to war with the US about it."

"So why are we here?" she asked.

"I don't really know. We? We French, I think, like to buck the US and UK, and we still like to play at being a world power with these games. We send the Légion to occupy some of the small islands for Mauritius. And we do the same kind of thing all over the globe. Silly. But then the French scientists get to go, too, so there is, as you Americans say, an 'upside,' yes?"

The sun was setting off the port beam and they fell into a moment of silence, except for the hum of the engines, and the faint sound of the sea being parted by the aged hull. They both looked out at the deepening horizon against a cloudless sky—it was easier to see out the door than through the windshield.

"Strange that there's a Chinese guy with the expedition, isn't it?" she said.

"Is it?"

"I mean, what's he doing?"

"He's another scientist, *n'est-ce pas*?"

"How far is this?" Skye asked, changing the subject again, and pointing with one finger to the dot they were headed for and at Diego Garcia with another. Jean Claude looked at her with renewed curiosity.

"Let's say a hundred nautical miles—115 miles, 185 kilometers?"

Ha! There was no reason for him to frame it as a question. Who are you, he was asking, and what do you want?

Well, Skye thought, let him wonder. He liked her, there wouldn't be any trouble there. And maybe a bit of mystery was exactly what was needed to keep him on her side. It wasn't sexual, clearly, which made it easier. He humored her because he was curious, and so curious he would remain. He was curious because he was a watcher—he spent his life more interested in watching people chase their dreams than in chasing any of his own. And he was living his dream already, anyway, tramping around the seas of the world. His watching was congenital, the way he was made. He recognized in her, she could see, the same fascination with figuring out the whys, the hows, and the wherefores of other people's actions. But his enquiry was disinterested, hers was not—he saw no use value in what he learned, whereas she investigated only that which could help her. He was all R, and she was R&D and product-to-market.

"Thanks, and *à bientôt*," she said, and gave him a little salute. "That's what you do when you leave the bridge, right, you salute?"

VIII
Frank

FRANK PULLED ***GOD*** *Sees* up to the dock in Antsiranana, the biggest town on the northern coast, down the bay from where he had first landed. Two men grabbed his lines and looped them over cleats. He killed the engine, adjusted his bumpers, and shut up the cabin. The harbormaster promised to see to a bottom cleaning for the ship and Frank found an absurdly expensive resort on a nearby atoll, Nosy Anko. The resort arranged to pick him up by helicopter at the tiny local air strip—yes, it was that chichi, it had its own helicopter for ferrying guests in from wherever. He walked off his boat with his backpack and two duffels containing all his clothes. A car was waiting at the end of the dock to drive him to the chopper. The old part of himself recoiled at the price, but he was ready for a touch of luxury. He had been a long time at sea, and he had too much money anyway. No matter how much he gave away, and how much he spent, he still always had a colossal amount of money piling up, always more than the last time he checked.

The money was, in a way, Dmitry's. After Dmitry had worked for Frank—he had been eighteen then, Frank twenty-seven and just getting started in the construction business—Dmitry had gone back to the UK, did his university studies, and then started his life in banking, eventually siphoning off many millions for himself of the billions he handled. He used Frank's passport to open some bank accounts, which were just rainy-day funds, he told Frank, for his wife and kids. When Dmitry's scams were about to implode, and the Crédit Lyonnais building where he worked exploded in a firebomb, Frank went hunting for whatever money might be in there: the accounts were insurance in case anything happened to Dmitry, and something had happened—Dmitry was gone. Frank found tens of millions of dollars under his own name in several banks, Dmitry having made him an unwitting accomplice to his money laundering. Anyway, long story short, Yuli was fine, Dmitry, it turned out, was still alive and still filthy rich, and Frank ended up keeping a small share of the money. Even that small share was a lot, enough to give half of it away and have too much left over.

His ritzy bungalow was on the beach, cantilevered over the water, and outfitted with his and hers bathrooms, for all the good the second would do him. Three different outside balconies were perfect for three different times of day. The bed was large enough for Gargantua. He handed off his clothes, except the shorts and T-shirt he had on, to get them properly laundered for the first time in months. He opened a bottle of Austrian Riesling from the refrigerator, poured himself a glass, and went out and sat on one of his balconies.

As he relaxed into a cushioned lounge chair, he had a thought that he had had many times over the years, sitting in the lap of absolute luxury, in one of the world's fanciest resorts—that this high-end living was very little different than his life on the boat, except that the bed was bigger, and the bathroom was bigger, and the towels were nicer. People paid very good money to live for a week the way he lived every day, on the water in dazzling locales, on his own schedule, with fresh seafood almost always available, and, when he stopped here and there, fresh, superb fruit and vegetables, too.

But then he had the follow-up thought, which he had also had many times. The reason you never find single people in a resort like this is that they are made for couples, for groups of friends, for families. A single guy in a fancy resort was a loud announcement of loneliness, an advertisement of his dysfunction, a horrible reminder of the ways life can go awry. This resort had seventeen villas, with one, two, or three bedrooms, ranging from $5,000 to $15,000 a night. People who can spend that kind of money, many of them recognizable from their film roles or from newspaper stories, don't want to leave their social life to chance. And even the non-famous people avoided him in places like this, because he wasn't of their tribe—they were the tribe of the hooked-up, the married, the familied. At dinner or breakfast or the bar, nobody wanted a random third wheel, and most people ate at their villas anyway, served by private chefs and butlers, each suite perfectly cloistered, plantings and walls and screens strategically isolating them, the view of the ocean unimpeded, the view of everything else perfectly blocked.

All of this, Frank reminded himself, was one step down from billionaire-land, where everything happened at private villas, with rock stars and Russian oligarchs playing polo with their friends behind a wall, all of them flying in and out on a private airstrip. The one-tenth of 1 percent were as cordoned off from the 1 percent as the 1 percent were from the cruise-ship tourists. It didn't make Frank feel any better about the extravagance when he did this kind of math, but he did it.

He recognized early in his accidental life as a rich person that the only company for him in these places were the bartenders and waitstaff, the people at the front desk, and the occasional gardener or worker, although many of the last usually didn't have much English. The staff interaction was all corrupted, of course, by the tips they lived on and that he was happy to spread around. But it was social intercourse, nonetheless, and he was happy for it.

Thinking about all of this, he decided to ask for dinner in his villa rather than brave any kind of public dining room. He ordered from the front desk and went into one of the bathrooms to wash up in a round stone shower the size of a farm silo, after which he put on the hotel's silk robe and went back to sit facing the beach.

"Is this seat taken?" a woman asked, which was shocking, because he hadn't heard anything, and funny, since he was alone on his own balcony.

At first he thought it must be his dinner arriving, but she was carrying nothing. She had light auburn hair with a lot of sun or however those blond streaks happen in women's hair—European, young, maybe under thirty, he guessed, and she looked like a casting director's idea of a surfer, in a bathing suit and sarong.

"You what?" he said, incoherent in his surprise.

"You're my new neighbor," she said with a Spanish accent, more Madrid than Barcelona, he thought. "And you are the only other person on this whole island not here with his wife, mistress, both, or whole family, so I thought I would say hello. I always forget how much it sucks to be at one of these places."

"I was thinking the same thing myself!"

"Well then invite me in for a drink."

"You're already here. Inviting you seems redundant. I'm having the Riesling from the refrigerator. It's pretty good. Glass?

"It better be good, for these prices." She flopped down on the outdoor couch, kicked off her flip flops and pulled her feet up. "Who can afford this *mierda*?"

He looked at her and saw he was out of his depth, had no idea what was happening.

"I'm sorry, is shit too crude? Who can afford this place, though, I'm serious! $6,000 a night? *Jijijijiji*. That makes an expensive week! You don't look like a banker." She looked him up and down. "What are you, a bad boy Rockefeller? Did you invent TikTok?"

"No," he said, laughing. And how could he explain it? "Nothing like that."

"Uh, huh," she said. "The silent type? Well, I work for a living, and I haven't had a vacation for a decade, so I'm trying to amortize it in my head and say it's like I'm paying $500 a night for each vacation I didn't take for ten years. But wow, really, who are these people?" He realized he loved the way Spanish people said wow—like it had an extra vowel. She didn't seem old enough to have had ten years of diverted vacations, and at the same time she seemed much older than him. He was at sea.

"They live on people's misery," he said. He wasn't sure where that came from.

"And a poet," she said. "Pour me another."

They had a few, and he became a bit loquacious, after all. Without too many details, he told the story of his friend, who he thought had been killed but who hadn't been, the story of his ill-fated love for his dead-but-not-dead friend's wife, his ridiculous enamorment and even more ridiculous heartbreak, his swearing off love forever. Even as he talked, he knew he would regret it.

"You're a romantic," she said.

Frank smiled slightly; he felt his face flush a little. "Yeah, I guess I am," he said, shrugging.

"It's not a compliment."

"Oh . . ."

"You realize this is stupid, yes?"

"Yes, I suppose . . ."

"This hanged-dog, mopey thing you men have—you know women don't like it?"

"They don't . . ."

"Of course not! If we don't like you already, it is just pathetic, and annoying, creepy. If we do like you, it is still pathetic and we want you to just be a man and say what you want to do. Don't be a moony little boy."

"Okay."

"I'm sorry," she said, clearly not sorry. "But that is the truth."

"Yes, I know you're right, and it isn't exactly news. But this is not an act, not manipulation, or anything—it is just a feeling, just a feeling that happens. And like I said, I am over it."

"You see? Like a baby—feelings just happen and you cry, you have a temper tantrum. Pah! And over it? I don't think so! Who is this friend?"

She really was quite lovely, and there was no animus in this as she said it, no attempt to make him feel bad or guilty or stupid—even as she was calling him stupid—no judgment, in a strange way. Plus, at this point he was drunk, having had so little alcohol for so long. They had gone onto the next bottle, and he had some inebriate distance on himself, as if they were discussing someone else.

"Just a guy." He looked at her—how could he explain Dmitry, the deep perversion of him, the weird hold they had on each other, or maybe didn't . . . "He was a kid when I met him. I was building a house—the first house I built—I was a contractor—he was a narcissist—but compelling, you know?—also a crook—handled money, when he was in a bank—investments—a banker for the worst—of the worst—a pig, really—"

He was drunk, speaking in phrases instead of sentences.

"And where is this just-a-guy now?"

"Donknow."

With a start he saw that she was quite attractive, that he had become interested, and maybe he had even been leering at her. He immediately quenched that, and cursed male perversity, the weird alchemy that turned insult into arousal. He tried to focus back on the conversation.

"Well," he said out of nowhere, trying to take charge of his scattered thoughts. "I'm glad you stopped in. I have been very much alone." And with the alcohol-lag, he only heard how stilted and odd that sounded after a beat. "I don't mean that in a moony way!" he added quickly. "I haven't talked to anyone for a long time. I only recently remembered I liked it!" He did his best to make this sound casual and collegial, devoid of implication. He had a sense he failed.

"Okay!" she said, getting up. He knew her okay was pointed, but he wasn't sure how. "Glad to hear it. Ciao!"

And with that she was gone as fast as she had come in.

IX
Alain

ALAIN KNEW SOMETHING was up because the birds were quieter than usual. He stepped out of his tent and saw, offshore less than a clip, a big old gray ship, with rust stains down its sides, dropping an anchor. As he washed up and shaved, he could see that they were readying a boat to send in. He'd have visitors. Good, he thought, maybe I'll stow away and go AWOL.

A half hour later, the boat having been lowered with a winch, four people motored toward the island. He checked with binoculars and saw that one of them appeared to be a woman. The ship looked a million years old, but its boat was newish and had a big outboard, so they were making good time toward him. This must be the oceanographic survey. Interesting. Company. He looked around, and yeah, he should pick up. Funny how thinking about someone else seeing his camp made it all look even sadder and more derelict than it already did. He gathered up the detritus, straightened out the stuff in his tent, and threw fresh lime in the toilet pit.

There were three men and a woman. They must have good charts, because they knew where to beach—it wasn't obvious—and they threw Alain a line as they slid along the rocks. Two of the men looked like the scientists he had been told were coming—intellectual hipsters, environmental activist-types. One, with a white streak in his hair, was the guy in charge and Alain pegged him as a bit of a dick. The other was a nerd with wire-rimmed glasses and a jacket with too many pockets, like a photographer or fly fisherman. The third man had a wind-carved and sun-beaten face and the vacant look of a lot of hard drinking in his days: a sailor. The woman was way out of place, good looking with a big head of reddish bronze curls, glamorous compared to everyone else, with no apparent reason for being there.

"*Bonjour,*" said White Streak, who then proceeded to give an introductory lecture on what was going to happen. His sigh suggested he thought the woman, who he introduced as an ethnographer, had no business being there, but he didn't come out and say it. The nerd would stay on the island for two weeks taking measurements and then they would pick him back up. The nerd and the sailor were pulling his tent and kit and supplies out of the boat and setting up his scientific equipment. White Streak lectured Alain about protocol, and as he was doing that, the woman peppered Nerdbait and the sailor with questions about every gadget and wire. She was cute and friendly, so they didn't seem to mind, although they got nervous when she touched things. White Streak was going on about all the critical dos and don'ts involved in the scientist's mission, but Alain wasn't listening. He was watching the woman, and he could swear she added one of her own pieces of equipment to the array the scientist had set up. White Streak noticed that Alain wasn't registering much of what he was saying and decided it was because he was a moron. As a result, he slowed down and became even more patronizing. Alain kept listening over his shoulder to the girl talking to the scientist. Maybe his wife was right, and he was nothing but a dog, sniffing after every new dish that passed his way. But he didn't think so—there was something off about this woman, something that didn't make sense. He was interested in what she was up to, not interested in her.

At one point the Nerd noticed her add another piece of equipment to his rig, and he started to object, but she flattered and teased him until he let it go. Alain glanced around and noticed her pulling a couple other small black boxes out of her bag. He instinctually looked away and caught White Streak's eye—the girl was breaking some rule and so Alain was on her side. White Streak was The Man, and French, so fuck him. He stayed focused on the man's eye and pretended to listen, making sure to keep the prig's attention away from the woman. She clocked this, and when, a few minutes later, he caught her eye again, she gave him a wink.

Finally White Streak was done French-splaining everything to him, and the girl came over.

"Alain, is it?" she asked. "Do you mind"—this was directed to White Streak—"if I ask him a few questions?" She had a way about her—she ordered the universe around while acting innocent and unassuming—and he was curious to know what her next move would be if White Streak said no. The Frenchman, though, just fluttered his hand in the air in dismissal and turned to the other men.

"I am done," he said, over his shoulder, as if that was important.

She looked right at the dick without saying anything until he walked away.

"Aren't you interesting," Alain said to her.

"You don't know the half of it," she said.

"Okay!" he said.

"French Foreign Legion, originally from—I'm going to guess—Madagascar?"

"That's right."

"How long on this godforsaken pile?"

"I don't know. Around 287 days."

"Not that you're counting."

"Not that I'm counting."

She got him to talk about where he grew up, how he ended up in the service—Alain gave her some bullshit about that, not the real story, and he had a sense she could tell. He told her, again in response to her questions—she had a lot of them—what his daily routine was like, how much longer he had on this detail, what came next for him, maybe military contracting, sure, and blah, blah, blah, again, him feeding her bullshit about the future. All the while he knew she had another agenda and went through the motions waiting for that to reveal itself. She knew it, too, knew he was waiting, and was quietly monitoring White Streak and the others while she asked innocuous questions. When the Frenchmen ran into a problem setting up the Nerd's equipment and they were all in a huddle, she wandered toward the water. He followed. As soon as the distance gave them privacy, she got personal.

"How much do you hate being here?" she said, quietly.

"You can see."

"You want out?"

"Of course. But as we say in Madagascar, '*ny atody tsy miady amim-bato*': an egg does not fight a rock."

"I mean out, out. I can help you disappear. Set you up with a new name, a new identity, a new country, a new job."

"I have kids."

"The new job would pay much, much better than this one, and we can pay to two addresses if you want, some for you, some for them. Both checks would be bigger than yours now. You'd be joining a new kind of Foreign Legion. A new kind of life. Someday you'll be able to tell your kids about it. But not for a while. Not until a few statutes of limitation run out."

He looked at her to see if she was kidding. She wasn't. Okay. Fuck it. Was he going to be a loser all his life? No.

"I'm in. Maybe."

"Maybe?"

"I'm in."

She handed him the two small black boxes.

"These are memory cards—replace them in the two instruments I added to the array—I know you noticed me add them—look over there, do you know which they are?"

"Yes."

"Good. Replace the memory cards every 48 hours until I return. And be ready to go."

What the hell was this, exactly? He didn't know. Did he care?

"All aboard!" White Streak yelled, like he was invading Normandy instead of getting a couple of coworkers into a dinghy. The sailor was already there, ready to push off. The woman ran over and hopped in, they shoved off, and Alain watched the boat recede. He kept watching until they reached the big old tub of a ship, got winched up and the boat secured, and climbed out.

He turned to the Nerd. It was just the two of them now, for weeks.

"Okay," Alain said to him. "Who are you?"

X
Mónica

SHE HAD WATCHED the American guy, Frank, come in with no real luggage, looking like he needed rehab.

Maybe you could clean him up, get him a haircut, and he wouldn't be so bad—nice chin, nice eyes—but what is wrong with him? Who comes to a $6,000-a-night resort in a dingy T-shirt and worn-out shorts, lugging beat-up duffel bags? Alone? Six months out of grooming? What is all that? Some Howard Hughes *loco* gonzo billionaire madhouse *caca*?

She went to his bungalow to find out. She drank wine with him, staying at one glass to his two, curious. He said he was "retired," that he lived on his boat, spent no money to speak of most of the year, and so didn't mind splurging now and then. It didn't add up. She looked up the boat—a Scorpio 72—and, fully rigged out for the kind of travel he said he did, it was a million-dollar boat—sorry, ship, as he corrected her, except that, as she told him, it would always be a boat to her. So okay, he sold the house in California and traded it for the boat, and he sold the construction business, or so he said, but what would that mean? A bunch of tools? There was a lot he wasn't saying. She knew exactly what kind of cash you needed in the bank to blithely drop thirty grand on a week's lodging. She had that kind of cash, almost, but she couldn't drop it as blithely as he was doing. She wondered if there was something else going on, if maybe he was on her side of the law. His not-completely-thought-out beachcomber front might just be a ruse, a badly chosen alternative identity. Maybe he was on the lam, a serial murderer, Ponzi schemer, or some other kind of con man, staying a few feet in front of the slammer by looking hapless on purpose. That would make sense. She decided to find out.

After a few glasses of wine he didn't make a move, with her sitting there in what was quite a nice bikini, recrossing her legs now and then for his benefit, leaning forward as she grabbed the bottle of wine and letting the bikini top go a little slack. He didn't even acknowledge the possibility of a move, which translated, she assumed, to either (a) gay, (b) pedo, rice queen, or other fetish, or (c) who knows, but something was not quite right. Men between the ages of ten and ninety didn't ignore her, but he did. Even the gay guys acknowledged her, gave her the thumbs up. This guy was fishy.

Yes, there was the story of the long-lost love, the sad, sad story of his idiotic crushing on his rich friend's wife, and maybe that was all there was to it—he was merely an extreme case of male longing, a nincompoop like the rest of them, only worse.

And speaking of nincompoops, Eamon wouldn't stop calling. She'd have to get back to him. No sense triggering her own personal WWIII until she was ready. And she wasn't ready. She needed more bank. She needed *al carajo* money. She needed to have *screw it all, buy a yacht, and sail around the world* money. Or maybe she didn't. She could always get whatever she wanted. She wasn't worried.

But the more she hesitated, the more she had to face the fact that maybe, despite it all, she wasn't quite ready to retire. She did love the work—if she ran a construction company like the beachcomber guy, yeah, she'd retire, too. But her job? Every care in the world taken care of by other people, travel around the globe, life or death excitement with every assignment? It didn't escape her notice that even now, as she was supposed to be on her first vacation since forever, she couldn't suppress the desire to work, building a file on this guy Frank, seeing what makes him tack and jibe, as if she was casing him for an assassination. The next thing you know, she thought, I'll be checking his phone . . . And like a sleepwalker she found herself outside his villa, hacking into his phone while he slept. It was way too easy, which meant either this was a dummy phone meant to mislead people like her, or he had a virtually nonexistent online life. She downloaded everything and went back to her own villa.

It *was* a fabulous villa she had, and she had it on her own hook. Fresh water pool, saltwater pool, big stone shower, crazy big bathtub, enough room for a small regiment, everything perfect, fresh flowers in all the vases, local woodcarvings, and museum quality, not hotel-room junk.

She looked at his GPS tracking and saw that he had, in fact, sailed around India as he said, had stayed at an island off the coast of Yemen for a month, which he did not mention, and had recently arrived by sea in Madagascar as he said. The Yemen bit, a hot war going on—that was something to figure out. Over the last few months he had done some bank business, sent a few emails, all friends and family, uninteresting *how are yous* and *everything good heres*. Vanilla. And that was it. For a cover story it was too boring. If it was his real life it was even worse. The most recent flurry of online activity, such as it was, involved searches for a boatyard and a resort in the last few days.

Eamon. She had to call him. Why did his jobs always need to be done *immediately*? The answer was they didn't. Yes, all situations are fluid, and *the only way to guarantee that your information is accurate is to act on it immediately,* as he told her over and over, *before the situation changed.* The situation. Where you are situated. Where the target was situated. By now Eamon would have traced her here, to this situation. She had to call him.

She pulled out a new phone, stuck a SIM card in and looked at it. Let's pretend, she said to herself, that you want out now. What's your move? Do you tell Eamon you want out? Do you try to make a deal? Or do you disappear as best you can? He was a worthy adversary. He let her know, whenever he got the chance, that he was on to her every trick, that he knew where she had been, what she had done, even when she thought she had covered her tracks. But last night she checked, and Eamon hadn't sent anyone to her storage unit in Paris, which means he didn't know about it, and so her go bags were waiting, freshened just two months ago. *Jejejeje,* tomorrow for that. Now, just call. She set up a VPN that would place her in Santiago, Chile. It would be evening there, good. She rang him.

"Chile?" he answered. "Really? You are so predictable. I say you are still in Madagascar."

"No," she said. "But *claro,* you are right, not Chile, either."

"Are you ready to stop being a dick and get back to work?"

"I am not being a dick," she said. "I am being a human being. I need a little down time like anyone else."

"Since when? Look, stop it, okay? Stop being a brat. I have something for you."

She had a lot of respect for Eamon. He was a true psychopath and had killed fifty people with one bomb blast, he said. And now that he was in management, so to speak, he had become a new kind of ruthless, had mastered everything there was to master about electronic surveillance, security, and communication, and had an intimate knowledge of IT systems around the world, or, more likely, had a whole staff of people doing it all, she really had no idea. She didn't know who he worked for, didn't know where he was, didn't know his setup, didn't know his *situation.* They had met only once after that first year, in, yes, Santiago—that was sloppy of her, a glaring tell, to use Chile, and she realized that that slip-up was proof of how nervous she was—her, *nervioso!*—how not in control she was. And Eamon would know exactly this, damn.

"Okay," she said.

"Okay? That's all you have to say? You bugger off on me and sit eating thousand-dollar lobsters, and you can only say *okay*?"

Jajajajajaja. It occurred to her, not for the first time, that he acted like her pimp. Berating her as part of a system of control. Psychological IT.

"You don't have to make me show you my belly, you know. You don't have to act like a pimp with a mouthy whore."

There was a moment of silence. He knew how to use that too.

"Stay ready. We're talking hours, not days. When you get a bottle of wine delivered to your room, call me on a new card."

He hung up.

And not for the first time, she thought that *of course* she was a whore to his pimp—he made her use her body for what he wanted her to use it for, and what he wanted was considered horrible and disgusting by straight people. It was both empowering and degrading. She got whatever money he decided to give her—he was the real contractor, and she was just help. It had always been so much money that she never asked for more, never negotiated, and by the time she decided she was worth more, he was ahead of her, and already offering more. He kept her on the longest of leashes most of the time, so long that she barely remembered she was on one. She supposed he fantasized that, like Nikita and Villanelle, she was half in love with him. At first, thinking of herself in those roles was helpful; everyone needs role models. But over time she felt more and more disgusted by the idea. They were both psychos, both violent sociopaths. She was not. She had been driven to violence by violence—first the violence of her step-father, and then the violence of the state—because putting someone in a prison like that is a daily form of violence. But she was not violent by nature, she was sure. She had ended up in a violent profession because at the time it was her only real option. People who end up working in sewage plants don't love human waste, they end up there out of economic necessity. And yes, she had learned to take some pleasure in the deeds, but anyone would. People do. That's why there are war atrocities and gangster massacres—once you do it, you can't undo the knowledge of the thrill. It's why people hunt. And much of the pleasure was what anyone felt exercising a high-level skill—it's why people play chess. But she was not a violent person, not a sociopath. She was no Villanelle, and not even a Nikita, a misfit who needed revenge. She, Mónica, was, in fact, peculiarly normal.

Anyway, she couldn't blame Eamon for having his little daydreams. Given her background, daddy issues wouldn't be out of the question, after all, and it was the perfect Stockholm Syndrome set-up. Funny, though, the idea of her being in love with him. When she thought of him as a person, she felt nothing but repugnance. As a player in her field, a certain amount of respect, maybe. But love? Please! And now that she wanted out, she'd be happy to put a bullet in his brain at the earliest possible opportunity. She wouldn't want to stab him—too much contact, too intimate. But a bullet, yes—she didn't want to be looking over her shoulder forever.

XI
Skye

"**MISS PETERSON,**" **DEVRY** said. "Please follow me."

Okay, she thought, power move. To the principal's office we go! Ha! She had been chatting up one of the crew in the engine room, a Malagasy guy who called himself Pablo, and she smiled at him and said she'd be back as she turned to follow, walking out to the port side and then up the gray rusty stairs to the bridge.

Devry held the door for her—being a woman she couldn't be expected to have the strength to open her own door—and Jean Claude turned to look at them.

"Jean Claude, can we have a few minutes?" Devry said without attempting to make it sound like anything but *get out.*

Jean Claude raised his very large eyebrows, but stood up, checked his computer screen out of habit, grabbed his bag, and walked out, nodding with a wink to Skye. Devry motioned her to sit. When she did, he sat on the table in front of her. Classic power move again, like he had read it in some management technique bestseller a decade ago. Pitiful.

She sat smiling up at him. She wasn't about to help.

"Miss Peterson," he said. "I have tried to extend the hospitality of the ship to you as a guest of the company, but I need to establish our ground rules." She wondered what movie he thought he was in. "Some of the crew are concerned about all the questions you are asking about equipment and processes. Can you please explain why you want this information? The crew are not authorized to make this information available."

"I'm sorry, Monsieur Devry, I am doing what I always do, what I was trained to do. I interview people about their lives, which means interviewing them about their work. There is nothing to worry about! I am not an inspector for your insurance company! Or for your competitors! I won't be selling any corporate secrets."

"There are no corporate secrets, Madame!" Okay, she had been promoted from Miss to Madame. Or was that a demotion in his world? Either way, the talk about trade secrets had made him nervous, which it was supposed to. "This is a scientific expedition."

"*Bien sur, Monsieur.*"

"*Bien sur*. So why do you want to know about the lifeboats?"

"Étienne is in charge of the lifeboats, yes—I was interested in what that meant to him, what it meant for his workday."

"It means nothing to his workday. We haven't used them in years, and I hope it stays that way."

"Yes, in fact I learned that today. They are taken out and painted once a year, yes? And when was the last time they were used?"

He harumphed, making a big show of how little time he had for such things as he pulled a logbook off one of the shelves on the back wall—he was the kind of guy who could never say he didn't know something.

"This only goes back three years, and you see"—he pointed, running his finger down the page to check—"there is not a single use."

She did a quick scan.

"Thanks so much for that! Again, I am only interested in the daily routines and the lived experience of the people who work on the ship. I don't really care about the lifeboats. Only the crew's daily life. I'm sure you know the work of Margaret Mead or your own Claude Lévi-Strauss? This is what we do, we study daily life. I am truly sorry if I inadvertently overstepped my bounds." One part snob-appeal with the name-dropping, one part conciliatory *mea culpa*. He would retreat to smugness to avoid admitting he hadn't read the anthropologists, and the apology would let him think he bested her in the fight. Result: he would leave her alone for a while.

"I would thank you to not interfere with the crew as they are trying to work."

"Of course, *bien sur*, and the last thing I want to do is interrupt their work—my research is about their work, after all, and I would be a bad researcher if I did not let them proceed unimpeded—a little too much Heisenberg principle. Which reminds me, when you have time, I would love to interview you, and if possible, shadow you while you work?"

Predictably he waved this away.

"I don't know when that might happen without impeding things, as you say."

But as soon as he said that, she could see him imagining himself as the hero of her story. She gave him a three count to save face and then it came.

"Perhaps some evening, when the day's work is mostly over, we could talk as I work on my daily reports."

"That would be very helpful, I am very appreciative, thank you, *merci, monsieur*."

He wasn't a dunce; he suspected he was being played, and so he grumbled as he left. That was good for her. The last thing she wanted was him feeling comfortable and droning on and on about how important he was. She wanted to give him more reasons to avoid her.

Jean Claude came back in as Devry left.

"Have you been a naughty girl?" he asked with a wink. He sat back in his chair, checked the screen.

"Would you expect anything less?"

"Ah! No, no."

"I am disturbing the crew."

He smiled. They liked each other. And he was no fan of Devry's. "I don't doubt it," he said.

"I wonder," she said, "why I should care."

She would, she decided, need to work on that logbook when the chance presented itself; that is, when Jean Claude was not around.

"I wish I knew," Jean Claude said, "what exactly you are up to . . ."

"Ha! But that would rob me of all my mystery, and you would no longer be madly in love with me. We can't have that."

"No," he said with a chuckle. "We can't have that."

XII
Frank

THE NEXT MORNING, one of the young men from the front desk was at his door. Frank looked at his watch. It was 10:00 a.m.

"Yes?"

"Mr. Baltimore, I am sorry to disturb, but there is a message for you—the harbormaster at Antsiranana called to say that everything is taken care of."

"Thank you." So it was time to make a decision or two. Huh.

"And Mr. Rakotomalala, the manager, was wondering if you would be staying on after today?"

"Yes, I'm wondering the same thing."

"Sir?"

"I'll stop by the desk in a few minutes."

"Thank you, sir," he said, bowing as he pulled the door closed after himself.

For the first time, Frank found he was feeling hesitant to go back to sea. He wasn't sure why—the resort wasn't much good to him. Aside from the woman who stopped by his room last night, whose name he didn't even know, he hadn't had a real conversation with anyone. Whatever rich people were staying in the other villas, he hadn't seen them, and wouldn't. The staff was trained to be so circumspect you couldn't have a satisfying conversation with them either, beyond pleasantries—anything else made them uncomfortable. If he was going to stay ashore, it shouldn't be here.

He thought about Kennedy and Lulu, his almost-step kids, out there in the world working jobs, Kennedy in green energy, Lulu living the starving artist life, although she was, thanks to him, literally a trust fund kid. He had lived with their mother, Tracy, when they were all poor, and he'd stayed in touch with them ever since. They rarely talked these days; he called on birthdays and left messages, sent chatty emails once in a while and got some in return. The oddness of their relationship had long since stopped being an issue—he was nothing to them but one of their mother's ex-boyfriends, and not even one with much longevity, albeit the guy who ended up rich and paid for their colleges and nest eggs. He had long since resigned himself to marginal status. He was just glad they were doing well.

There was nothing from either of them in his email now, but there was a cryptic note from their mother. Tracy was often cryptic. He had always had trouble, in the year or so they were together, figuring out what she was saying, which was undoubtedly one of the reasons for his lack of longevity as a boyfriend. She was hardest to understand when she was trying to get him to do something for her, and he sometimes thought it was a form of self-defense, that she was so unsure of herself she needed to hide what she wanted. But what did he know? The note just said that he should call when he got a chance, nothing important, no particular reason, no hurry. With Tracy, that often meant she was anxious. He'd been avoiding it for the last twenty-four hours, not because he minded helping her out when he could, but because he dreaded the struggle to get her to come out and tell him what she needed. She would have to make him feel bad, first, by accusing him of purposely misunderstanding her, and then, when things felt utterly doomed, and it was clear that he was an emotional wreck, she could allow herself to give in and let him know what she wanted. It wasn't a terrible mill to be run through, but it wasn't fun, either, and it touched off his PTSD each time. Still, if he was heading back to sea, best to call her now.

First though, the front desk. Maybe he'd stay two more days; it would give him an extra day to get the call to Tracy made, and, for whatever reason, it felt like a good idea to give himself the extra time on shore. He walked out of his villa and down the misted, arched floral walkway to the front desk.

"Mr. Baltimore!" the manager said. "Rudy said you were stopping by."

"Yes, thank you, Mr. Rakotomalala." The formality was the exact opposite of what he was looking for, in general, but it seemed like the kindest thing in this situation—it made the manager happy to have everything by the etiquette book. "I would like to stay two more days if that is possible."

A man in a chef's toque came out of the kitchen with a cart, and on it a bottle of wine in an ice bucket and two glasses. He wheeled it over toward them. Odd, Frank thought, it's a couple hours before lunch.

"Of course, Mr. Baltimore, we will love to have you stay, but I'm afraid the villa you are in will not be available—would it be okay if we moved you to a new villa? We have a wonderful one, with also a sea view, very similar, except without the stone shower. I can show you?"

"Of course. No need to show me, I'm sure it is fine."

"Oh, please, if you don't mind, I would appreciate you viewing it. I was asked to deliver this wine myself, as a personal favor, and it is on the way to your new villa, would you mind if we made a very quick stop?"

He agreed and they headed back down the arched pathway, and at the villa next to his, the manager asked for *one moment*, wheeled the cart up to the front door, and rang the bell. The surfer woman from the night before answered the door. She looked over and saw him.

"This is from you?" she called to him.

"No, I'm afraid not," he said.

"Good, then come help me drink it."

He promised to be right back, went and saw the other villa, almost identical to the one he was in, and agreed to the change. He and Mr. Rakotomalala smiled at each other, Frank complimented him on running such a wonderful establishment, and they headed back up the path toward the reception desk until Frank peeled off, went back to the mystery woman's door, and knocked.

She opened it with the two glasses in her other hand.

"This is ridiculous, but I don't know your name," Frank said.

"That is right. Come."

She turned and led him to the back patio and pointed to one of the lounge chairs. She sat in the other. The ice bucket was between them and she pulled the bottle out, poured them a glass, and dropped the bottle back in the ice.

"Prost!" she said, caught his eye, and held it.

"Cheers," he said.

"You sailed here."

"Almost, yes. I'm berthed in Antsiranana."

"Good. I need a boat."

XIII
Skye

SHE DIDN'T HAVE the best tools to work with, but she managed with the pens and erasers she could scrounge. The log now showed a total of nine lifeboats instead of ten, and since they had not been put into use for the three years the log covered, the revisions were minor. Good forensics would show the edits, but who would look that hard?

She had shut down the power to the onboard cameras one night, and while it was out, she repointed the ones on either side of Lifeboat #10 so she could launch the boat without it appearing on any of the screens or tapes. She loaded most of her gear into the boat and waited for the return to what she now thought of as "her" island. She had had Étienne, a kid sailor from a small town in the Dordogne, show her, step by step, the procedure for launching the lifeboat from the davit arm, how to return the davit arm to its closed position, how to start the engine, how to retract the lines, and how to pilot the boat, all of which she could easily do solo. Étienne was exhilarated to be at sea, and he had learned everything he was teaching her in the last year, so it was all new, and he was not at all surprised that she was fascinated by the details—he was, too. And since she was putting everyone through the same step-by-step explanations of their work, making the cook show her how to use the electric mixer and the dishwasher, making Jean Claude explain all his software to her, trying it all herself, nobody found her interest in their work suspicious. Getting hands-on experience, she explained to them one by one, was the only way to write well about the life of the ship. One thing she had going for her was that almost to a man and to a woman, they had zero interest in what she was writing, zero interest in writing in general, and zero interest in her, except the usual passing, hormone-based curiosity she was expert in attracting and deflecting. She sometimes wondered what it would be like, as an old woman in her forties, no longer causing a buzz among the sexually alert, and if she would miss it. She also wondered what it would be like to be one of the va-va-voom hypersexualized young women who really made a scene when they walked in a room, but that wasn't her. She was the girl-next-door type, although maybe prettier than most, not threatening to anyone unless she wanted to be. For most of them, she was more like a pet than a member of the team—not being a professional sailor or an oceanographer, she was not a full human to them. She was unremarkable, predictable, and at worst underfoot, and they sometimes enjoyed her following them around like the family dog, wagging her tail and letting them lead the way, and then, once she shut down any sexual interest, they let her be.

She had downloaded all of Jean Claude's navigation software, so she could study the charts at her leisure. Her island was fifty-five nautical miles southwest of Diego Garcia, and roughly twenty southeast of Island X, as her unimaginative boss had taken to calling it. It was in waters simultaneously claimed by the British Overseas Territory and Mauritius, as was everything north of her island. Since the oceanographic expedition's research area was south of the line, once she lost sight of Mr. Devry's ship and made her way a few miles north, she was sure to never see it again.

The only dicey period would be the first twenty minutes getting away from the ship. From Jean Claude's bridge, at a height of twenty-five feet or so above the water line, the horizon was around four miles away, so she could disappear in less than a half hour.

She would head straight off the stern, which was much lower, and she would be a speck in half that time. She would need a little luck for the first ten or fifteen minutes, but chances were that anybody looking off the ship would be checking out the island they were approaching, not the opposite direction, where there was nothing to see but the blue horizon.

If the captain was less of a prig, she was sure she could disappear and nobody would give it a second thought, the basic French fear of bureaucracy ensuring that even the few nosey people wouldn't say a word. But Devry was a wild card. He was a coward, so he wouldn't want to report anything that would get him in trouble, but he was also a quisling, and his terror of looking insufficiently slavish to his superiors would be at war with his fear of drowning in acres of bureaucratic mud. There was no telling which would get the upper hand.

She made her way to the bridge in the dark and found Jean Claude dozing in his chair.

She sat across from him, and he opened one eye and smiled.

"I will miss your company," he said, sitting up and straightening his shirt.

"Am I leaving?"

"Given the fussing with the logs and your lessons operating the lifeboats, I'm guessing yes."

"Well," she said. "This makes it easier. I was debating whether or not to take you into my confidence and it seems you already are."

"Am I in your confidence enough to know what you are up to?"

"You know the old saying: 'then I'd have to kill you.'" They smiled at each other, but it was perhaps not, she had to admit, the wisest use of humor.

"I wish I knew if you were with the good guys or the bad guys," he said.

"Yes, I wish I knew that, too. I'm with, well, my current employer—that's all I can say."

"And your current employer is not a university."

"No, I'm afraid not."

"Are they white hats or black hats? Like all Europeans my age, I grew up on Westerns, and I need to know who to root for."

"You know that is not how the world works, Jean Claude. It never did. The white hats were settler-colonialist genocidal maniacs."

"Don't get sophistic on me."

"Then, sophistry-free, let me say that I don't always know how to do the ethical computation myself in this case, but on a strict us-them scale, yes, we are the good guys."

"Hm. Not a rousing endorsement."

"No."

"I thank you for the frankness."

"It is not without ulterior motive."

"I presumed."

"I am leaving, and it would be best for everyone, Jean Claude, if I could just disappear. I assume Devry will be happy to not have to write a report, especially for something this strange, me disappearing in the middle of the ocean. There are now nine lifeboats in the logs, and nine lifeboats on the ship, so clearly I did not disappear that way. Since your next stop is in the Comoros, it makes sense that I would leave the ship there."

"But you are not leaving the ship there."

"No, before that. Best you don't know exactly where."

Jean Claude thought about this for a moment.

"You remind me of my director," he said. "One of the things I appreciated, right away, when I first worked for him, was that I could never be a director. I saw the way he thought. Everyone around him was a tool in his toolkit. He was not abusive, or inhuman—he was, like you, very charming, and easy to talk to, 'easy-going', as you say. But for me, it was not possible to always think of the people around me as tools, to have an always-strategic view of life. It seemed exhausting to me. It was not exhausting for him—he was invigorated by it. Again, like you."

"I don't see you as a tool, Jean Claude!"

"No, of course, not alone; you could not be effective if you did, and he could not have been the great director he was if he did. But I was a tool for him nonetheless—that is okay, that is what I signed up for, that is what being the soundman is—and I am being employed as a tool by you now. I can accept that, *ce n'est pas un problème*. So, what will you direct me to do?"

"Well," she said. "First, I cannot deny any of that." She looked him in the eye and realized they would never go back to their easy camaraderie. Casualty of war. He was very smart, and very sweet, and she decided she would think about what all this should mean to her later—it had been a while since she had taken stock of what she was up to—but for now, she did need to give him his direction. "I have loved our time together," she said. "I hope you have as well. What I need is for you to believe something."

"To believe something . . ."

"Yes, I am going to my room at some point tomorrow night, because I won't be feeling well. I need you to believe that I was ill in my room—as far as you know—from tomorrow night until we reached the Comoros. Perhaps you can even bring food and drink to my sickroom."

"Do I bring food and drink to your sickroom or do I just believe that I brought food and drink to your sickroom?"

"I would appreciate the added realism of you bringing food and drink. I won't be able to eat anything, I'm sure, but the drink you might want yourself, leaving the empty glass."

"This also is why I was never a director. The attention to visual detail."

"If all goes well, Jean Claude, I hope we will see each other again."

"Yes, my dear, you are still young enough to have such hopes and not be ridiculous in them, but I am quite confident this is our last act. Would that it were not so! But long life helps one recognize how one's wishes are independent of the inexorable unspooling of time."

"Not a director, but a wordsmith."

"Hardly, *ma cherie,* only an old man with an old man's unwanted wisdom. People leave and they don't come back. That's life."

"I hope to prove you wrong."

"Yes! You can hope! What does the poet say? 'Hope is a thing with wings.' It flies away, too."

"Feathers," she said. "A thing with feathers."

"*La même chose,* or as an American I heard said it—'same difference.'"

XIV
Alain

ALAIN SET THE alarm on his watch so he wouldn't miss the 48-hour window, and had a neat stack of the cards, dated with a sharpie, although she didn't ask for that, and given the big-time spy feel of the whole operation, he doubted they needed it—he was sure they were all date/time coded anyway. He tried reading the memory cards, using his laptop, but all he could see were vast lines of code and numbers he couldn't make heads or tails of. Spy stuff.

Who was this woman? She didn't vibe military, but if she was an anthropologist, he was Haile Selassie. He'd never met an anthropologist, but he was sure they didn't offer people new identities for clandestine data harvesting, or new well-paid jobs without a full background check and some other basic tests—she didn't even know if he could read. She was American, so CIA? Or who knows who was who over there—FBI, NSA, CSI, SVU, NYPD, DIA? He knew his information was from TV and YouTube, not reality, but his first thought, in any case, was that she was from some initialed part of the US government. He wasn't a nitwit, and they were less than a hundred miles from Diego Garcia, and so whatever she was up to had to have something to do with that place. Maybe that meant she was a spy for someone else—Russia? China? That would be deep. He could see that the Russians or the Chinese would be smart to have an American doing their dirty work for them—a Russian doing what she was doing would be too obvious. A Chinese doing it would be too obvious. Both would be pegged spies in an instant. But an American—a young American woman—might just be who she said she was. Nobody's first guess would be that she was a Chinese spy.

What would that mean for him? That she was offering him a job as a Chinese spy? It was too far-fetched. If she was, in fact, working for the Americans, maybe it was even stranger: why would they be spying on themselves? He had watched a prodigious amount of American television—working as a guide for tourists meant that he had six months on the road and six months of sitting around each year. He did odd jobs in the off-season, although not as many as Angela wanted, and his band played a gig every other month, but the rest of the time he took care of the kids while Angela was at work and they weren't in school, and he watched TV. He watched TV a lot of the time when he was watching the kids, too. He was a multitasker.

The Nerd—his name was Dylan, and he was American—wasn't much help. He was fresh out of some university in Rhode Island, which the Nerd said in a way that Alain knew he was supposed to be impressed. Whatever, it was better than any university he'd been to, which was none. The Nerd had learned to speak French at his university, but spoke English all the time, like the American he was, effortlessly at home with his neocolonial hubris. He had studied something to do with ocean ecology, and even though he was only twenty-four, this wasn't his first expedition. He had the sparse, scruffy, untrimmed beard and unkempt, uncut light brown hair of a hippie, and he dressed like a homeless person, but he was exacting about everything else. He was tricked out with state-of-the-art camping gear, and he was the kind of guy that had everything in protective bags that fit neatly in larger protective bags, and his underwear and socks in packing cubes, everything top rate and completely anal compulsive—again, whatever. He was a decent enough guy, 100 percent focused on his research.

That research, he said, was for the survey the team was doing, but he also was making a number of his own measurements having to do with shifts in prevailing winds, which he would then cross-analyze with the data that other scientists were gathering about changes in ocean currents. He was very proud that he knew some of those scientists, had met them at conferences. Alain nodded as the Nerd recited their names. Their work was the most globally significant now underway for understanding the full impact of climate change, he said.

"We are doomed, you know," he said at one point.

"I know I am," Alain said, and he wasn't kidding.

"No, seriously, bro. The hurricanes, the floods, the fires? We're going to see an unbroken string of major fucking weather events from now on—superstorms, massive natural disasters. Arma-fuckingeddon."

"Huh. Nothing we can do? That's it?"

"Theoretically we could slow it down. But we won't. Mankind is fucking over."

"Well maybe that makes my life easier."

"Is that supposed to be funny?"

"No." He considered just not talking, but then, like an unexpected burp, he said: "So what do you make of this Skye chick?"

Dylan looked at him squarely. One of the things that happens when two people are holed up in tight quarters like this is that they stop looking at each other. It's polite, really, since nobody wants to be watched all the time, and looking straight at someone is a kind of demand, or at least a request—it's best to look a bit to the side. Sometimes you break the code because you need to really check in. Alain understood Dylan wanted to know what was driving him, why he asked.

"This isn't high school," Alain said. "I don't want to know if I should ask her out on a date."

This relieved the Nerd. He thought for a minute, and then inexplicably, he got cantankerous.

"It's not fucking science, what she does," he said, breathing heavy, his face red. "They call it 'qualitative social science'. It's qualitative, it's social, but it's not fucking science."

"Okay."

"I'm sorry," the Nerd said. "It pisses me off. And they get oodles of research money. Fuckers!"

"She seems trustworthy, though, don't you think?"

"For someone whose entire professional life is a sham? Or do you mean because she set up those two pieces of equipment? Whatever. She's probably recording our conversations. She'll transcribe all 300 hours of it, then she'll quote two sentences. Don't worry. Nobody reads what anthropologists write except eleven other anthropologists, all of whom will ignore anything we said, anyway, and will only write about what is wrong with her theory."

"No, I mean really, as a person?"

Dylan looked at his face again, and this time Alain met his eyes and did a quick raising and lowering of an eyebrow, as if to say, it's okay, no funny business, just curious, no worries.

"Yeah, she seems cool enough," Dylan said. "She was actually interested in my research."

Maybe she was interested in the Nerd's research, what did he know? But he doubted it.

"Do you think she's CIA?"

Dylan laughed. "What would the CIA want with our rinky-dink expedition?"

"You don't think it's odd that she is so pretty? Too pretty to be doing this, no offence. And suspicious that she's sneaking around with equipment? That she's going around the boss man?"

"Boss man?"

"Yeah, White Streak. Isn't he the boss?"

"Yeah, I guess he is. He's not the scientific director, only the captain of the ship. And everyone goes around him. He's too much of a pain in the fucking ass. It's simple math. If it costs twenty minutes to do it without him, and it costs an hour and twenty minutes to do it with him, then, duh. We all go around him when we can. And what does 'too pretty' mean?"

The Nerd wasn't going to be any help here. He had a slight autistic vibe. He found people not as interesting as data, not entirely worth his time.

"Yeah, well, that's an interesting question," Alain said, because why not. "She's just very pretty. I mean, too good looking to be an academic."

"I don't judge women on the nature of their physical appearance." He said it like he had learned it in an HR-mandated course. Or at college.

"Okay." Alain got up and slipped into his tent for the night. They'd dispensed with any formalities. Action was announcement, and there were no surprises. There were no *good mornings* or *good nights*. They went about their day then went to sleep and did it again.

Alain lay back in his tent and thought again about what it would mean to be whisked off and given a new identity and a new job. Where would they put him? It would have to be somewhere not in Madagascar, and he had a moment of panic. The Americans and Europeans all thought that Madagascar was African, that the Malagasy were Africans like the Shona, Ibo, or Ndebele. What the hell would he do if they tried to settle him in Kenya with some tribe of cattle herders? What if they threw him into Somalia? He would stick out like a sore thumb. He would insist on Europe. Or America.

And if he was going to be a spy, would they at least give him some introductory course, some basic training? Spycraft 101? It was very much not part of his *Légion étrangère* training. They made it clear that you were there to be a grunt, and a grunt you would always be.

The main thing he'd have to work out with this secret agent was the money. How were Angela and the kids—and, he supposed, Raissa and her kid, too—how were they all going to be taken care of? Maybe she could fake his death and they could get the Legion's pension payments—it wouldn't be quite his salary, but it would be a monthly payment forever. Maybe Skye could get them American military pension money—that would be five times as much, and then he could live on it and they could, too. That is, if Skye was working for the Americans. Or something similar if she was working for the Russians or Chinese. Maybe she's a double agent and she can get him money from both sides. Haha. Maybe she worked for a gangster outfit—Russian gangsters?—or the Saudis . . . He had no idea.

Was he ready for this? Was he ready to never see his children again? His wife? His, what, mistress? Skye had said *someday,* that someday he'd be able to see his kids again. What would that mean in the meantime? He liked the idea of being presumed dead—part of him loved the thought of his wife weeping at his funeral, he had to admit. Maybe Raissa weeping at his funeral, too. And part of him loved being freed from all those guilt-inducing ties forever. But at the same time, it was a life sentence he was giving himself. He might never be able to step foot in Madagascar again. Maybe he should ask for a cash payment for keeping quiet and be done with it. Stay on this godforsaken island, as she called it, serve out his time, and go home. If that was even possible. Maybe she would have him killed if he asked for that.

Then he got to thinking about the crazy world that had been revealed to him. How many people around the world does this happen to? How many people get offered new lives at the drop of a hat? One agent, in one forlorn place, had decided to spend the thousands and thousands of euros, dollars, rubles, whatever, that it would take to move him to a new place, guarantee his silence, and train him for a new job. How many other people had she done this for on this one mission? Times how many missions? Times how many agents? Thousands and thousands—hundreds of thousands?—of people living under assumed names, funded by the US, Russian, or Chinese governments. The whole world sprinkled with these bribed accomplices. How could they even afford it?

Which gave him a chill. Wouldn't it be cheaper to feed him to the sharks? Get him on a boat out of there, slit his throat and dump him overboard, make it look like he went AWOL? Angela and the kids would get nothing . . .

And he ran through everyone he knew—were any of them on their second identities, or even third identities? What about Raissa? She said she was from Antsirabe, but was she? She never talked about her family or friends she left behind—although, to be fair, Alain hadn't talked about his family with her, either. It wasn't that kind of relationship. It followed the code of the illicit, which was like witness protection: nobody has a past, keep any threatening reality at bay, cosplay at an alternative life.

But then again, this wasn't witness protection she was offering, it was a job. It was an illicit job, somehow, secret. He was to be a secret agent of someone. The US government had the Army, CIA, FBI, NSA, CSI, SVU, NYPD, DIA, LAPD, Navy, Air Force, Marines, Coast Guard, National Guard, gendarmerie, state police—what were a few more clandestine agents for a machine that big?

And how fucked up was it all? These horrible people running around the world perverting people with their inexhaustible capital, subverting anything and anybody in their way, these neoliberal, neoimperialist, neo-slavers buying us all up, a person at a time. He was enraged and confused in turns, because the more he thought about it, the more he realized he was in over his head, that he was in a political drama over which he had no control, and the more he realized, too, that he would have no way to know what was happening to him until it was too late. Maybe, of course, it didn't matter. He was already sold. There was no going back. They were dangling something way too seductive. A fresh start.

If it all worked out, this would be his salvation. If it all worked out, he thought, while turning on his too-thin mat on the hard ground, he would, at the very least, be able to take a god-damn hot shower and eat food that wasn't fish. At least, if nothing else, he would be able to sleep, after long, long last, in a god-damn bed.

XV
Mónica

A YEAR EARLIER, she had been sent to kill a coder, and—this was a big no-no—she had met up with him first. Eamon was apoplectic, and she had lied and said that he had caught her snooping around his apartment, that she had become friendly in self-defense. But in fact, she meant to meet him, did it on purpose. The coder had built a system for Eamon's boss, and had thereby made himself the weak link in the organization's security system. Before she dispatched him, she had him build her an encrypted cloud storage unit on an Icelandic server with a 99-year lease and no notifications allowed. It had an unbreakable firewall and a triple-check authentication system that was unhackable. The coder was very proud of it. They spent a week as a couple in love. It was fun. She felt terrible killing him right away, but at least he went out satisfied with his work. And satisfied in love, too, up to that last minute when he saw the knife in his belly, and maybe even after that—she wasn't sure.

It was reported in the papers as a robbery. All the extensive computer equipment for his business had been stolen, and she had it crushed in a junkyard, inside the car she had used for the week. Eamon had to admit that it was perfect, police looking for thieves in the hacking world. She spent the next few weeks reconstructing every job she had done for Eamon, writing up the hits one by one in as much detail as possible, attaching screen shots of her communications with him, and although not all of them would provide sufficient evidence to stick him with murder charges, plenty of them would. It was her last-resort safety move, and she had an email set and ready to go to police detectives in a dozen countries, and that would be sent in two weeks unless she rescheduled it, which she did every couple of days. There were only a very limited set of scenarios in which she could use the threat, and they all had to do with running out of time. If the gun was to her head and the killer was in countdown mode, she might have to use it, and if she did, it would only buy her a little time. Once the threat was made, Eamon would dedicate the rest of his life to hunting her down and killing her. Which meant, of course, that her only real option at that point would be to kill Eamon. And he would be forewarned, knowing that killing him was her only option, and a victim forewarned is a very difficult target. It would be better to kill him now, of course, but that would require her being sure she never wanted to work again, sure that she was done with all of that.

Much better, for now, that they stay friends. Maybe go into management with him? She could even offer to help in the field for tough cases now and then. Like an old dentist that cuts his practice back to two days a week, then one day a week. She'd ease out of it.

The minute she said that to herself she could hear his reaction—silence. Who was she kidding? Bargaining with the devil was just stupid.

This case, and the one before it: both vics worked for Darkwater. She could go to them. She could imagine Eamon scoffing at the idea, but that was always his reaction. He was a scoffer. Mr. Reality Sandwich. But Darkwater was big, they didn't mind killing people either, and if she worked for them, she'd get their protection against Eamon.

Of course, Darkwater's protection hadn't helped the last two vics one little bit.

This last one, the guy at the campfire, was completely out of his element—you could tell he wasn't an outdoorsman, that he wasn't out there for the midnight beauty of the baobab trees outlined against the moon. He checked his phone constantly and puffed so hard on a cigar that his head stayed shrouded in smoke. One of his two bodyguards had built the fire, and the same one had built his tent. The other was the perimeter guy, the better job, to her thinking, since you didn't have to cater to Smokehead every few minutes. Each of the bodyguards had approached the poor lost girl with her camera and the helpless air as if they had never had a day of real training in their soon-to-end lives, both more than willing to be her knight in shining armor and point her back to her hotel. As she dispatched the two of them, the vic stayed glued to his phone the whole time, sitting in a folding camp chair. As the CFO at Darkwater, if he'd been attending a dinner in Saudi Arabia, he would have had a security detail and support entourage of a dozen people, minimum. What was he doing out here with just two guys? And who was he chatting with? How could he explain to anyone why he was here? Why Madagascar? And not just Madagascar, but a twenty-hour drive from the capital? Of course, the vic hadn't done that long drive—that was for her and maybe the bodyguards, while he was shuttled in by helicopter. The helicopter would come back for the bodies, she supposed. No doubt he was talking to his wife or his mistress, explaining why he would be late for dinner. Eamon must have had real dirt on him, and dirt the guy didn't want people at Darkwater to know about, hence the bargain basement security detail. Maybe he was embezzling. Maybe selling secrets.

The CFO had been at Darkwater since the beginning with Fred Prinz, and after Prinz "retired"—everybody guessed he still called the shots—he had been promoted to the top spot. He didn't answer to anyone but Prinz, and, to a lesser extent, the Board of Directors, and so if he was hiding from anyone, it was Prinz or the board, or both. Bringing this dude to a campsite in Western Madagascar was classic Eamon: lure someone to the far ends of the Earth in a doomed attempt to protect themselves, and thereby confuse every police effort to make sense of what happened. The press and the detectives would spend immense amounts of time trying to figure out why he was there rather than who had killed him. And at the same time, if she knew Eamon, there was a message encoded in the spot, too. And that would mean a message for Prinz or the Board. Madagascar would mean something to them.

She was doubly curious now. What was Mr. CFO protecting so hard that he would agree to this? And what did Madagascar have to do with it?

There were two kinds of people, she had decided some time ago. There were those who, when death is looking them in the face, think—what? why me? what did I do to deserve this? She found these people comical. Not a single one of them had any right to ask that question. Leave aside that 60 percent of them cheat on their spouses—and in her subset of vics, more than that—and that 90 percent cheat on their taxes, drive over the legal limit for alcohol and over the speed limit, all of which was less salient than the fact that a hundred percent of her vics, every single one of them, was complicit in gross economic inequities of myriad varieties and complicit in destroying the planet with their climate-devastating consumption. She didn't kill poor people. The dead were all rich, and therefore all guilty. They had no right to ask, *why me*?

And then there were some—a minority, by far—who saw death coming in her eyes or hands and thought, okay, here it is. I expected it, and if anyone deserves it, I deserve it, so okay. She had respect for these people. And if she could, she made it go faster for them.

Mr. CFO was in the *why me*? group, which was one reason she wished, and would always wish, that it had lasted a little longer.

XVI
Frank

THE YEAR THAT had changed everything for Frank—the year he had followed Dmitry to Asia, had fallen in love with Dmitry's wife, left everything in the US behind, become rich, and dropped into the depressed state he was emerging from—was losing its grip on him. All of it was starting to fade from his mind, succumbing to the entropy of memory.

And speaking of memory, he said to himself as he walked along the beach in front of his villa, I have to call Tracy as soon as I'm back in the room.

"The thing is, Franky," Dmitry had said to him once, many years earlier. "Memory is so often wrong because it is combinatory. We may have images stored in our brain cells, but when we play the slide show back to ourselves, we never know how the slides have been shuffled while we were asleep, like a box of photographs that have been rifled dozens of times. For instance: I can remember sleeping with those three delectable girls the first summer I took the Green Tortoise across America"—and the frailty of memory aside, Frank could hear exactly how the Liverpudlian said *Americur*—"but which one did I sleep with first? Actually, that's a bad example, it was definitely Sally, but who did I sleep with second or third?"

When Dmitry was holding forth like that, he loved torturing Frank by using misogynistic examples and he loved asking rhetorical questions. Dmitry lived to make people uncomfortable. Frank would sometimes counter the rhetorical questions with rhetorical questions of his own: "Was it the one with the lower self-esteem?" he asked that time.

Dmitry would ignore these, or comment on them but continue his harangue unflustered: "Good one, Franky! But we—that's the editorial we, don't accept substitutes!—we all have self-esteem issues, don't we? Look at me, Franky, I have self-esteem issues, don't I, as you always remind me."

"I do."

"Yes, you're always reminding me that I have too much self-esteem. I mean, not directly. Never directly. I mean it wouldn't be passive aggression if it wasn't a little indirect, right?"

Dmitry had launched into this minor oration, Frank remembered, as a distraction from something Frank had accused him of—was it the loan he hadn't paid back? Was it the pimping he was doing when he was supposed to be working for Frank? He couldn't remember. "As you always like to remind me, Franky," he went on. "Our thoughts have feelings attached, and so do our memories, and the thing that changes the most is the feeling, not the image. The image that we get nostalgic about—our first bicycle—that image doesn't start out nostalgic. The morning after we got our first bicycle, we don't wake up, remember we have a new bicycle, and feel nostalgic about it. No, we feel pride of ownership, we're ecstatic that we now can lord it over Billy down the street, who for so long had made fun of our bicycle-lessness. I should say, in passing, Franky, that I have no memory of receiving a first bicycle. I do remember having one, but it wasn't much of one, and I don't know how it came to be in my possession. The bicycle nostalgia is an illustrative case out of whole cloth, not the result of an actual memory."

It had been a long time since he had thought about Dmitry's endless discourses, back in the wilds of Connecticut, as they built that house, the real start of his construction business, back when Dmitry's criminality was embryonic.

"The point is this, Franky: memory is a very blunt instrument, even though it never feels that way. We often say, 'I don't really remember', or 'I can't remember', but we also say, 'I remember it like it was yesterday', and 'I remember it all so clearly.' Because when we do remember something, it always feels either irrefutable or horribly hazy. I went with a friend to Morocco, and we were driving into the Sahara. I wanted to see the big dunes, the *Lawrence of Arabia* dunes along the Algerian border—don't, don't, Franky, tell me T.E. Lawrence was not in Morocco, everyone knows that, and your pedantry is so unattractive! Anyway, like everywhere in Morocco, people were offering to guide us, and I thought, okay, makes sense, don't do the Sahara without a guide, but my friend Sean was even tighter than you, Franky, and couldn't stand paying the few dirhams it would take to get us a guide. He kept saying, 'How hard can it be, Dmitry? We head south until we see the dunes. It's not like we can miss them. There are 40,000 miles of them!' My friend Sean was using what the poets call hyperbole, Franky, the Sahara is not 40,000 miles across."

One thing Frank couldn't quite remember anymore is why he found these interminable stories of Dmitry's, with their profuse deviations and stoppages, interesting. Maybe he didn't. Maybe it just passed the time through the daily, stupidly repetitive two-man jobs required to build a house. That day they were putting 4 x 8 sheets of plywood sheathing on the roof rafters, and so it was like having talk radio on, nothing else to think about except lining up the boards and nailing them down.

"We passed a young man named Mohammed—it is easy to remember that because most of them are named Mohammed—and we asked him if we were pointed south, and instead of answering that, the boy Mohammed said there was no way for us to get where we wanted to go without a guide. Sean screamed,

'Ballocks!' and drove on. The kid chased after us on his bicycle for a mile, sweating and grunting, but keeping up with us because the so-called road was so potholed and cracked that we were crawling along, and *he* knew we would eventually need him. We ended up stuck at the top of a ridge, with no choice but to turn around and find another way down, when it became clear that yes, we needed a guide. We surrendered, Mohammed handed his bike off to a little kid who appeared out of nowhere, and he got in with us. It was many hours before we finally got a glimpse of the dunes. The point of all of this, Franky, is that in a pub, six months later, Sean told the story to some mates and said that we got a guide who first made us follow him a mile to his house so he could hand his bicycle to his little brother, and then guided us to the dunes. I objected, saying that's not how it happened at all! Who was right?"

He didn't, of course, want an answer. Frank went down and started handing up the rest of the 4 x 8s they needed to finish the roof. It was hot, heavy work.

"I'm sure you wish we were at an end to this excursion into the philosophy of memory, Franky, but last year I had an odd experience. I went to visit the council flat where I, as a wee lad, had lived in Brownfield, East London—this was before I got the imaginary bike I was now telling you about—and walked up to the door. A typical dumpy council flat mum came to the door—oh don't look so glum, Franky, I know you find my class-based stereotyping distasteful, and I agree it is distasteful, like so many things—but anyway, she asked what I was about. 'I used to live here,' I said. 'Did you, then, my big strapping lad?' she said. 'Well,' I told her, 'I wasn't so big or so strapping then. I was just a wee lad.' She said, 'Come on in, then, wee lad, I suppose you want a look around.' And Franky, I do believe she wanted the big strap, *if you catch my drift.*" He always turned on a James Cagney gangster accent when he used Americanisms. "But I went in and saw the door to the cupboard, and thought, of course, *this is exactly what*

I remember! And the doorknobs, and the windowpanes, all came flooding back, absolutely the same as I remembered. There was a Formica countertop in the kitchen, of a specific pattern, with boomerang shapes in it, and there were knife marks scratching it up, and I remembered them! Each detail was another Proustian madeleine, and my whole life came back to me in a rush of, well, nausea, I suppose you'd have to call it."

They finished nailing the last piece, trimmed it off, and Frank looked at his watch, trying to figure out if he had time to take on the next job, and whether that next job should be the soffits or the flashing and tar paper on the roof. If Dmitry had been a better worker, paying more attention to what he was doing and less to his own blabbering, they would have had time for the soffits. But given that Dmitry was all he had, he called it a day and started packing up the tools.

"And since you are wondering, Franky, why I took us down this particular memory lane, I will tell you the two reasons. The first, and less important, is that I comprehended that I could not have recalled, in a million years, even if I was being waterboarded in one of your CIA black-ops hideaways, *any* of those details. Not the cupboard doors, not the doorknobs, not the Formica, not the knife marks. But seeing them in front of me, I recognized them, I saw that they were indeed stored in my memory, no matter how inaccessible they might have been moments before. What does that say about memory?" He paused. "That's an actual question, Franky, feel free to answer it if you can."

"And while you tell me the second reason, can you put your tools in the truck?"

"The second point I wanted to make is this: I was in the wrong flat."

"The wrong flat."

"Yeah. As I was leaving—council mum protesting that I should stay for 'tea'—I looked up at the number above the door, and it was

21. We lived in 27. They all had the same Formica, the same layout. I was fervently moved *à la Proust* by being in someone else's flat."

Frank had been reading a lot of stuff that was over his head at the time—Nietzsche and Freud—and he was a sucker for any ontological speculation that came his way. He wasn't sure if what Dmitry was talking about counted, but these monologues made him think, and it made the relationship feel valuable. Later, it occurred to him that the ideas he was enamored with—ideas of the absolute relativity of good and evil, of the ego's boundless ability to defend itself—had enabled Dmitry, or would have if he needed any enabling, as he set out on his criminal career of grisly capital extraction.

He wasn't sure why that particular memory—his memory of Dmitry's memory—had popped up. Perhaps his new-found sense of freedom from the mess of that eventful year, from the entanglements and betrayals, the exaltations and degradations, had allowed him to entertain a reminiscence or two, but still, why that one? Telling this fascinating woman who had wandered into his life—crazy that he still didn't know her name—the story, or a pared down, no-incriminating-details version of the story, the night before had him thinking about it more than usual, he supposed, and made him realize that yes, memory is an odd beast. One of the things he had concluded was that whatever he remembered of the experience and whatever he had concluded about it: all of it was unconscionably wrong, indubitably mistaken, horribly inaccurate, and so, of what use were the memories? They weren't even a guide to what had actually happened.

And now he was about to set off on a new adventure into the unknown, since this woman needed a "boat." His only consolation was that he was under no illusions about her. It was clear she wanted his ship, not him, and he wouldn't go down that farcical road again, anyway. As she had said, to call him a romantic was not a compliment. Amen, sister. Learned the hard way.

"Wah, wah, wah," he said out loud, a habit he'd developed to snap himself out of spirals of self-pity. She wanted to go up toward Diego Garcia. Well, great, he'd always wanted to go himself, and if the US Navy didn't torpedo them along the way, maybe he'd see it. He felt his freedom. He even felt free enough to let his self-surveillance go slack, to throw caution to the prevailing winds.

XVII
Skye

SHE WAS PRETTY sure that Jean Claude would cover for her, or, at the worst, plead ignorance. So the official story would become that she left the ship when they docked in Moroni, in the Comoros. Yes, the captain would explain, she took everything with her, she told us nothing, and we don't know where she went. That is, if anybody asked him. Like all tiny tyrants, he was a coward, so he wasn't going to volunteer anything unless pressed. And it was very unlikely anyone would press him, unless the mission went south, in which case, really, who cared. She'd be dead.

And it was even less likely that anyone—save the captain, who knew they spent time together—would ever ask Jean Claude about her, ever. He was merely the navigator, after all. The captain would be left to scratch his head about it in private once in a while. And boom, done.

Nothing would link her to the disappearance of the French Foreign Legion soldier from a pile of rocks south of Diego Garcia. That, anybody with a brain would think, had to be the doing of the Americans. They must have convinced the young soldier to go AWOL, and who could blame him? A solid year sitting with nothing to do in the middle of the ocean? Of course he left when he could. The whole affair would be unnewsworthy, ignored, and then hermetically sealed in top secret files, impregnable to anyone trying to meddle.

The expedition was looping back through the northeastern outposts of the expedition, picking up all the scientists and equipment they had deposited a week or ten days earlier from each of the small islands. When they got to what she now considered *her* island, the ship shuddered to a stop, dropped an anchor, and lowered a boat to starboard with Devry and Étienne in it, Étienne driving, to go pick up the Nerd. Skye had loaded her boat with purloined rations and water, extra cans of gas for the engine, two full sets of scuba gear, and all her stuff. She waited until she heard their engine rev and get underway, then slipped out of her room, dropped her lifeboat on the port side and stowed the davits. She lowered herself to the boat, pulled the leads in after her, started the engine, and headed directly away from the island, keeping the ship between her and Devry. The ship cooperated and dutifully pointed into the wind, so anyone manning the bridge with Jean Claude faced the island and was blind to her receding boat. She barreled full speed until the ship became a speck and then disappeared. An hour or so after leaving it, she saw on her phone that the tracker she had left on the ship was moving. They were headed to the next outpost, to the west. In another forty minutes she came back to her island, landed, and greeted Alain, who was, thankfully, glad to see her. There was a one in three or one in four chance he ended up with cold feet and wanted out, but she had guessed right—he was ready to roll dice.

"Here," he said, handing her a plastic box, "are your instruments." She took it. "And here," he said, holding out a smaller box, "are the cards."

When she reached for them, though, he pulled that box away.

"Problem, Alain?"

"Yes," he said. "I would like to trust you, but I'm not sure I do. Maybe, given everything you know about me, I have a right to know more about you, and about the mission."

"But then I'd have to kill you," she said, giving him her most innocent smile. This time it landed, and he laughed.

"That's exactly what worries me. I don't want to give you any ideas, but it would be easier to kill me, wouldn't it?"

"If I was going to do that, I could kill you now and take the cards."

"But you don't know if the cards are actually in this box."

"Well played. But look, I was serious. You have basic military training, and you have pluck and smarts—and you have SCUBA training, weapons training—"

"Wait," he interrupted. "Who told you that, about SCUBA training?"

"Come on, Alain, I've read your file. You would be valuable to us."

He thought about that for a minute. It did make more sense.

"Okay," he said. "Who is *us*? CIA?"

"You know that if I was, I would have to say no. No."

He looked at her, and decided it was a fruitless endeavor.

"You're not going to tell me," he said, more to himself than to her.

"Not yet. You aren't AWOL yet, and you haven't committed any crime. Therefore, you don't have all that hanging over your head. That makes you a liability. Soon, your status will change, and with it my ability to tell you more."

"I get it. Once I'm AWOL I would need you." They apprised each other, and he curled his lip but said, "All right, then. What is the plan?"

She sat on one of his two camp chairs and pulled a laptop out of her backpack.

"I am going to spend the next few hours analyzing this data and sending it in. Then we pack up whatever you're taking with you and head north. We have one stop to make in the middle of the night, where we will do a scuba job for a couple hours—recon, nothing violent, we hope. Then we'll head northeast to Diego Garcia, where you will get processed and sent off to your new life. A regular day at the office."

"NSA," he said.

"I could tell you, but . . ."

They looked at each other, and Skye thought she was winning his confidence. He smirked. Yes.

"So right now, I know nothing," he said, "and I don't have a story anybody would believe. You could take me or leave me. But you say you want to take me. Yes, my training is worth something, but every American soldier has better. Why not just take your data and leave me here?" he asked.

She wanted to be honest with him and see how that would fly.

"Your ability to tell people I was here, what I did, and where I went, all militate against leaving you in the wind."

"But I'm just a loser Malagasy nobody cares about. You got what you wanted. Go."

"Well, you haven't actually given me the cards yet, so no, I haven't got what I wanted. But once you have, what if the French police or Interpol come and ask you what happened to the girl who stole the lifeboat? What will you tell them?"

"Like you said, they would think I had sun stroke. And say I go with you, and I resettle with a new identity. What if the police in Australia—I wouldn't mind going there—ask me?"

"They won't. And if you told anyone the story, they would think you were off your meds. You were on a pile of rocks where? And she was CIA? She show you ID? And she took you where? Why? It doesn't hold together very well as a story. Plus, you are not going to resettle so fast. We want you to work for us. By the time you are done, the police won't be an option. And of course, you won't want to go to them, because you will be set up, solid. You won't want to put it all in jeopardy. What we worry about, in this business, is people with nothing to lose. We want to give you enough that you have plenty to lose."

He considered this for a beat. Then he handed her the box with the memory cards. She immediately got to work downloading them.

"Kind of crap technology," he said.

"Tell me 'bout it."

"You do realize you contradicted yourself, right? You can't leave me to tell a story, you say, *but* it's a story nobody would believe? And by the way, I don't think that's what 'bout it' means anymore."

"The data is good," she said, ignoring him. "I've got it loaded. We move in ten."

The data downloaded fast and easy, and she ran it through her program. It was clear Darkwater's hunch had been right—somebody had been very busy not 50 miles east, and she knew what reef that meant. It was one they had considered building on themselves and the US had nixed it. The old joke about military intelligence—leave it to the Joint Chiefs to decide they would rather give space rent-free to a contractor like Darkwater—even on a place with land as scarce as Diego Garcia—than let them out of sight for a minute. As if that would control them.

And she had a very good idea, too, what outfit had to be colonizing the place. Time to go see what they were up to.

XVIII
Mónica

THIS FRANK GUY would do. After the first day, with his laundry done, he started dressing more like a normal adult than a down-on-his-luck, long-in-the-tooth skater. Whatever worries she had had about him abated, and she realized he wasn't a perv, just a gentleman, really—so rare she had forgotten they existed. He wouldn't be a problem.

They met at the helipad, which was nothing but a lawn with a white circle of lime on it, like the ones used on sports fields. The hotel had put her two bags and his two on a golf cart that was there waiting; she carried the bag she wouldn't want anyone to look in, and he carried nothing. He really was a kind of beach bum after all, it occurred to her, just a very rich one.

"You're sure this works for you?" she asked, knowing the answer.

"I'd like to know more, but I've freed up my calendar for the next week or so . . ."

"I'm so very sorry to make you rearrange things."

"I was kidding," he said.

"Yes, I know." He was slow like that. A little dumb and kinda cute wasn't a bad combination, better than real dumb and handsome, or very smart and anything. Eamon was very smart, and a putz.

The chopper took them the twenty minutes to Antsiranana, a sleepy port town, where Frank opened up the *God Sees Everything*—she thought the name was a bit creepy, but hey, not for her to say.

She stowed her stuff in the second largest stateroom while he settled with the harbormaster. She found an empty compartment he wouldn't stumble upon for her weapons bag and the rest of her go-stash, setting her empty duffels on top of them, unpacking the clothes and toiletries and strewing them around like she was loose and at home, an open book. She went back on deck to wait for him, and checked out the dinghy suspended from the stern, happy to see it was a serious dual pontoon boat with a 150-hp Yamaha engine, all that she would need. The navigation gear was extensive and, like everything else on the boat, it looked top dollar and brand new.

She sat back and took an inventory. She could use a shag, but he might not serve there—nice guy, but no apparent get up and go. Still, he was game enough to take a woman he'd just met on a 1,500-mile sail through the middle of the Indian Ocean, so he had some gumption. She'd see about all the rest. He was sufficiently incurious about what she was up to, or at least kept most of his curiosity to himself. Good enough for her. The less he asked, the less likely she'd have to kill him. Although to be honest, she knew she'd probably have to kill him anyway.

She could hear him saying goodbye and thank you to the harbormaster before heading down the short dock. He stepped into the cockpit, turned on the inboard engine.

"Ready?"

"Should I get the lines?"

"Ah! Crew! I knew this was a good idea," he said. She hopped off, untied the ship fore and aft, stepped back on, giving a little push out, and went to coil the rope. He headed toward the mouth of the bay.

"So, you've been on a 'boat' before."

She looked at him straight-faced, instead of saying, *come on, you can do better than that,* or *do I look like a girl that's never been on a boat?* Sometimes it felt like he was goading her into mocking him, but maybe he truly was, as he said, out of practice as a social being. She let the jape die and said, simply, "Yes."

"Right. Stupid. You're sure about the coordinates, right?" He was punching them into his system. "I keep coming up with a 75.5 degree heading to Chagos."

"Yes. You should head 79.4."

"To Egmont Islands?"

"No, one farther south."

"Okay," he said, worried. "We can't get too close to Diego Garcia, right, or the US Navy will shoot us out of the water."

"No worries, we'll stay outside the patrolled waters," she said.

"I don't suppose you want to tell me how you know all this . . ."

No, she didn't, but she said: "*Jajajaja*. I know it's asking a lot, Frank, but trust me. I do know what I'm doing, and we are perfectly safe." A lie, but who is perfectly safe in this world? Nobody. "Besides, the US recently left Afghanistan, right? Maybe they'll just get up and leave Diego Garcia before we get close." He smiled at this, which was a good sign. He wasn't worried, except in some theoretical way, and she could continue to jolly him along.

"Well, then, let's hoist and set the sails and relax." He pulled the sail cover off the mainsail, and she grabbed the one off the mizzen. All the sails were on motorized winches and he raised the mizzen first and set it on a slight reach. She coiled the halyard while he raised the mainsail, and again when he raised the jib, and she was going to pull in the sheets but decided not to look too competent, and instead waited for him do it. Then they were truly underway, and it was a handsome ship, moving graceful and fast in the steady breeze. He futzed with the sails, as a good sailor would, and didn't seem to care what she thought about it. He wasn't—and she was grateful for this—showing off, just working out of habit. He checked all his instruments, clicked on the autopilot, and sat back. He gave her the distinct impression of someone who, like her, had had to learn how to relax, and so she said it.

"You had to force yourself, at some point, to learn how to relax, didn't you—"

He laughed. "Yeah, it didn't come naturally. I managed when I was younger with pounds and pounds of weed and gallons of wine to look relaxed if I got comatose enough. But I can get myself there unaided now, with a little effort!" he pulled the jib sheet in slightly. "And now, because I think this wind will hold steady for a couple of hours, I'm ready to sit and enjoy it. I have, as you say, learned how."

She would have thought that after all those months sailing the oceans, this would get old for him. But for now, for her, years since she had been in open seas, it was exhilarating.

"I love this!" she said.

"Good," he laughed. "Because 'this' is what we have, give or take a change in the weather, for the next five days and nights."

She rearranged her seat cushions, laid back in the shade thrown by the mainsail, and put her hat over her face. Was this really the best way to do what she needed to do, or was Eamon right that it was an incredible waste of time, and that this Frank would become a new problem for her? Maybe, she told Eamon, but in any case, she needed to get to the islands, and a flight was impossible without leaving a strong trace, especially with so few people coming and going. She would need a fast small boat in the Chagos, and getting one there would result in *somebody* becoming a problem, and maybe more than one person. Here was a guy who had everything she needed—a way in and out of the archipelago without anybody else being the wiser, a way to hit the small islands, even scuba gear. She'd gotten Frank to volunteer that back at the resort. Given all the unknowns on this crazy job, a second set of hands might be necessary. And then, the perfect getaway. She could get rid of him in the middle of the ocean and sail to port herself.

She found she had drifted off, under the slow rock of the boat and the soft whoosh of wind, and when she woke, the sun was setting.

"Rested?" he asked.

"Yes, and hungry."

"Good, I made a batch of fish stew." They ate, without talking, except she gave a few compliments—the soup was surprisingly good—and they both, it seemed to her, were realizing they had quite a few hours ahead of them.

"So this is your life, most of the time, except without me aboard," she said.

"Not quite. I don't spend this much time on the open sea," he said. "I like to hug the shore. I like to see life floating by, instead of nothing but water."

"Of course."

"Of course? Maybe. I've met a lot of people, though, who love this, for whom this is the ideal. No land in sight in any direction: this is what they live for, and they put up with coastlines for as long as it takes to load up with supplies and get back out here. But I love cruising in and out of bays and inlets and estuaries and coves. I hope you like fish."

Fish? She looked at him and thought, not for the first time, is he simple?

When she didn't say anything, he did what men do, blabbed about himself, saying he had fallen into a routine—congee for breakfast, leftovers for lunch, and fish however—depending on the catch and what he had in the larder—for dinner. But he would be happy to let her wreak her will in the kitchen anytime she wanted.

"It would be nice," he said, looking off.

"You don't know my cooking."

"No, I'm sorry, I was thinking about what you said earlier. It would be nice if the US left the Chagos."

"We're going to talk politics?" she asked. "Should we defund the international police?"

"Yeah, you're right," he said. "What do I know? Except that I do, in fact, know first-hand how horrible some people can be. There are sociopaths out there."

Si lo dices. “This is still about your friend with the beautiful wife?”

“I never said she was beautiful,” he said, but like he knew how lame it sounded, because of course she was. “But yes, him and his clients. He invested money for Putin, for Mugabe, for the worst of the worst.”

“Nice account,” she said. “Putin.”

“That’s what he said. But enough. *Basta*, right? Long gone. I came into the resort,” he said, “because I woke up one morning and decided I was ready, after my long mopey solo pity party, to see people again. It never occurred to me I’d end picking up a hitchhiker.”

“Had you been passing many of them by?” She was glad to see he knew what a dope he was to feel sorry for himself.

“It may have been that I wasn’t quite close enough to shore to see their thumbs.”

“I suppose talking to one person is an improvement over talking to none,” she said. “But don’t you have friends that you talk to on the phone? Family?”

“Not really,” he said.

“Poor sad boy!” she said. She wanted to know what her exposure was going to be, and if she needed to 86 his phone.

“Yes, I know, you’re right to tease me, I’m very lucky.”

“Why lucky?” she asked. “You built a company and sold it, right? Where’s the luck?”

“Not that simple,” he said. “But that story’s for another time. I’m going to clean up, check the weather and call it a night.”

“Let me clean up,” she said. “Show me where everything is.” It was all going to be fine. She would just need to remember to meditate. She wasn’t used to this much interaction any more than he was.

XIX
Alain

SHE WAS RIGHT, Alain knew as they motored away from the island across calm seas, heading a few degrees north of due west. He had done it. He had gone AWOL, and his status was irrevocably changed. Everything he knew was gone. He would be court-martialed if he ever went home, and so home was gone. The kids were gone. Angela gone. Raissa gone. His family, friends, gone. He was exuberant.

The boat zoomed along at full throttle, and the air rushing by felt great. This American spy should have been very scary, like a cinema villain, but for some reason she wasn't, sitting toward the bow, her thick copper curls thrown about by the wind. He felt like he had joined a cult, following the leader blindly into the unknown, shorn of all previous connection. And he felt the kind of calm they say comes over cult followers—in severing his relation to his former world and relinquishing his will, he felt no anxiety, felt no compunction to figure out what to do next or how to do it, or whether or not he should be doing it. He was enjoined and he was free. This is what most of the guys in training camp felt—they were calm and happy when they submitted, and he couldn't for the life of him understand it at the time. Back then, he felt nothing but constraint, constriction, contraction, and he bucked against it all day and tossed and turned about it all night. He wanted to kill his drill instructor. The other guys, instead, wanted to be the guy's best friend—no, worse, his devoted servant. Now he got it. They had turned over the driver's seat and relaxed into being passengers. They didn't have to worry. They only needed to do what they were told. How had he never discovered this, that obedience wasn't a prison, that it was a kind of freedom? Now, even though he was at the tiller, and he was holding the throttle, *she* was driving them forward, he was a mere appendage, an adjunct, a tool. And for the first time he could remember, he didn't have a care in the world.

She was on her phone, a satellite hookup, typing away.

"Do you have internet on that thing?" he asked her.

"Not like that, no."

"Spy stuff."

She smiled at him. He was the anti-Spartacus. He was ready to row all day.

"So I don't suppose I can . . ."

"No." She smiled again.

He could see that sometimes she was texting with someone, and sometimes she was looking at a GPS map. The GPS seemed pretty useless, of course, since there was nothing on it but their own dot moving against the blue.

Four hours later, the sun getting low in front of them, she motioned him to stop.

"Let's lay low here," she said, "until sunset."

Okay, why not. She threw a drag anchor over the side and he killed the outboard.

"There is no island out here," he said.

"You're sure?"

"Believe me, I studied all the maps. I calculated how long it would take me to swim to every piece of land within a thousand miles."

"Okay, well, we will see. In the meantime, try to get some rest," she said. "We'll need it."

She laid down abeam, her head on one pontoon, feet reaching the other, and used a towel to shade her face. He liked the discipline, her ability to be on point one minute, shut down the next. He followed suit and took up his own post parallel to her, his hat over his face. He hadn't really rested for days, and he fell asleep immediately. He twitched a couple times because he was falling into a dream, and it weirded him out, some assignment he was late for, something he was going to get in trouble for missing, and it startled him half awake, at which point, he thought *this is a dream*, took a deep breath and start slipping into the dream again. When he woke a third or fourth time it was dark, and Skye was typing on her phone. The dreams had had something to do with the women in his life and therefore were angsty and full of dread, but he liked the sight of this woman taking care of business.

"Up and at 'em," she said, sometime later, still dark. He had fallen back asleep. "Let's go ahead on the same heading we were on for another hour or so."

He started the engine as she pulled in the drag anchor, and they were off. Forty minutes or so later, there were lights on the horizon about ten points to starboard, and she motioned him to reorient in that direction, palm flat and vertical, and then to slow down, keeping her palm flat but horizontal, moving it up and down.

"Take it down to about 1,000 RPM."

"I have no idea what that means."

"Slower." She looked straight ahead at the lights. "Slower. Idle speed. Okay, there."

They puttered slower, and it made sense—the engine gave off a low murmur instead of its high whine. When they looked to be two or three kilometers offshore of a small atoll he had seen on the maps, uninhabited, she had him kill the engine. She threw the drag anchor off, stood up and took off her clothes. Under them she had on a bathing suit, and she pulled a wetsuit on top of it. She tossed another to him. He shrugged and stripped down to his shorts and put it on. She shouldered on a set of scuba tanks and he followed suit. Fins, masks, regulators.

"Follow my lead," she said.

"*Javolt*," he said. Some habits of insubordination die hard.

She laughed, maybe to show him insubordination was useless.

She leaned over, opened one of her bags and pulled out two spear guns. She handed him one.

"We going to go after dinner on the way back?"

"No," she said. "But they might come in handy."

He couldn't tell if she meant that to sound ominous, but it did. She showed him how to work the gun. She handed him a wristband with a depth meter and some other functions, an Apple Watch-like screen, a compass, and a couple other buttons, and she walked him through those, too.

"We are going to swim under the surface until we get a thousand meters off. When you see me dive, follow. Then we'll approach at a depth of ten meters until we hit the shelf, and slowly come up along the bottom. When we're close, we'll stop and surface. You'll tread water, always ready to dive, and keep an eye out. I'm going ashore to set a couple instruments and take a look around. Once we leave the boat, no verbal communication. When we're moving, a finger pointed down means go down ten meters but keep moving. A finger pointed up means surface. A fist means wait. A finger down followed by a fist means go down ten meters and wait. Repeat the signals to me."

He did. She checked her tanks, his tanks, and their regulators.

"Remember the red panic button?" she said, pointing at his wrist band. "You are going to float just offshore and keep an eye out. If you see any human being besides me, doing anything, anywhere, on land or on water, press the red button and go as deep as you can. If you hit bottom, head away from shore until you can float down at ten meters. Wait there for me. If I'm not back in twenty minutes, head back to the boat. Your watch has a readout, but I won't have time to type if things go south. We are swimming due west to the island, so watch your compass and swim due east toward the boat.

It shouldn't drift too far in that amount of time. Stay down at ten meters for the first half to evade the sonar system they have set up. I'm not sure we would trigger it anyway—they are really on the lookout for big boats coming in—but better safe than sorry."

She was chipper, not at all worried, and he decided okay, I can stay chipper, too. She sat up on one pontoon, her back to the water, and he got on the other. She put in her regulator, rinsed out her mask and slipped it on, he did the same, and then she let herself fall backwards into the sea. He followed.

She took off at a pretty good clip and strobed her flashlight once every four or five seconds. Helpful, for him following, and smart, since it would look like random phosphorescence if anyone happened to notice. After a while she turned to him, finger pointed down, and they resumed at ten meters. After a while, when she pulsed the flashlight, he could see the bottom, and soon after that, they were at it, pushing off the rocks, coming up higher. He tailed her as she followed the contour and when they were close, she held up her fist. He stopped, but she kept going. He surfaced, pulled up his mask and treaded. He could see lights on the land, but whatever they were lighting was hidden by the foliage along the shore. He saw her, through the gloaming, come out of the water, leave her tanks and flippers behind a big rock, take her speargun and head to the foliage line. He could see, now and then, movement among the scrubby birdlime trees and naupaka shrubs and was pretty sure it was her, and so didn't hit the panic button. Then, nothing.

How does a woman that young get this competent at everything, and stay so sure of herself? he wondered. American. Being American made you invincible. He checked his pressure gauge and had plenty of nitrox. He was having no trouble staying afloat with a slow paddling of his fins, but the tension was growing on him. It had been ten minutes since she landed.

Then he saw her again—he hadn't noticed her emerge, but he saw her pick up her fin and tanks and disappear again into the foliage. Hard to figure why she would do that unless she was afraid someone patrolling would come across her gear. He put his mask back on and settled lower in the water, bobbing up to look now and then.

Her twenty minutes was up. Just then his wristwatch lit, and there was a message—*go to boat.*

Fuck. Now what? He headed back along the bottom the way he had come, swam at ten meters until he thought he was a kilometer away from shore, then surfaced to see if he could spot the boat. Nothing. He swam further, due east, under the surface, popping his face up to look now and then. What had happened to her? She had time to message him—does that mean things were not too dire? Was she coming back to the boat? How long was he supposed to wait? They had not discussed what he should do if she never showed up. Was he supposed to get the hell out of there before daylight? Why else wait until dark to come here?

And if she never showed up, he guessed he would have to go back to his shitty little island, back to that miserable black hole sucking his youth away. His new life evaporated, the old rushing back like a massive mudslide. And what was he supposed to do with the boat, her stuff, the wetsuit, the scuba equipment? Sink it offshore? If they found any of it, would he get charged with stealing it all? With her disappearance? With her murder?

Why did he agree to all this? Was he being the same kind of blockhead as always, doing whatever some woman asked him to do? He was AWOL. He'd missed his first satellite check-in call, his life was ruined again, and he was stuck in the middle of the Indian Ocean with no job, no money, no way to help his family, nowhere to go, no future, no plan, no pot to piss in, no luck but bad luck. He looked back toward the island, which was a low haze of light on the horizon, and he didn't have to look around to know there was nothing else as far as the eye could see. Maybe, just maybe, this was all a ploy to get a free ride to this island, leave him to deal with the boat, knowing that his only choice was, what? To return to his post and forget it? As she had said, nobody would believe any story he told them.

He found the boat, grabbed it, threw his gear in, and climbed on. He was slowly hatching a plan. It had been almost an hour, and there were at most two more hours of darkness. He would motor back to his island, pull the boat up on shore, and leave it and the wetsuit there, and when the Legion came to pick him up, or the Nerd's crew came back looking for her, he would say he had no idea why the boat had been left there. She and someone else had come in two boats soon after the Nerd left, probably as part of the scientific expedition. He had no interest in such things, so didn't ask anything about it. After they'd been there a while, he had gone to sleep in his tent. They must have left when he was sleeping. He had no idea why or where. When he got up in the morning, one of the two boats was gone, the other still on his beachhead. He had no idea why or where they went. He liked it. It was a solid story. He pulled off his wetsuit, checked his gas level for the outboard, and switched it on.

Right then a flashlight shone in his face, scaring the shit out of him. It went out, and he could see the woman was approaching the boat. She grabbed the side, slipped out of her tanks and handed them up, peeled off her fins and mask and threw them on board, and lifted herself up.

"Leaving so soon?" she asked.

XX
Frank

THE PREVAILING WINDS were strong and steady, and he only hopped up once during the night to trim the sails. He had developed an internal alarm over the years, and when the sails began to luff he could feel it. He would snap to and fix them, pretty much in his sleep, and fall back into his pillow a minute later. On his way back he noticed a light on in her room and wondered if she slept with it on or was up at 3:00 a.m. He didn't wonder long, though, because he was asleep in seconds.

He barely needed to touch things in the morning, everything steady as could be, and he went into the galley to put on coffee. He assumed she wanted coffee, but figured it wouldn't go to waste anyway, so filled a French press. He put together pancake batter and fired up the griddle, put a saucepan of milk on the stove and whisked it. He looked up to see her watching him.

"You'll make someone a very good little wife one of these days, *una buena ama de casa*."

He laughed. He had been trying to remember who she reminded him of, and it was a drama critic he had dated briefly, years ago. He had moved to California to be with her before it quickly fell apart, and so she had, in effect, changed his entire trajectory, despite how brief their relationship was. He often wondered what life would have been like if he had been ready for such a formidable partner—he wasn't—wondered if her worldliness and sarcasm would have toughened him up and made him into a better, less muddle-headed person. Maybe. Maybe not.

"Pancakes?" he asked.

"Sure. I was at Buddy Guy's club in Chicago once, and when he was introducing a song he saw me, and said, into the microphone, 'Well look at you, sugah! I want to bring you home and make you pancakes!' Do you think this is what he meant?"

He laughed, and said, "That is part of what he meant! Coffee?" He poured her a cup and pointed: "Milk in the fridge, sugar here."

He poured out some batter, and they small-talked a while. He felt a slight luff, went up and corrected the sails, and they sat with their coffee while the pancakes cooked, everything a little tense since they were still strangers.

"You're from Spain," he said.

"Most Americans assume Mexico, but yes, Spain."

"Did you want to get any more specific than that?"

She took longer than expected answering, and he again wondered what he had gotten himself into. He flipped the pancakes.

"*Jajajajaja*," she said. "You are not stupid, yes? So you know that my life is a mound of secrets. Who I am is a secret, or a lie. Where I live is a secret, or a lie. My profession is a secret, or a lie. Would you like me to tell you some lies?"

"Well, I suppose. We have several more days outbound, so we might as well tell each other lies. Beats silence." He plated a couple of pancakes, handed them to her, and passed a bottle of maple syrup.

"I would have thought you liked silence, given your monk's life all these years." She buttered the cakes, poured syrup on them, and dug in.

She had a very healthy appetite, Frank noticed. "Yes, silence when I'm alone is quite nice. Silence with another person is oppressive."

"Okay, touché. So here, as you Americans say, is the deal." She finished off her cakes and took a swig of coffee. She looked squarely at him. "I am an assassin. Yes, I kill people for a price. I am, in theory, open for business wherever it comes from, but in practice I have only one client. I have never met the client, but I know he or she exists, or they exist, and I work with someone close to them, take orders from that guy, who I have met once or twice, and he, or someone who works for him, does a lot of my logistics—plane tickets, apartments, hotels, et cetera. I would say I have a kind of love-hate relationship with him, but really he is just a dick who makes my life possible."

Okay, Frank thought, that is very specific and probably all true. "Okay," he said, trying to keep it light. "Fair enough. I can see why you might not want to volunteer that on first meeting someone, I get it. More pancakes?" She shook her head *no* and he went on. "I, I may as well say, am not an assassin," he said. "But in my work as a marionettist, I do kill quite a few people."

"A marionettist. Is that what you call it?"

"Yes, or marionette-puppeteer. I like to put on shows about history, primarily Burmese history, and that requires quite a few battle scenes."

"So you make them shoot each other? Do you do the sound effects?"

"Not shoot. Much of this is longer ago than that. They use swords, and lances, that kind of thing. On horseback, which makes it much more difficult."

"And whole armies . . ."

"Yes, I am quite good."

"This is a very odd fantasy profession. Assassin? Everyone wants to be an assassin. But Burmese marionettist? Strange choice."

"It was the most exotic profession I could think of. I don't really want to do it, but I have a friend in Bagan—do you know Bagan, the ancient temple city in Myanmar? I spent time there while the *God Sees* was being refinished and refitted in Rangoon, and I sat out the worst of the cyclone season there. I stayed pretty much to myself, in a small upscale hotel, but over the years I came to know a few people, including a young woman who put on a marionette show in the evenings in the hotel's garden. Her name was Kyine, and she was a genius at this, and yes, it is a very peculiar art. She had battle scenes with warriors on horseback and yes, sound effects, and great lighting effects, too. But the extraordinary thing was the way she could make her wooden characters go through the most intense emotions, make the horses gallop elegantly, a flurry of string-pulling at superhuman speed. She was only in her twenties, but she had learned her craft from her mother and grandmother, as her father had learned to play his instruments from his own father—oh, yes, her father did the music for the show, and most of the sound effects. I liked to grab a beer and watch their show—their only steady customer, since everyone else came to see the show once and never again, just appreciating the novelty of it. And of course tourists don't know the history, and so they can't follow the story." He was babbling, he knew, but she had just told him she was an assassin.

"Is this how you learned most of your history, from puppet shows?"

"Yes, I know, it all sound preposterous, but I can't tell you how sublime it is. Did you ever see the movie *Being John Malkovich*? No? That is great at showing how amazing marionettes can be, and Cameron Diaz is—"

"Wait, it is a movie with Cameron Diaz as a marionettist?"

"No, John, what's his name, Cusack. You really have to see it. Or go to Bagan, and see Kyine. I'm sorry, I'm talking too much!"

He had almost said *Come with me to Bagan,* which would have been so wrong—problematic in so many ways—that it had tripped him up. Why *had* he almost said it?

"No, go on," she said. "Kyine is your girlfriend in Bagan?"

"No, nothing like that." He looked up at her and, as usual, she was studying him.

"And you," he asked, because if she was going to go there, he was too. "Boyfriend?"

"No. I live in Paris now, you know, the city of love. But no love for me. French men I don't like."

"No?"

"Yes," she said. "They are good for the sex. But they are big babies. Their *mamans*, their mothers, they love them too much."

Frank didn't know where to go with that, so he let it be.

"Marionettist," she said. "So you like pulling strings? You like being the controller? Hm. Don't they call it manipulation, too, what a marionettist does?"

"Maybe, but I don't think that I—wait a minute, what? How can I be the bad guy? You're an assassin!"

She looked at him so strangely then, after his light comment, that he thought, holy fuck. She is an honest to god assassin.

XXI
Skye

"**WHAT DO YOU** mean, leaving so soon! You told me a half hour," Alain said to her. "I waited more than a half hour in the water, got your message, and I've been sitting here for an hour. I figured I had to be back home by daybreak if everything had turned into a mess."

"Yes, my bad, and I guess I was being cocky. I never told you what to do if I never came back—it never occurred to me that I wouldn't be back." She watched him receive this, and sure enough, admitting she was wrong made him feel better. "But home? Think about it. That island is no longer home, never will be again. We're heading due south." She pointed. "Rev 'er up!"

"Due south," he said. He sparked the Yamaha and pointed south. "Idle speed?"

"No, crank it."

He did, got it planing, then corrected with the compass. She could see he was still worried. It had been a mistake not to give him orders for what to do if she didn't make it. A tactical error, in that it had eroded his trust. She was going to have to do some work.

She looked at her wrist and said, "Okay, now, due east. We have about four hours. Do you want me to get us some grub, or do you want me to steer?"

"I'm good," he said, looking straight ahead. Yup, she had work to do.

But then, how could she explain it all? She had been having more than a misgiving or two about what she was up to. This was normal, she assured herself, an emotion more than an analysis, a temporary feeling that would pass, and change, and be replaced by something new. She could wait out any moment of doubt, self-doubt, mission-doubt, and find herself on the other side of it, self-possessed once again and confident. A college course, a psych course on emotion, taught her this. They read Sartre's little book about emotion. "Why does an infant cry?" the professor asked. Because it wants something. Is it thinking that it wants something? No, it is only aware that it is crying, that it is unhappy, yes, perhaps, but even more aware of being immersed in the emotion of the moment, feeling the tears, the intensity of its own breathing, the hormones touching each other off all over, the bodily feelings of that emotion rather than the thought-content of the emotion. It has very likely forgotten that it is crying because its diaper rash is bothering it. It is now crying because it is crying. If help comes, and its diaper is changed, it will eventually stop crying, maybe not immediately, but as soon as its attention is attracted to something new. Does it stop crying because it is being rescued from its distress? No, and this is why it continues to cry while its diaper is being changed, continues crying, often, even after the change. It is not until it attends to something new, something that is accompanied by a new feeling, that it stops. And sometimes, of course, the baby can be distracted, given a new object of attention—even as rudimentary as a rattle—and forget its distress. Its distress is replaced by a new set of sensations, and thus new feelings, and the crying is forgotten along with the diaper rash.

The clincher for Skye was when the professor said to think about the way nurses give injections—they pinch you on the other arm, or pull on your earlobe, and distract you from the jab, give you something else to think about, refocus your attention away from the puncture. In the same way, we can always replace one emotion with another. If you are worried, and I slip on a banana peel in front of you, he said, you laugh. For at least a moment, your clenched jaw and furrowed brow are replaced by laughter. People tickle babies for the same reason. It is emotion-replacement therapy.

In the time it took to remember that professor's lecture, her self-doubt evaporated. She knew the only thing to do was take Alain part way into her confidence, relieve his worry by making him feel like a colleague rather than a beleaguered assistant. She had pulled a salami and loaf of bread from her supplies, cut them in half, and handed him one of each.

"About eighty clicks east," she said, "we will go introduce you to the company."

"The company?"

"Yes. I work for a military contractor, and we have interests in the area. That is why I am here. Why we are here. The work on the island we just visited is being done by one of our competitors, and I was sent to check on it, see what they were up to."

"And what were they up to?"

"I wish I could say."

He looked at her askew.

She laughed. "No, really, I wish I could say. I can describe what I saw, but I'm not sure what it means."

As she guessed, saying that she didn't know made him happier. He was a man, after all. A woman who is lost, who can't figure something out, is always more comfortable for them than one who can figure it out and knows where she is. And Alain carried a wounded vanity—why, she didn't know, and didn't need to know—but whatever it was, it made him even more susceptible to stratagems like that. She didn't like that she was the white person manipulating a person of color, a guy dragooned by poverty into the colonial army, no less—but she needed to think about the mission first. Always the mission first.

"I'll know more after I download to the rest of the team."

"The team?"

"Yes, you'll meet them as soon as we land. And they'll meet you. You are now part of the team."

Alain had been a rugby star, she had read in the file, had vaulted onto the Madagascar national team from high school, and had been headed to the Olympics when an injury ended his glory days. He had adjusted pretty well to life out of the limelight, marrying his high school sweetheart and having a couple of kids, working as a tourist guide, which gave him more English than most, and it was all going well for him until he got his kid's kindergarten teacher pregnant. He did what her psych professor suggested and traded his feelings of guilt and shame in for feelings of daring and adventure with the French Foreign Legion. That was a year ago, even less. She guessed his sense of no longer being on any team at all—he was off the rugby team, off the parents-of-school-kids team, off the civilian team, and he made it clear he didn't feel part of the Legion team. So assuring him he was on her team was the smart move to make.

But it wasn't enough, she saw right away. He wouldn't look directly at her, and had wariness written all over his face.

"You hate the French, right?"

"Christ, how do you know that kind of shit?"

"It's in your Foreign Legion file, which, of course, we managed to hack."

"It's in my file?"

"Do you think that when you scream 'Fuck you, you fucking French cow!' at your drill sergeant that it doesn't go in your file? You were kind of famous in your class for hating the French. I'm sorry to tell you that a couple of your fellow recruits reported you, too."

"Yeah, I can guess who. There are always some ass-kissers around, right? The Cameroonian, for one."

"Right, for one. Anyway, it's why we liked you for this job."

This did not compute for him right away, in part because he was still stuck on getting reported.

"It wasn't Motumbo or Abdul, was it?"

"I don't remember the details."

"Fuck. I would hate it if they ratted on me. The rest of them, fuck the fuckers."

"Your English is really good."

"I watch a lot of TV."

"I can tell. Anyway, the company I'm investigating—the people on that island?—they are French."

He nodded. Okay.

"Well, a French–Indonesian company, mostly, international, but headquarters in Jakarta and Paris."

"Okay, I get it, you read my file, and yes, I will admit I like the idea of fucking with them more, now, knowing they are French, than I might otherwise. An easy screw to turn."

"Good," she said. "Good."

"But how, exactly, are we going to quote-unquote fuck with them?"

"We'll work that out with the rest of the team."

And sure enough, she watched him settle down to the idea that he was part of a team.

"The rest of the team," he said, trying it on.

It was like some poor little Dickens orphan being taken in by a real family. He was still wary, but relieved. People are so easy, she thought. And me? I am so good at what I do. So good. And I am, in my own small way, righting the wrongs of the colonial era. And *that*—the feeling she got when she thought that—that was the warm and fuzzy right there.

XXII
Mónica

SHE NOTICED SOMETHING very strange in her interactions with Frank. The night before, after he had checked the ship's course and its sails, and everything was squared away, he said goodnight and went up to his room in the front. She looked around, and felt something wasn't right. She was, what? Upset? Unhappy that he had left her? Or something. She couldn't quite put her finger on it. Then she realized that what she was feeling was loneliness. What? He left to go to sleep, and she felt lonely! *Qué bicho raro,* she thought, what a strange bug I am. This guy? Why this guy?

Maybe she was just horny, she tried telling herself, but she knew that wasn't it. Maybe it was because she was considering getting out of the life, solving the final problem, thinking about going normie, trying to be a regular person. He was such a regular guy, after all. It was annoying. It was stupid.

The last time she remembered feeling lonely was in prison, when she was surrounded by women she hated, down to the very last one. Murderers always have a special status in prison, and were given a certain respect—especially compared to the drug mules and cartel flunkies that made up most of the women, or to the few embezzlers, for instance. And it mattered how the murder happened. One woman had poisoned a John because he hadn't paid her what he owed, and she was respected, but not as much as any of the women who had stabbed husbands who beat them.

And the women whose stabbed husbands died got more respect than the ones whose husbands lived. And for some reason, killing an abusive stepfather, like she had, counted more than killing an abusive husband. Okay, she'd take it. And having cut off his dick and balls and stuck them in his mouth as he bled out—that made her a legend, turned her into royalty. The fact that she was only seventeen, that she was a prodigy, added to her celebrity. She still had to defend herself and watch her back and all that, but so did everyone. Otherwise, she reigned supreme.

That status didn't ease the loneliness—in fact, it made it worse. She thought the people who respected her for her act of pure rage were idiots. She knew that the women who got busted ferrying drugs or weapons for drug lords all had their own problems, but still, *a lo hecho, pecho*—they made the bed, sleep in it. Did the crime, do the time. Done is done, spilt milk, *pah!* And this, along with the exalted rank they had bestowed on her, made her despise them all. She watched them all hooking up—prison made everyone lesbian except her—and thought *how pathetic. Who would want any of them? Yuck.*

Jajajajaja, she said to herself. *Don't blame the victims!* The victims were so much of the time their own worst enemies—everyone knew that—but the victims were victims, and she was the queen of the victims. She understood all this at that young age, because—*¡cómo no!*—she wasn't her age. And in prison she also came to a fateful conclusion: she was going to have to become, through years of attention, dedication, and peerless execution, exactly the exalted creature they had mistaken her for. She would conquer the alienation created by her ersatz coronation when she claimed the crown for real. She didn't yet know how she would do it, but she knew she would. That is why she was so ready for Eamon when he showed up. When he said, *we see great things for you, for your future,* she could say, *¡claro! So do I, maybe better than you do.*

All this was exactly why she found her current conundrum so

galling. She'd been in lonely land and come out of it fine, only to end up here? Droopy in the middle of the ocean.

She and Eamon texted, using their encryption programs, which helped keep *him,* at least, from being too annoying. She always hated it when he answered a serious question or challenge without missing a beat, like he knew all the answers before the questions were invented. Slowing him down made him more bearable. He knew more about what he called the problem—the job was always *the problem,* the problem that existed in the *situation*—than he had before, and he was as persistent as ever at getting her to spill the beans on how she was getting to the destination, the *destination* being the place where the *situation* would be defused and the *problem* solved. He launched in, from his first text, with his old chestnuts, but she was not in a mood to humor him this time. He said what he always said, that if she didn't tell him everything, he couldn't protect her. That made her laugh. She texted:

> *Well, have you been here? Have you ever been in the middle of this bloody ocean? Because nobody and nothing can protect you here. There is no cover, no way to run, nowhere to hide. If someone wants to get rid of me, all they need to do is put a hole in the yacht and put a hole in its boat. They could send a drone from Diego Garcia and get it done in under an hour.*

She loved watching him, in her mind's eye, wait for this torrent of words to end and get de-encrypted.

So, you're on a yacht, he texted back.

Pyrrhic victory.

Did you think I swam here? she replied.

Why are you being like this? he asked.

This?

You know I don't use the word "cunt" lightly, he wrote.

I don't know that you use it all. I'm disappointed you do.

Can we get back to work?

I'm at work. What are you doing?

And they went on like that. A complete waste of a million-dollar encryption program. After a while, he texted:

You know that I love you.

Too late, I've found someone else.

Exactly what I was wondering.

Acch, she thought. *¡Hijo de puta!* How could he know? But this time, she wouldn't fall for it. Of course, he had no idea.

Yes, I found a puppy. She's adorable. But she's afraid of the helicopter noise.

She was elated that it took him longer than usual to respond to that. Ye olde double double. He taught her that.

The old double double, he texted.

Jajajajajajaja. Why not SEND me some fucking information instead of trying to get it out of me?

He was silent for a while. Good. She pulled the SIM card and threw both it and the phone overboard.

XXIII
Alain

THIS SKYE CHICK was hard to figure out. She was his best friend, now, because who else? And she was offering him a new life. But only if he became a zombie doing exactly what she wanted. When he had straight-up asked her why he couldn't just go back to his island, serve out his time, and go home, she had said "Look, you are already in our reports, and you saw we hacked the Legion? Don't you think the Legion can hack us? You want to go home and wait for the knock on the door hauling you in for a court-martial? Besides, *we* don't want you getting hauled in for a court martial, and not out of the goodness of our hearts—think about that."

She let it sink in as they motored east, toward Diego Garcia. She had been perfectly clear: the option to pick up his former life was dead and gone, or else he was dead and gone. He'd prefer the former. But it was a shaky foundation to build a relationship on, especially given his anti-colonialist rage. She was playing with fire. Did she know that?

"Look," he said. "I'm on board with the *team* and everything, you've got to let me do something besides be *Driving Miss Daisy.* Don't keep me three-fifths."

"Fair enough," she said. "This only works if you don't feel exploited, I get that. I understand your anger—"

"I'm not sure you do."

"I'm not saying I have lived in your shoes, experienced your position, felt your pain, or been tied in your knots. I'm saying I recognize the validity of your grievance. You are being offered a place on this team *because* you have that rage, not despite it."

"Okay." He did, in fact, like that.

"We want you to focus that rage outside our coalition, not inside. The minute you focus your rage inward, toward me or the team, is the minute our deal is null and void. But in the meantime, I get it, you don't want to feel like you're being treated like a servant—nobody does—but right now there are two jobs to be done. One, coordinating with base, and two, getting there. What would you have me do differently?"

"I want to be in on the action."

"Yup. Too much TV. But, like I say, I get it. You want to feel useful. And you need to know what we're doing, okay."

The rival company, she explained, was building a man-made island on that reef, because it wasn't a real island, but a submerged reef known as the Centurion Bank. Okay, well, he thought, that explained that. He knew there was no island there. They were constructing an enormous energy facility, she said, converting ocean currents into electricity, which would supply power, through underwater cables, to Diego Garcia, the Maldives, the Seychelles, and beyond. *But,* she explained, that was just a cover for what it was really all about. The energy project was real, but they were only building it to provide cover for what would end up being the world's largest private military base.

"Darkwater? Wagner?" he asked.

"What about them?"

"That's who is building it?"

"No, a new competitor. GreenCon. Darkwater doesn't need it. They're set up on Diego Garcia already. Wagner hasn't made its move here yet. These are some new assholes."

The new assholes, GreenCon, had not just their green energy corporation, she explained, but a mad, mad investment portfolio, and were deep enough in the security clearance world that they had received permission from the UK, US, and Mauritius to go ahead with their base. Mauritius did it for a check—a lease deal—but the UK and US were both feeling a need to offload as much military budget as possible, since both governments were hostage to the budget hawks on the right and the antiwar activists on the left. Disguising military investment as green energy investment was the ultimate dodge for the left, and a tiny part of the military savings would pay for it, making the deficit scolds happy.

Or so she said, and it hung together pretty well, as far as it went. Who she was working for was still a mystery, and what she hoped to accomplish, too. He pushed her on that. She gave him more claptrap about the team—he was part of the team and would get more fully "integrated" (really? "integrated"?) as they went along.

"Okay," he said, in a way he had taken to lately, freighted with hesitance and doubt, but sanguine. She smiled at him to say that she got that. He was being played, for sure, but for the moment he was down with that.

What he needed was to have things taken care of in Tana, and she promised that they were working on having him declared dead, which meant death benefits for his wife, and his own paycheck would be to his new identity. In the meantime they had already sent his wife and Raissa messages from a certain Lieutenant Macroone, his supposed superior. The lieutenant was a French aristocrat with a monied family, and he had been so fond of Alain that he had endowed an annuity for each of them (the fake lieutenant asked Raissa and Angela to be careful not to mention this to anyone, including each other, as it would create tax and other problems for the Frenchman and his family, and might imperil the legacy). They would each be receiving a thousand euros a month, which was more than Alain was sending, more than he was making before he left, with an additional amount deposited in an educational account for each of the children.

He was so relieved when she told him this that he could have wept. He felt himself the hero of a romantic tale, going into hiding like a heroic spy, a secret emissary for god and country, so dedicated that he was willing to leave his home and wife and children (and mistress) behind, sacrificing his own happiness for the greater good, tossed forever on the lonely seas of duty. He looked up from this little reverie to see Skye looking at him with a wry smile on her face. He smiled back, his eyes glistening. He was ready for his mission, even if it was only, for now, driving Miss Skye.

Eight hours later, they approached Diego Garcia. Two US Navy PT boats met them and escorted them in. They pulled up to a dock where they were relieved of their boat and belongings and taken in for search and review. They were put through body scanners and asked to follow a young soldier, a US Marine, who took them down to a Jeep, driven by a second soldier. A double airstrip took up much of the available land, and the rest was occupied by radar domes and a collection of buildings, all the same Cold War vintage, all painted the same military gray or beige. The Jeep took them out of the central base, onto a long road with ocean on one side, the lagoon on the other. Most of Diego Garcia, like many atolls, was the rim of a volcano, and very thin, often not much wider than the road. They drove a mile or so until they came to a wider bit of land that been built up more recently, the buildings the same military gray, but shinier and more impressive. Marines and sailors of different ranks went about their business, which consisted entirely of walking from building to building. The Jeep stopped in front of large doors. Skye got out and he followed her. She entered a code at the door, and it popped open.

Inside looked more like a corporate office than a military installation, and nobody was wearing a uniform. A large set of raised chrome letters against the wall read *DARKWATER*, and so one major mystery was solved—at least now he knew who he worked for. A woman got up from an overlarge wooden reception desk and asked them to follow.

She turned to Skye as they walked and said that "they" were expecting them. He didn't know how that was possible unless Skye had managed to message them. He didn't remember her texting for the last hours. Maybe they were tracking her.

The receptionist opened a door—again, wooden, expensive-looking, like in the offices of fancy law firms and investment banks he'd seen on TV, and the conference room behind it was the same. Six men sat around the table, and all stayed put except one, who got up and welcomed them.

"Well done, S.T., and you must be Alain." He put out his hand and Alain shook it. He tried to remember from the TV shows what he was supposed to do. "Come, sit," the man said, motioning to a couple chairs. He took one and Skye the other. "You can call me 'Chief.'"

"Alain," Skye said. "This is HQ for us, headquarters, and this is Chief's control staff. They'll introduce themselves, and then they'll ask you a few questions. Nothing too serious, just a way for us all to get to know each other."

They all took turns introducing themselves, and he immediately forgot the names and initials—a couple went by initials—as soon as he heard them. One was in charge of IT, one was liaison to this, one liaison to that. None of what they said made his own role much clearer. Then they asked him questions. Halfway through it, he realized that they knew the answers to all of them—where was he born, when he joined the Legion, what his last assignment was—and so what exactly were they looking for? To catch him in a lie? Maybe. To see if he took some initiative? Maybe.

"Okay," he said. "You have my file, right? That's what Sk—S.T. told me. So why are you asking me these questions? Is it a test?"

"Well, yes and no," the Chief said. "We're testing you, sure. We're testing the file, too. But, good, we'll move on to more interesting questions. If you had to hire two people to help you complete a project, who would they be."

"I don't know. What project?"

"A top secret, lethal project."

"Lethal?" He thought about this briefly. "For me, or for the people I hire?"

They laughed. "No, for your target or targets."

"Well, to be honest, I was hoping you were going to give me a few spy school classes, get me ready to answer a question like that."

"Is that why you're here? For spy school?" asked the guy whose name was T. something.

"You tell me. I'm kind of hoping, in fact, that when you all are done, it'll be my turn to ask the questions." He was trying not to sound defensive and sullen, but it kept getting harder.

The other guy with initials instead of a name leaned forward. "Do you hate the French?" he asked "Or do you hate all white people?"

He thought for a minute.

"For most of my life it was the same thing. The only white people in my life were French, except on TV. It doesn't make sense to hate people on TV."

"What about us?" the Chief asked. "We're white."

"Look, racism is racism. If you walked around the lake at midnight in Tana, you would be mugged. They wouldn't care if you were French or not. It would be enough you were white."

"And you?"

He laughed. "Yes, I wouldn't care whether you were French or other white if I was going to mug you. But I am not a mugger. I worked as a guide for tourists, and tourists are mostly white or Asian. Both are assholes most of the time. Do I think they are assholes because I am racist, or because they are, in fact, assholes? Probably both."

He found, as he was talking, a certain calm. Nobody had ever asked him this kind of question, and these people—they were at the neoimperialist, capitalist, heart of the whole thing, protected by the humongous military power of the US. He might as well tell them. Sometimes, working with the tourists, when they treated him like their servant, he would start to get furious, but then step back and say, hey, they are just people, and they don't realize, like the Bible says, what they do. He often wondered how they would react if he turned to them and said, *look, I am not your fucking dog, I am not your fucking slave, you pigs, you are no better than me!* They would blink, uncomprehending, hurt—they think they are being so nice, because most of them are very polite and faux-friendly part of the time at least, even half the time, most of them. But these Darkwater guys: they asked the question straight, and they were not about to feel hurt or pissy. They weren't going to feel betrayed, or alarmed. They asked, they wanted to know, so okay, he would tell them. And he felt tranquil, unruffled.

"Yes, I hate white people. All of them, all of you. In theory. But not in practice."

Without missing a beat, T. asked, "What kind of man leaves his wife and child behind?"

His first thought—well, his second, his first response was a wave of shame—but on its heels he thought *what kind of man asks a question like that.* By some kind of miracle, he wasn't feeling the same kind of kneejerk, antiauthoritarian rage he usually felt. Maybe it was because he had thrown his life away for a second time and he felt free, or maybe because he felt so out of his depth that he was untethered to his former self, or maybe, in fact, it was because he felt not out of his depth at all. Maybe he was having the examination he had always been waiting to take. Maybe he was so ready for this that he had earned the right to be calm.

"A man whose options have run out," he said. "Or a man who needs to reshuffle his options. And you all: are your wives and kids here? Or did you leave them behind?"

They laughed at this. It was as if he had made a good joke about the Australian rugby team in a bar, and his mates were slapping him on the back. How very, very strange, he thought.

"So, what is the point of all this?" he asked. "Group therapy?"

They laughed again.

"In a sense," Skye said. "Yes."

None of them disagreed with her.

XXIV
Frank

FRANK WOKE, HIS face and shirt damp with sweat. He was above deck, in his hammock, but the air was still as a corpse, not a wisp of wind, and even at 9:00 a.m., the low sun was hot. The wind had died in the early hours of the night, and that had sent him above deck.

He dove into the sea to cool off, wondering how in the world he had slept so late, and as he climbed back in, he saw his skiff was gone. It hung from two davits off the stern, easy to lower to the water with an electric winch, but tied in securely so it wouldn't jump around in rough seas, and there hadn't been any rough seas for months. He had checked on it when he picked up the ship in Antsiranana, and it was secure. He dried off and went below deck. He checked her room to see for sure what he already knew, that she was gone, too.

He remembered that he'd gotten up around 2:00 a.m., when the wind had died down, turned the engine on, and checked the autopilot, seeing that they would be arriving at her coordinates soon after sunrise. He had felt dead, dead tired, and wondered how much wine he had had, having trouble focusing and climbing into his hammock, which he did instead of going back to his room, since he knew it would get warm without any breeze. That was the last he remembered. Strange. When she killed the engines, he should have woken up—his body was trained to react to the ship.

And if she had started the outboard, he would have jumped up, too. *If* she started it—why did he qualify it? Of course she started up the outboard. She was gone.

He looked at his charts and saw that they were indeed at her coordinates, with only the slightest drift easterly. She had been watching and killed the engines when they arrived. They were sixty miles or so west of Diego Garcia. If she was going there, why did she leave from this far out? Was she sneaking in? Was that even possible? If she had clearance, there was no reason to leave the ship here. He was confused.

He dove in again, and floated. A tiny breeze had picked up, which helped with the heat, but not enough. Who *was* this woman? Interpol? CIA? Or Russian? KGB, FSB, was it, or SVR, or some new acronym? Or was she working for a Russian or Saudi oligarch? Or a drug kingpin? And what was she doing here, in the middle of the Indian Ocean? If she was, in fact, an assassin, who could she kill here? There is a part of the Arabian Peninsula called the Empty Quarter—this was emptier.

He pulled himself back on the ship, made a cup of coffee, and sat under his shade. It was a hot sun. He noticed he was feeling like dozing off again, which never happened, not in the morning, not right after coffee. It began to dawn on him—she had drugged him. That's why he was drowsy, that's why he was so dead tired in the middle of the night, why he wasn't awakened by any of the things that normally would sit him up.

He looked at his charts again, and saw, some fifteen clicks north, a tiny island in disputed waters. It was the size of a football field, high enough to make it on the map, but doomed to disappear with another few years of polar melt. It was the only place she could have gone, but what could she possibly want there?

Then he must have dozed off, the first daytime nap in his adult life, further proof that she had slipped him a mickey, and was awakened by the sound of the outboard motor approaching. He wasn't sure what to expect, but to see her radiantly waving as she approached was not it.

She expertly turned the boat and threw him a line. He lowered the falls, and she attached them fore and aft and climbed aboard. He ran the hoist pulling the boat out of the water to hang from the davits, lashed it down, and did all of this without looking at her.

When he did, she was watching him with her smile, as usual. He didn't find it charming for a change, but irksome.

"Why?" he asked.

"I needed to do a little reconnaissance. I didn't want to wake you."

"And so you drugged me."

She just looked at him, with the same small smile.

"I think," he said, "our revels now should end."

"Revels?"

"Whatever. Where do you want me to drop you?"

She didn't say anything, just walked on board and went to her room.

Not exactly what he wanted, but he had no idea what he wanted. The nearest inhabited places, besides Diego Garcia—which was not an option since you needed security clearance to approach—were the Maldives, five hundred miles to the north, or the Seychelles or Mauritius, both over a thousand miles away. And so the Maldives it was. He set his instruments to Malé, the capital, turned on the engine and hoisted the sails. There was scarcely enough wind to help, but enough.

This *wasn't* what he wanted—it was anticlimactic in every way, and so deeply unsatisfying an ending to this story that he wondered what the hell he was doing. He tried to remember where he was and what his plans had been when their paths crossed, and it seemed a lifetime ago, even though it was a matter of days. He had been watching himself change before they met, watching himself decide that it was time to become a social being again. Watching himself wake up from his bad dream. Maybe, it occurred to him, maybe the problem was simple. Maybe he had forgotten how to do it, how to be with people. Forgotten what it meant to let other people have some control over his life.

But of course that wasn't the problem! She slipped him a roofie! This is not about his failure to relate, about him afraid to relinquish control, but about her being a whacko (maybe) assassin (maybe) who had no compunction about knocking someone out and stealing their boat! She brought it back, but still. Why was he making excuses for her? He had been thinking, as they were on that long reach for the last few days, that even if he was being the same kind of imbecile he had been in his previous life, ready to be at the beck and call of any woman who gave him a modicum of attention, this was different. When he moved in with Tracy, he was sexually intoxicated, and when he moved to California to be near a woman who didn't want him, or when he basically moved to Jakarta for ditto, he was being, as The Assassin had put it, a "moony little boy," and he deserved everything that happened to him. This time, though, he was not being stupid, he was not pulling the wool over his own eyes, he was not even trying to get together with her, not trying to hook up, not trying to fall in love, not even close.

He knew that empirically it might look otherwise. It wasn't normal to sail someone you don't know a thousand miles, to navigate your way to an uninhabited atoll in the middle of the ocean for no other reason than that a beautiful woman asked you to do it the night you met. He knew it looked bad. He knew the fact that he added the *beautiful* and *the night they met* to that description was a bit of a tell. And he knew that, if the past was any guide, he was not to be trusted in these matters. He knew less than he should at this point in his life. It was cold comfort, but at least he knew that, knew he didn't know.

"I realize I owe you an explanation," she said.

He jerked his head around, surprised to see her. "I didn't hear you come up," he said. A basic assassin skill, he thought, coming up behind someone without making a sound. She was standing there with a bottle of white wine and two glasses. She could even pull out a cork without making a sound.

"Come, let's have a heart-to-heart," she said.

"You have, as they say, a lot of explaining to do, so go ahead. Let me see you do heart-to-heart."

"*Jajajajajaja.*" It was her version of *yeah, whatever.* "Look, I'm working. I was sent here by the man who hired me—"

"So, this is a job, good, I knew that. You work for who?"

"You wouldn't know them," she said, pouring out two glasses of wine. "I could tell you a name and it would mean nothing. And the man who hired me works for someone else—my employer is just the fixer. I could tell you who I think Mr. Big is, the man behind it all, but again, you wouldn't know him, the name would mean nothing, and it's really just a guess on my part, I don't really know."

"So not the CIA, not the KGB."

"The KGB doesn't exist anymore, but no." She handed him one of the glasses of wine, but he waved it off.

"I'm not ready to be roofied again, sorry." It sounded cranky, maybe, but he didn't care. "And I usually don't drink wine before breakfast."

He waited. She waited. She was used to people getting nervous and talking, but he wouldn't give her the satisfaction. They sat. She sipped her wine. He poured his over the side and put the empty glass down. She pushed hers toward him, poured a new one for herself in his glass. He didn't touch it. She gave up and resumed.

"My employer had information that a certain person was in this area, a person who was bent on disrupting—"

"Wait. The name. Try me."

"Eamon."

"Ay-mon."

"E-A-M-O-N."

"That's a first name or a last name?"

"Do you know anyone by either?"

He thought for a moment. "No."

"First name. Eamon's employer, this unidentified personage who is in effect also my employer, wanted this certain person neutralized, and knew the person was in this area, very recently."

"Neutralized."

"Yes. I didn't mean to say that, but yes."

"So, you *are* an assassin."

She looked at him, again with that small smile. "Yes," she said. "I told you that. But really, I am a fixer. Sometimes assassination is the only way to fix things."

"So you are a fixer for the fixer."

"Exactly!" she said brightly.

"So why did you drug me and take my boat?"

"Right, I can see how that might bug you."

"Might bug me."

"Isn't that what you say? Anyway, I did it because I thought you'd still be asleep when I got back and not be any the wiser."

He liked the honesty but didn't see any reason to mention that.

"If it turned out that the situation was what we thought it was, and assassination was the only fix, then to have you, in the extremely unlikely event that you were questioned by the police, be able to say that I was on the boat with you since we left Madagascar, this would be better than you saying, yes, she was on the boat except during the hours when you suspect she murdered someone. You see, it would be better for me, safer for you, easier all around."

"Safer for me."

"Easier for you. Sometimes my English—"

"Your English is fine. So you killed the personage."

"The personage was not where we thought she was. In fact, nobody was where we thought they were."

"She."

"Yes, don't be sexist."

He sat, uninterested in parrying that since it was just part of her arsenal of deflection, guessing she had purposely said "she" as misdirection. He wondered what this all meant for him. He was lost. He knew he was lost.

"Okay, sorry," she said. "But I don't do this, you know? I don't tell people what I do, why I do it, who I do it to or for, how I do it. Not even my employer knows most of it. The control of information is essential to me, essential to my continued existence. I would be dead or in jail or both if I didn't control information, and I can hardly believe I am blabbing all this to you. It hurts me."

"Hurts you."

"Yes, literally hurts. I am in pain. I do not do this."

"But you have hardly done anything! Hardly said anything. I know nothing. Someone named Eamon Johns or John Eamon—"

"I tell you, it is first name."

He suspected she dropped her articles and mangled her tenses just to muddy the waters.

"Someone named Eamon hired you to fix something in the middle of the ocean, and surprise, there was nobody in the middle of the ocean. You tell me things, but still I know nothing."

"You know more than anyone in the world about me, right now, except Eamon. And you even know things he does not know."

"What would those be?"

"You know that I am losing my shit, that I am losing control of my information. If Eamon knew I had given you his name, he would have us both killed as soon as humanly possible. And that would be soon."

He could see she was getting upset as she talked, red in the face. He was feeling shakier, too. She threw down another glass of wine in a big gulp and continued. He downed half his glass.

"*You* know, because I told you, that the situation was not what Eamon assumed—*he* does not know that, yet. *You* know I am on your boat. *He* doesn't know that. *You* know where you have pointed this yacht, and not only does he not know that, I don't even know that!"

Now she was really hot, seething, even.

"I—" he started to say.

"You are infuriating!" she growled, throwing her wineglass into the sea.

"Hey! I—"

She stood there, breathing hard, even redder in the face.

"You have really pretty eyes!" she blurted out, furious, turning and heading into her stateroom.

That was a stumper.

It made him feel, although he couldn't name it right away, incredibly lonely.

XXV
Skye

SHE HAD BEEN right about Alain, right to bring him in. He had stepped up big time, and in vetting him, the team had found a vein of iron. He was solid.

When they asked him if he was racist, he said yes. When they tried to goad him, he goaded them back. They had been expecting a hick, and were surprised when he gave as good as he got. It reminded her of those stories in Ellison's *Invisible Man*, when the characters surprise the whites by being two steps ahead of them. He turned the tables and told them they had to show their cards and be straight with him. They more or less were.

She had her usual room, on the fourth floor, a little larger than a standard four-star hotel suite, with a balcony overlooking the lagoon. The first time she was there, she had told the Chief that it seemed odd to her, like a security breach, that the balcony had a glass door and that the room had floor to ceiling windows, and he said that if they were attacked, it wouldn't matter how many windows were open. They would get attacked by barrages of missiles from warships and submarines, or maybe a nuclear device. It would be Armageddon, he said, not a shoot-out. They put Alain a few doors down. She was sure it was nicer than any room he'd ever stayed in. On the tourist beat in Madagascar, the hotels had tiny rooms or dorms with shared baths for the drivers and guides, even at the fancy places. He would have to appreciate the relative luxury.

She had known he would do better at his interview if she didn't coach him at all, that he needed to feel like he was being his own person, and it had worked beautifully. He had passed with flying colors and she had an adjutant again, six months after losing Bernard. Going forward she could be much more efficient. She had taken a huge risk pulling this untested guy into service without prior authorization, so she had been on the line in that meeting, too. His success was her success.

She couldn't decide what her next move should be with him. For some people, a bottle of champagne would be the cement, but she thought it could backfire with him. It might suggest that she hadn't been confident enough, that this hadn't been exactly what she expected. She could see him looking askance if she showed up with a bottle. Celebrations only work if the celebrant thinks it's called for. She sent him a text on his new phone (monitored, no calls or texts to Madagascar or to anyone from his past) saying *well done* and setting up a meeting for 9:00 a.m. That would make him feel right. Sanctioned, accepted. No ceremony.

The next order of business would be to train him on the midget sub, get reports on the latest satellite images, and get to work destroying GreenCon before it went any farther. The team made it clear that the execution of Darkwater's CFO and his two bodyguards in Madagascar the week before was a sign that things were only going to get worse if they didn't act fast to make them better.

At 8:55 a.m., Alain was in the assigned room, and a commander of the submersible division came in to walk him through the essentials of the Shallow Water Combat Submersible. She watched as the commander explained the basic physics of the machine and the control panels. She jotted down the central facts. Alain followed everything closely, but even though they had left yellow pads and pencils on the table, he was not taking notes.

"You're not going to take notes?" she asked.

"I don't learn that way," he said.

"No. Wrong. Everyone learns that way, and everyone learns better that way. All it means when you say something like that is that you haven't learned, yet, how to learn that way. And as in all things, the easiest way is to learn by doing, so take notes."

He looked at her, then pulled a pad next to him and picked up a pencil.

Good. Chain of command. Discipline upheld. Good.

And she could see that he was jazzed by this turn of events. It wasn't spy school exactly, but then again it was, in a way. And he had exactly the right attitude now—ready for new ideas, no illusions, no resistance, no god complex, no mission beyond the mission.

Her favorite part of his interview was when they asked why he thought they were taking on the risk, why they were bothering to bring him onto the team. He thought about it for a good long minute, looked at each of them and at her, and said:

"Well, I suppose it is because I'm expendable."

They all sat there, knowing the truth of it, of course, but not admitting to it yet, and he went on.

"Right," he went on. "You could use any of these American boys you have snapping to attention and saluting you all over this island. But when they die on some pile of rocks in the middle of nowhere, you would need to explain all of it to their next of kin, and you would need to justify it to the chain of command, and it might get on the news, and all of it could be a big problem. Especially if what you were doing wasn't all legal and above board. Me? I'm 100 percent deniable and 100 percent expendable. I can see from the look on your faces that I'm right."

They all sat, not objecting to a word of it.

"Ask me again," he said, "why I'm a racist."

She was so proud of him she almost applauded.

XXVI
Mónica

***JAJAJAJAJA,* SHE THOUGHT** to herself, I am making a mess of things.

They were headed to the Maldives, and she was uncharacteristically uncertain about everything. She *could*, she knew, feed this guy to the fish and take his boat where she needed to go. Or she could seduce him into remaining her willing chauffeur, which would make everything else she needed to do easier. She could, she thought, trying it on, go away with him and start disappearing. She could convince him to sail somewhere unexpected—Tasmania, The Gambia, Montevideo—or even that island he raved about, Socotra, off the coast of Yemen. He could be the perfect ticket out. Maybe that's why she had such strange feelings for him. She had twisted him into a savior.

Still—and the more she thought about it, the more she was convinced this wasn't a rationalization on her part, wasn't a wish-fulfillment fantasy, but a fact—she could be his savior, too, if she decided to be. He had been completely shut down, had turned into a hermit because he was so damaged, and she could bring him back into the land of the living. She could take him out of the land of the living, or she could reintroduce him to it. It was up to him. Or, if she was being honest, it was up to her.

She knew she should meditate and stop worrying about everything. But she decided this needed sterner stuff. She ate three

Oxys and rummaged through the galley until she found a bottle of hard stuff—bourbon, as it turned out. Frank was up in his hammock and wanted nothing to do with her, which made her feel like she did on her first day of prison—alone, hopeless, doomed. She couldn't wait for the pills to hit, and the bourbon was the perfect accelerant.

She had gotten massively high before she stabbed her stepfather, and she still thought of that as the smartest move she had ever made. Everything bad in her life sprang from him, everything good from killing him. She had snorted a big pile of heroin when Eamon had given her a night to consider whether she was going to accept his deal or not. Maybe that one didn't count, since she knew she was going to accept the deal before he had even finished making it. But prison had made her cagey, and she told him she needed to sleep on it. So yeah, maybe that one didn't count. She just wanted to get high, she might not have easy access to heroin on the outside.

And maybe that was what was happening now—maybe she just wanted to get blotto. Who cared? She poured herself a triple and went back to her room, bringing the bottle. She knew from experience that a decision would be made, one way or another.

XXVII
Alain

DARKWATER WAS LIKE being in the Foreign Legion—there was a clear chain of command, there was lethal force behind everything, and there was an agreement that everyone on the inside was fundamentally different than everyone on the outside. But it was also like civilian life, in that you didn't have to salute, you didn't wear a uniform, you in theory had your life to yourself when you weren't working. In practice, on Diego Garcia, that meant little since there was nothing to do. He wasn't interested in going to the enlisted club to drink with the US soldiers, and although he worked out in the gym every other day, he wasn't going to join a pickup basketball game or learn to play squash, handball, or tennis. He had to spend time studying—websites, the PowerPoints and PDFs he was sent by instructors, his own notes—to keep up with everything they were trying to get into his brain. But the rest of the time he spent like he did at home, watching TV.

He had been out in the Submersible, the SWCS, a few times, and he wasn't sure how much of the excitement he felt about it was a boyish fantasy thrill—going down in his own personal submarine!—and how much of it was pure terror. The sub was an aluminum cylinder eight feet in diameter and three times that long, like a tanker truck on the highway, a clumsy-looking thing that could carry a total of eight people, they said, but was claustrophobic, even with only the two of them and an instructor on board.

The mission, as he put it together, was to return to the man-made island they had visited in scuba suits and when they got there, blow it up. Blow it down, in effect. He was learning how to attach explosives to the piers the island was built on—they assumed, that is, it was built that way; they didn't have any actual intelligence about the structure. To deal with that he had learned five different detonation patterns for five different possible structures. But in any case, the idea was to cut it off at the knees and sink into the ocean. They would start to do mock drills underwater in the next day or two and be off in their sub shortly after that. The sub was battery operated and only had a twelve-hour range, so they would get close to the island by piggybacking on a larger sub, courtesy of the US Navy, then cut loose, do the job, and rendezvous with the mama sub after the deed was done.

Skye joined him for some of the instruction. She knew most of it already, but the sub was a new piece of equipment for her, so she did the in-water training with him. Since they would be on the mission together, it was important that they get comfortable with who opens what door and who closes what door and all that mundane stuff, as well as with the sequence for setting up the explosives, and then the sequence for detonating them. In the water, comms would be minimal to avoid detection—they'd want to be able to execute without breaking silence.

He marveled at the US military industrial complex, how one company got to use the massive US military might to go after their competition, to literally blow them out of the water. Something was profoundly corrupt, but as they say in the military, these were all decisions made above his paygrade. He never again saw any of the "team" that interviewed him, although Skye apparently did. Again, not his lookout.

At times, though, his curiosity got the better of him and he had to ask.

"These French guys—"

"Who?" Skye interrupted.

"On the island."

"French and Indonesian in corporate structure, but like us, international personnel."

"Anyway, we, the *team*, we want Darkwater to annihilate this rival company, I get that. And I'm starting to understand that it's all like a Mafia movie. You go onto someone's turf and there's gangster wars. We're in a gangster war. But who is the law? It's Chagos Archipelago, so UK says it's UK, Mauritius says it's Mauritius, and America runs everything from Diego Garcia. So, who is the law? Doesn't somebody, eventually, come and break up the fight? Doesn't the other company go to Interpol, or the UN, or EU, and get help?"

He watched Skye think about this. He had learned that she always put everything she heard and everything she said through a filter, asking *how does what he just asked help me?* and *how can my possible answers help me?* But he was okay with that. He factored it into his interpretation of what he asked and how she answered.

"Darkwater has a tricky balance to keep. It wants business from the US and from the UK, and so wants them both to be happy," she said.

"Well, if it has nothing to be afraid of, why sneak around with pretend ethnographers, why sneak ashore and have submarines send frogmen in? Why not send a couple warships in and bomb the fuck out of it?"

"Darkwater succeeds as a business by being hidden, behind the scenes, covert. Every time it is in the news, it is bad for the company. Everything, especially everything like this, everything gangsta, has to happen as quietly as possible, with as much deniability as possible. When warships move, there is a record—the people monitoring such things see them in the satellite imagery, and it becomes public record. Deniability dictates. It is why the governments use Darkwater to begin with. And it's why Darkwater uses me."

"What do you mean by that?"

"I don't work for Darkwater. I'm a contractor for them. So are you. Have you looked at your bank account? The deposits are not from Darkwater."

"But from their payment service or something, no?"

"No, from some shell corporation hidden fifteen layers back in the international banking system, routed through countries that make a living hiding transactions. Darkwater can deny ever knowing us. We are very much off the books."

"But they are supposed to be supporting my family—that was part of our deal. How do I know they are?"

"Give me five minutes," she said, and went out of the room.

She came back and pulled up images on her phone of the checks his wife and Raissa had cashed, with their signatures on the back, and images of the bank accounts for his kids, with the balances. They were making good on their part of the bargain, and he saw that the payments were from yet another entity, something called the "Macroone Family Fund." He was behind the curtain, and although he wondered if he would ever have a normal life again, he also wondered if he ever wanted one. Maybe he and normal were never going to get along. Maybe he was a low-down dog, and it was his nature to sniff around the other dogs. On the other hand, maybe he was, in fact, the star of a Hollywood movie, a real-life Hollywood movie, going undercover and underwater to blow up the secret island lair of the bad guys.

Maybe. Maybe not.

The thing that kept him from feeling good about it all was that he had no idea who the bad guys were, and even less who the good guys were. Most people want to be one of the good guys if possible, and he had a nagging suspicion—or more than a suspicion—that both sides of this war, where he had found himself a foot soldier, were bad guys.

Then again, he thought, he might be able to live a happy life as one of the bad guys. He might prefer it. Most bad guys did, it seemed to him. It's the role that gets top billing. Tony Soprano, Walter White, The Godfather, Dexter, Stringer Bell, Lupin—the stars were the bad guys.

He'd still like to know. He'd like to know if he was standing on a rock, on jelly, on a cloud, or on sand. And he'd like to know who he was standing there with. Skye was great, but she was a cipher, too. Did she have a moral compass, or just a tactical one? What percentage of what she told him was true? What had she decided not to tell him? When he found out, would he like it?

And who was she, really? He knew nothing about her except what he had seen. She was American. A college kid. Or an expat, a child of expats? For all he knew, she grew up in Saudi Arabia and went to the American school there. Was she gay, straight, something else? Did she go home and tell her parents what she'd been up to? Did she go home to a lover and talk about her exploits? Did she even have a home?

Maybe not. He didn't.

XXVIII
Frank

WHEN HE WENT down to make coffee in the morning, he found what looked like a poem on the counter.

Abro los ojos por la mañana,
Y recuerdo,
Te vi en mis sueños.
Me emociono, y
Todo mi cuerpo se endurece,
se curva y te busca.
Y te espera.
Y te espero.

Something about opening eyes, something about emotions and bodies, something about hope. He opened his laptop and typed it into Google Translate.

I open my eyes in the morning,
And I remember,
I saw you in my dreams.
I get excited, and
My whole body hardens,
it curves and looks for you.
And it awaits you.
And I wait for you.

Okay. A love poem. He tried googling some lines from it to see if it was a famous poem, and the first line got a lot of hits, as, duh, it would. Lots of poets and songwriters over the world had opened their eyes in the morning. The last two lines got a lot of hits, too, but not exactly like that. It was that last couplet that got him thinking it was a famous poem. It was so elegant. *Y te espera. Y te espero.* Google should have left it parallel: *And my body awaits you, and I await you.* He was right, *espero* can mean *I wish,* or *I hope,* too, not just wait. *And my body yearns for you, and I yearn for you.* The rest of it in Spanish, too, was much more poetic than Google's version. *Se curva y te busca*—the parallel construction, again, so elegant. Maybe it was a famous poem, in fact, but she was not remembering it correctly, which was why it didn't show up in his searches.

Sitting next to the poem was his bottle of bourbon. Empty.

Okay, so she got drunk and wrote a love poem. He wasn't at all sure how he felt about that.

He put on the espresso pot and thought that there was a time, not too long ago, when he would have been overjoyed to have this woman's attention, and her affection, even if drunken. But he felt freed from a cruel master, as Socrates or someone said about sex when they aged out of it. He felt a tug in this woman's direction, but not enough of one to overcome his revulsion for the whole romantic ethos. He put some milk on and watched it until it came to a boil. They'd passed over the equator in the night, and the sun would be hot. He poured a café au lait and went above deck with it.

He realized that he wasn't ready to think everything through, that he was in a holding pattern, waiting to land. He would think about it all once things were back to normal. And normal meant back to his wandering life, his monkish life just off the coast of whatever country he happened to be passing.

The breeze was fresh, and the ocean had yet to be stirred up by it. Again, nothing but watery expanse in every direction. Not his favorite place to be. There was something about the open ocean that mocked him. He felt like it was saying, yes, Mr. Baltimore, you are nothing, you are a speck of nothing, and you move all day for what? To be in exactly the same place, to be still looking at the unbroken horizon, to be still in the middle of nowhere, to see nothing new, to be nowhere.

He wondered, again, about the poem. It was still very early, and so when, exactly, had she "opened her eyes in the morning"? Not this morning. It had to be someone else's work. Or else she wrote it at least a day earlier and had drunkenly shared it. Or wrote it for someone else and was reusing it. That made more sense—the hand was steady and neat. It didn't look like the work of a drunk person. And it didn't read like that, either.

Oh, well, he thought, not his puzzle, not his problem, at least not yet. They'd be in Malé by evening, and he'd say goodbye to all of this, and never, ever see her again. Then he could figure out what he thought, what it all meant.

XXIX
Skye

IT WAS TIME. Alain turned out to be a fast learner. He knew when to take initiative and when to trust her. They were a good team. When they met in the conference room in the morning, she got right down to it.

"From what I could see, there were only a half dozen people on the island, at most a few more. Our systems don't show any increase in activity since then. Three of the four buoy-based monitors I placed when we were there are still operational, so I think it's safe to assume a wave got the fourth, but that they are unaware we paid them a visit, and that there is no new activity to speak of." As she said things, Alain gave a nod to each check. "*If* all we were going to do is blow the thing up and leave, we could go tonight."

"If," he said.

"Yesterday, I got word from the chief that they want the tidal turbines to survive the attack. And then today the word is no explosives at all. The new thinking is we don't blow it. We chase them out, we take over, we defend, and we continue to build. The US and UK want a paramilitary base built there, and they don't care much who does it, as long as they're known entities. And Darkwater is the devil they know."

"Our mission was to blow it up. If we don't blow it up, there's no mission."

"Right in a way, but no. New mission. We'll be the front end.

Take the place, sweep it, and hold it until a full force arrives. You have experience holding an island against all comers."

He laughed. "Easy when there are no comers."

"We go in—me, you, an IT guy, a comms guy, four of my security guys, and a pilot for the second boat—all of them off the books like us."

"Does Darkwater have any actual employees?"

She ignored that. "We sweat whoever we find there to give up their codes and anything else they can tell us, we send that, and them, back to the team here for debrief, and then we await further orders. No sub, because we know we can get in before they are the wiser, the satellites will tell the whole tale, as will the comms shutdown, and we might need the boats to get out if things develop in ways we haven't foreseen."

"What was the whole thing with the sub to begin with, then?" he asked. She debated, for a moment, whether to respond to this. But again: settler colonialism, racism, she had no choice but to be square with him.

"We wanted there to be confusion about what had happened for as long as possible. Like maybe it was a gas explosion, maybe it was a construction flaw. Now, we don't care about that, because there will be no explosion, no structural collapse, it will just be a coup, a hostile takeover."

During Alain's interview that first day, they had reviewed his hand-to-hand combat training, always the biggest question mark with any new person on a team like this. She knew that there was never any choice but to wait and see, especially with somebody who had never been put to the test. J.R., J.T., and Ralf, who she was counting on for firepower, had been through it all—Iraq, Afghanistan, Syria—and she knew they could handle anything. No real worries there, save the normal. She, and all of them, were going to be in for a fight, and there was no telling how many of the people on the island were fighters and how many tech people.

There would be a fight, no matter what. Only a simpleton wouldn't be worried.

She called in the rest of the team and went through the plan step by step. J.T. and J.R. were both the full package—medic training, killers, smart, resourceful. The third guy, Ralf, they had picked, so he must be good. IT and Comms would hang back if there was fighting, but they would do their jobs. It was a solid team.

She dismissed them and asked Alain to stay. She knew he had seen plenty of action flicks, she said, but he hadn't seen combat yet, and so he needed to know a few things. One, nobody knows how they will react until it hits. She had seen big tough dudes who thought they were ready for anything go into shock in combat, unable to function. There is only one thing to do if that happens—he looked up to her when she said that, and she was glad that he trusted her to be straight, to show him the way. That meant she could count on him following her instructions when the crunch came. The one thing to do, she said, is do what other people on the team tell him to do. If he short-circuits, he won't be able to trust his own thinking, he needs to trust her, or the other guys. If they say get down, get down. If they say shoot, shoot. If they say run, run. Don't think about it, just do it.

"Okay."

"And one more thing. You know how, in buddy movies, somewhere in the middle, the buddies get mad at each other and stomp off and go their own ways? That would not, could not, ever happen."

He shrugged. Seemed self-evident to him. Good.

"But wait," he said. "You mean this isn't the movies?"

She made a face and didn't bother answering.

They all went off to pack and get ready to leave at 1600 hours in two boats. She was feeling a little strange, she noticed, and recognized the syndrome. She wasn't crazy about being a commander of a combat platoon. She liked the cowboy work, the Butch and Sundance, Smith and Jones work, the stuff, yes, that buddy movies are made of. Send her into hostile territory alone, with a driver, or even a partner, and yes, she was on it. But overseeing a group of other people felt like a huge drag on her freedom of movement. Alone, she was at her most creative. She didn't have to use some pre-arranged plan, hew to some set of predetermined signals and procedures. She could hot dog it all. And if she bought it, well, those were the odds. There was only strength in numbers until the bullet hits you in the face. And if she and her partner bought it, well, they were, as Alain put it, expendable. The bigger team meant they could win and lose. Bigger just meant bigger problems.

They boarded two boats, and four hours of motoring later, the sun had set, and they were within scuba range. She, Alain, and the five other guys checked their tanks and dropped into the water, leaving the pilot alone with both boats.

As they had arranged, they emerged from the water at fifty-foot intervals along the eastern side of the reef at 0045, shed their tanks and flippers, unlocked their weapons, and went in. She had seen a small part of the complex last time, and the rest was more of the same—concrete slabs on piers, the slabs at different levels, separated by short four- or five-step stairways, some enclosed, some bare. Several twenty-foot by ten-foot planters were filled with soil and already growing vegetables. Other smaller planters had young trees, the beginnings of an attempt to make the place look more like a real island and less like a WWII bunker. All this infrastructure was arranged in a crescent, following the shape of the reef, creating a small lagoon on the western side. Some free-standing structures were built from shipping containers, which she assumed were living quarters, storage units, and instrument and communications stations. The space suggested somewhere between five and fifteen men. If it was Wagner, it would all be men.

They came upon a lone sentry asleep in a lounge chair. Alain covered the man's mouth and grabbed his head, while Skye showed him her Glock and injected his neck with fentanyl. He went out with a whimper. Skye held up her hand and pointed to IT and Comms to stay there, and she, Alain, J.T., J.R., and Ralf went on to the sleeping rooms. At the first building, they eased the door open and went in as a foursome. They managed to incapacitate two men, again with fentanyl shots, without much noise, and zip-tie them to each other. J.T. poked his head back out to see if anyone else was stirring.

They moved, careful and quiet, to the second building, and again slowly eased the door open. A man screamed a warning before they went in, and he or someone else fired several shots in quick succession. Skye rolled past the door and shot at him three times. She had a silencer on, but he didn't, and when he fell, he crashed into the wall, taking a small table with him. The dead man's roommate dropped to his knees, put his hands up and yelled, "Don't shoot! Don't shoot!" Alain gave him a fentanyl shot in the neck and within seconds he slumped to the floor. They zip-tied him to the dead man, arm to arm and leg to leg. But the damage had been done. Whoever else was out there was alert and armed.

They pulled open the door and prepared to meet whatever was coming. Skye gave them directions with hand signals—J.T. and J.R left, her, Ralf, and Alain right. They dove out the door and rolled, and automatic weapons fire sprayed over them, coming from one of the higher slabs. They rolled farther and fired back, a barrage that sounded like it was from more than four guns, because it was—J.T. and J.R. were firing AK-47s from one hand and handguns from the other, and she was doing the same. Ralf shot with AK-47s from both hands. Alain was using the AK, and she made a note to explain the technique to him later, using multiple weapons to make the enemy think there were twice as many of you. Ralf went down and didn't get up. The rest kept firing into the night, with less and less return fire. When it stopped, a man yelled, "I surrender!" from the darkness. J.T. shouted at him, demanding to know how many men were on the island. "Nine! Us two and seven more. That's everyone." J. T. told him to come forward, and he did, supporting a comrade who was hurt. They handcuffed him and his wounded, bleeding friend, zip tied them to a railing, taped their mouths, then turned on all the lights they could find.

Ralf was face down on the slab. Skye went to him and checked his pulse. She shook her head. He was dead. She looked at Alain and could see—the new adrenaline on top of the old adrenaline was making him a bit woozy. Four of the island men were dead, the one she shot and three from the firefight. Four were incapacitated, including the one who was wounded and bleeding. One was missing.

They pulled the fentanyled men in and handcuffed and zip-tied them all together. J.R. tended to the bleeding man's wounds, and Skye got in the face of the man who surrendered.

"Okay, quick, who are you all? First, you, what's your job?"

"I'm the Comms guy!" he said. "I'm not a fighter!"

She called her Comms guy over to debrief him.

"Who's your bleeding friend?"

He and the bleeding friend both blurted out that he was an IT and electronics guy, a techie, not a combatant. She waved her IT guy over to do the same. They sat down with their opposite numbers and asked their batteries of questions, entering the answers into pads.

"And these three?" she asked, pointing to the three unconscious men, one dressed for sentry duty, and two in the underwear they slept in.

The two men interrupted each other to describe them as guys who did construction work, but that all were weapons trained and took turns at security.

"They weren't very good at it, were they!" J.T. said, with a laugh.

"Okay," Skye said. "We're going to do a debrief here, okay? You help us with what we need to know, and nobody else gets hurt."

The wounded guy realized he had a question. "Who the good goddamn are you?"

"We are the good guys, and we are going to give you all jobs if you want them. But first, download everything we need to know."

She looked over at Alain, and she saw his mouth fall open.

"Skye!" he said. "You're hit!"

She looked down to see blood seeping out from the leg of her wetsuit.

"Fuck me," she said, and felt wobbly.

XXX
Mónica

"**YES, I KNOW** Eamon, please do not be a dick," she said, sitting in her stateroom. "We don't have to do this *Killing Eve* banter all the time, you know. I am not going to tell you where I am."

"Okay," he said. "Then I'll tell you. You are in the Maldives, roughly sixty miles south of Malé, on the boat of a certain Frank Baltimore."

How does he know this? He can't guess this—how does he know?

"Cat got your tongue?" Eamon asked. He read off her latitude and longitude.

"What do you want?"

"I want you to turn around the boat—with or without Frank Baltimore—and head back to the Chagos. Tell me right now if that is going to be a problem."

"If it was going to be a problem, you are the last person I would tell, so I will tell you no, it is not going to be a problem."

She tried to think of where he could have picked up her trail. And even if he had somehow figured out that she left Madagascar with Frank, how did he know where she was now?

"You know, you're the one that keeps bringing up *Killing Eve*. I think maybe you are being difficult because you think it is sexy."

"That Russian girl had daddy issues. Do I give you the impression that I want daddy vibes?"

Idiot, she thought. But how did he know who Frank was?

Then she put it together. "You have a tracker on the boat."

"The installation has been attacked," he said, ignoring her. "I need you to go there and eliminate the current occupiers. There are six of them, armed, ready for trouble."

"Six? Doesn't sound like they're ready for a lot of trouble, but okay."

"Check in before you go ashore, and I will update the intel. We have a slight preference that Frank Baltimore survives."

"Got it." She didn't add *me too, also slight preference.*

"But the mission comes first," he added.

She went up on deck and tossed her phone and SIM card into the ocean. She did it in front of Frank on purpose, trying to get a reaction. She didn't get one.

"Can I ask a favor?" she said.

"Sure?"

"Can we lay up for a moment so I can dive in?"

He was a gentleman. He would never be able to resist a simple request from a woman. And sure enough, he turned upwind and let the sails luff.

"A quick one?" he said. "I want to get into the harbor before nightfall."

"Aye aye, captain," she said.

The whole idea was to give him one more look at what he was missing because of his ascetic act. She dropped her sundress to the deck and dove in wearing the bikini she had worn on the night they met. It hadn't worked then, but she'd caught him giving her a glance now and then since, and he was primed with a love poem she was sure he had google-translated. This was either going to work or it wasn't. It usually did.

She splashed around for a minute and then climbed up the ladder aft. She stood with her legs slightly apart and asked for a towel. He could not resist a quick look as he handed it to her. She stood in front of him drying her hair, giving him plenty of time while the towel was over her face for him to have a good gander.

"You used to make me coffee in the morning," she said.

"You used to serve me wine without a roofie in it."

He backed into a tack and let the sails fill again, putting them back on course.

"I'm sorry I drank all your bourbon."

He looked at her, and took her in, and couldn't help himself.

"You do not look like someone who drank a fifth of booze last night."

"Why, Mr. Baltimore, are you flirting with me?"

"No. Look, I'm sorry. It was a very nice poem. But, even putting aside the fact that I would be a complete idiot to trust anything you say, I'm not a romantic anymore, and so romantic poetry really doesn't move me the way it might have once upon a time. I spent a long time as some cross between a predator and a sucker, and I have no desire to be either anymore. You're asking me to take up a role that I no longer have any interest in."

"That's a very pretty speech, although it seems to me overly rehearsed, and besides, I think instead of wasting women's time in interesting ways you are now wasting their time in boring ways. But I'd like to put the rest of my answer to this on hold for a minute while we talk about something else."

He checked his sails and instruments—a kind of nervous tic of his—but didn't otherwise respond.

"I am in a very awkward position, in that my employer knows exactly where I am and who I'm with."

"Okay," he said, confused. "I didn't ask you to keep it a secret."

"He has a tracker on your boat."

"Meaning you put it there?"

"No. Listen, Frank, I need you to listen to me, please, right now. I have been trying to get myself out of this life. And I need you to understand what that means, okay?"

"Okay. But can you put your dress back on? It's distracting. And in exchange, I'll make us a coffee."

She stepped into her dress and followed him down into the galley, where he set about pouring water into the espresso maker. She talked to his back, which made it easier.

"My stepfather came on the scene when I was fourteen. He abused me, and beat my mother, from when he arrived until I was seventeen. Then I killed him. Then I went to prison. Eamon showed up and said he would get me out. He said he would get me out because I had shown real courage and fortitude in what I had done, and because it was clear I knew that sometimes, no matter how horrific other people might think it, you needed to look at your work like an artist does, with detachment, and because he could see I understood that sometimes killing someone was not enough, that sometimes you have to leave a message, too. He wanted to help me develop and refine those qualities and make a career out of them. It is very difficult, the first time you kill someone, he said, but the second time is easier, and the third time easier than the second."

"Is it?" Frank asked.

"Yes, but let me finish. I'm not used to doing this—not used to telling anyone any of this."

"Okay."

"Eamon worked for someone, he explained, that needed someone like me to work as a fixer. He, Eamon, had worked as a fixer for him for years, and so he knew—it was a great job, the employer was a great man, the pay was astronomical, and the hours easy except when you were on assignment. Then it was 24/7 until the job was done. They would have my sentence commuted, give me a new name and a new identity, and I would be free and respected by the few who would know me, and by the many who would know me by reputation, like the Jackal or the Iceman. And I would be respected by the people who would know nothing of my work, but see my expensive apartment, my expensive clothes, my obvious success and wealth. Did I think I would be interested in that? Of course I said yes. I would have said yes without the bling. Prison was horrible."

"And so you feel you owe him, or them—that you owe them something for turning you into a professional murderer. I'm sorry if I can't agree that you should feel obligated."

"No. Not obligated. I loved every minute of my new life. I did it my way, and I did it well. I am known—well, not *me*, my identity is still a secret—but my work is known as the best in the world. I am the new Iceman. They call me The Shining. After the twins."

"The twins?"

"I'll explain sometime. But the point is, Eamon and his boss, they got their money's worth. I think we're even," she paused, "but—"

"But?"

"I am not free yet. I want out, but you know how you get out of the Mafia? To get out is to die. There is no retirement plan."

"Okay." He poured their coffees, handed her a cup.

"I have been trying to figure out how to get out without dying, but I talked to Eamon this morning—"

"You talked to Eamon . . ."

She looked at him with a cocked eyebrow but decided to continue: "And I have to go back to Chagos. I've decided that it will be my last job, and then I am out, one way or another."

"Why not stop calling Eamon and get out now?"

"Because, as I told you, he has a tracker on this boat, and he will come and kill us both."

"We dump the tracker."

"Okay, where is it?"

"I don't know, of course. But can't we find it?"

"No. My guess is that it is in the fiberglass somewhere. Or in the middle of the engine. Or on the top of the mast. Or baked into your kitchen counter—sorry, galley counter. He doesn't put trackers in like the movies, where it is a magnet on your bumper, and all you need to do is look under the car to see its flashing red light. When we get to a decent port, I can scan for it and we can do the work to remove it—but we can't just remove it, and throw it away, we need to transfer it to another boat—if we just smash it, then they know, and they start the search right where we were. We give them a big advantage."

"We."

"*Jajajajaja*, yes, okay, I admit I don't want you to die, either. I'm sorry to be so pushy."

"But if they find me and you are gone, then I am fine, right?"

"*Oyoyoyoyoyoy*, don't be naïve. It is not attractive after twelve years old. Of course they kill you. They don't know what I tell you."

She looked to see if her fractured grammar had the desired effect, and it had.

"So, we put away dopey ideas," she said, "and you help me out of this mess, and I help you out of this mess, and—happy ever after."

He was looking at her now, and she could tell he was far from certain she was telling the truth, far from convinced that he was better with her than without her. She considered recrossing her legs, but thought that might be too obvious, given his current monkhood. He stood up, took their empty cups to the sink.

"I know, Frank. I know this is a lot to digest. Most people don't have to deal with this kind of thing—murders, spies, high crimes and misdemeanors, fixers, assassins. But it is the life I was dealt. I don't want any pity—it's true, once I was rescued from prison, I loved it all, loved it all." She was surprised, herself, at how wistful that sounded, and she watched him to see how it hit. He took it in stride. "I want you to try to understand. And to understand that I want out. And want you to not be hurt."

He rinsed out their cups, put them in the drainer, and said: "I am not a complete stranger to the criminal life. To high crimes and misdemeanors. To corrupt, horrible people. It is not even the first time I have been drugged by a killer."

Of the million things he might have said, she had to admit that was not one she'd seen coming. He didn't seem to be looking for a response to it, but instead headed back to the cockpit. She followed.

"I know I wrote you a love poem," she said when they were above deck. "But I don't need you to love me. You think you are over all that, okay, fine, and I thought I was over all that, too, that I was over it before it even began. So good. We can let it go, go back to square one. We pretend it never happened, that it was never an issue, and bingo, it is not."

"Okay," he said. He was trying too hard to not give anything away.

"But there is no reason for either of us to die. Help me keep us alive. You don't have to do much. Sail us back to the Chagos and let me do the rest. Then we can find the tracker, stick it in another boat that looks like this one at a distance, and we sail free and clear and don't look back. By the time they realize they are tracking the wrong boat, we are gone, we have new passports, new credit cards, new everything. I know how to do all this, no problem. We just have to stay alive long enough for me to do it for us."

He thought about this for a minute.

"Have you tried that?" he asked. "Not looking back?"

"Yes."

"Could you do it?"

"No."

He did that thing with his lips, a kind of smirk that said *whaddya gonna do?* and she felt a movement inside her belly. He did have very pretty eyes.

Jajajaja, she thought, I am going to fuck this all up.

XXXI
Alain

THEY PULLED OFF Skye's wetsuit. J.R. had been patching up the wounded guy, and Alain wondered what he was supposed to call him—his enemy? the other team? combatant? colonizer? competitor? J.R. turned to Skye and poked around her thigh and groin. She had multiple wounds, bullet holes presumably, and she had lost a lot of blood. J.R. used a pack of gauze as a sponge to lift off the blood, splashed alcohol on the openings, and then probed for the bullets. She gritted her teeth for a while but then passed out.

They heard a burst of gunfire from the other side of the island, and then silence. J.T. had gone in search of the last man. He texted that he had him. They also heard the engine from their boat approaching. J.T. must have summoned him, too.

"She needs blood," J.R. said to nobody in particular, and he wrapped her as tight as possible. He turned to Alain. "We need to make a stretcher." He had pulled a bag of blood out of his kit and was prepping her arm for the IV line.

Alain went into the second room and kicked apart a bed, brought out the two footboards and a blanket. J.R. threw him a roll of duct tape and he fashioned a crude stretcher. Skye could not die. Would not die. He wouldn't let it happen. He had no idea how, but he would make sure she pulled through.

J.T. came back with the ninth man in tow, and he turned out to be another one of the grunts, also now wounded. Alain guessed that with Skye out of commission, he might be in charge. The three guys they had spiked were coming to, and the team needed to know their next move. J.T. and J.R. glanced over at him. Yup, it was up to him.

"Let's get everyone in the boats," he said. "I'll stay on the island. I'll keep some water, rations, plenty of armament, and the radio gear. You get everyone to base."

They looked at him, at once relieved that someone had taken charge and dubious about him staying.

"Right, boss," J.R. said, without any sarcasm, and packed his gear away. He had the tech guy help him lift Skye onto the stretcher, and they carried her down to the boat.

"You stay alone, and without a boat?" J.T. asked, not so much in challenge as in pity.

"Yeah. S.T. and I were going to stay anyway, and she can return when she's patched up. You will have your hands full as it is." J.T. responded the way he always did—he looked straight ahead and said nothing, gave the slightest of nods, then turned and walked the wounded down to the boats.

The colonizers had built a decent landing zone, with two concrete piers, each of which could dock a large warship or a container ship, and a series of smaller docks for boats up to a hundred feet long, each made of a six or eight prefab plastic ten-foot squares. They took up a third or so of the lagoon and looked like they could house a small navy, especially with other ships moored offshore. Their two boats came around to one of the smaller docks, and Alain helped get them loaded, sending the one with Skye, J.R., and the other wounded off first, with its original pilot at the helm. The rest went in the second boat, the drugged combatants coming to enough to walk, re-shackled when they got on the boat, with J.T. at the wheel, a few minutes later. He was sure it was against the Geneva Conventions, because if the boat went down with the four guys in it handcuffed to each other, the last one cuffed to an oarlock, none of them would survive. But they didn't have that far to go, and the sea was calm. Alain watched them leave the lagoon and head back to the base.

He was taking a risk, he knew. If GreenCon sent a team, he was doomed, but his relation to Darkwater was a slender thread, and its name was Skye. Would she die? He felt, with a start, how bereft he would be if she did. And if she did, would he still have a job? She was the reason he was there, and he had a sense that without her, he was more trouble than he was worth. Staying out here was the one thing that gave him value. He would be their man on the ground. He decided that he had made the right call. Unless things went from bad to worse, he was better off, and more valuable, staying put. Skye, he said to himself, as if wishes could make it so, would not die.

Here he was again, he thought, only a matter of days since the last time he was alone on an island, watching as the sun set into the western vastness, eating freeze-dried rations, wondering if the future held anything for him but more ruination, more despair.

XXXII
Frank

FRANK STILL HADN'T called Tracy. He couldn't put it off any longer. He kept telling himself he had forgotten to call her, but he knew he hadn't exactly forgotten, he had just been avoiding it.

After offering himself his usual excuses for *why*—she was difficult, she wanted something from him, she had bad news—he had to admit that he had avoided calling because he didn't know how to answer the most basic questions. *How are you? Where are you? What are you up to?* When he asked himself any of those questions, he couldn't give himself a straight answer. And Tracy always knew if he wasn't being honest, always knew when he was equivocating.

No matter. It was time to buck up and do it. If the painful past was going to keep knocking on his door, in the end, he'd have to open it. He pulled out his VSAT antenna and mounted it to the deck. The Assassin, as he always thought of her now, was down in her stateroom, maybe hatching murderous plans with her Eamon, maybe mixing batches of arsenic, maybe making a dirty bomb, who knew? He hooked up the phone, checked the time—it would be early morning there, but Tracy was an early riser—and dialed.

"Hey, stranger," she answered.

It was unexpectedly warm and inviting.

"How did you know it was me?"

"Oh, sorry, no, I thought it was someone else."

"Okay." Awkward, maybe, but when wasn't it awkward for the two of them? "I'm sorry it's taken so long to get back to you. What's up?"

"What's up?" she asked, letting it hang for a minute, despite the fact that she knew he was calling because she asked him to. He remembered how agonizing it was for him—these questions that should be innocuous but always sounded full of implications that he was a horrible person, or at least doing something wrong. "Oh, right!" she said, "I forgot all about it!" sounding chipper and charming, which she was, most of the time. And as always, it made him rethink—had he just imagined all that implication? He used to assume she did it on purpose, these rapid changes of awareness and emotion, making him think she had ulterior motives, then proving she had none, showing that there was nothing but his own projection filling up the ether of her pauses. It struck him as very sophisticated flirtation when they were first together, when they fell in love—or when he fell in love, anyway. He wasn't sure if she ever did. "I just wanted to tell you that Kennedy ran into Dmitry at a green energy conference, and she wanted to talk to you about it. That's all. No biggie. What are you up to?"

Frank and Tracy did some small talk, which included nothing about what he was up to—he could count on her disinterest in his life, after all, to let that question go unanswered. Lulu was having an art show in a hip café in Brooklyn, and it didn't sound like much, Tracy said, but if he talked to her, he should remember that it was a big deal, that it was a real start for her. He was happy about that—and it did seem like a big deal to him—so it made it easy to end the call on a high note.

Dmitry Heald had both ruined his life and enabled his life. Frank knew that Dmitry's wife Yuli—the only person he had a more complicated relationship to—had become famous as a green energy entrepreneur and financer. It had crossed his mind, in fact, that Kennedy's path, once she got into alternative energy, might cross theirs. He had very, very much hoped not.

He hung up and dialed Kennedy. She wasn't such an early riser, but he felt he couldn't wait.

"Hello?" She had been asleep, throat full of gravel. He hoped she wasn't smoking.

"Hey, sweetie, I'm sorry to call so early, but your mom said you ran into Dmitry and you wanted to talk to me about it?"

"Oh, hey, Franky, yeah, oh, jeez, I'm barely awake."

He could hear her sitting up in bed and taking a deep breath.

"You want me to call back in a few minutes?" he asked.

"No, no, it's okay. And yes," she said, with one last throat clearing. "I was at a conference about harnessing tidal energy, and Dmitry's wife was one of the speakers. He came up to me, read my name tag, and asked if I remembered him. Of course I did, because he is such a bizarre person—you know that, right?"

"Oh, yes, I know that."

"Right. Anyway, he said something I thought was very strange. He congratulated me on my PhD, and then said, 'You know I paid for it, don't you?' And I said, 'No, I had a TAship, and Frank helped.' 'Yes, my darling,' he said, which gave me the creeps, 'but where did Frank get his money? From me.' I said, 'No, he sold his construction company.' He laughed and said, 'No, no, no, that was peanuts. His big money is all mine.'" She paused a beat. "What is that all about?"

"He is an evil man," Frank said. Maybe one day he should tell her the whole story. But not now. "And not to be trusted."

"Okay," she said. "We'll let the fact that that was a non-answer pass. He said one other thing. 'If you talk to Franky, tell him I'm watching him.' I thought, *holy fuck, what is that?* I just thought you should know."

"Ignore it, Kennedy, you can't trust a thing he says. How can he be watching me? I'm in the middle of the Indian Ocean."

"Huh," she said, but it was apprehensive, concerned.

"What?"

"That's where their latest project is, the tidal energy project."

"Ha!" he said, trying to make it sound light. "It's a big ocean!"

"Right . . ."

"Don't worry about him. He just can't pass up an opportunity to throw a wrench in someone's gears. It's who he is. He's a sadist. Don't take it personally. But catch me up, tell me what's happening with you."

He listened, distracted by this news of Dmitry. He paid more attention as she wrapped up, and then she told him about her sister and the café art show, that it was brilliant. A few minutes later she said she needed to get ready for work and he told her really, don't worry, glad you two are doing so well, and they both did the rest of their exit lines and hung up.

He started packing up the VSAT dish and saw The Assassin sitting, watching him.

"You were listening," he said.

She pretended to know nothing, asking who he was talking to, saying she had just sat down, didn't hear anything except him telling someone not to worry.

Maybe. But either way, he didn't want to tell her anything about Kennedy. It seemed only fair, given how little he knew about her, to keep some information to himself.

"Personal," he said.

"It's okay, you don't have to tell me—and you're right, it will make things a bit more even, since I don't tell you much about my personal life," she said, again seeming to read his thoughts. After all, you can say that to anybody at any time and they would think you had caught them keeping things to themselves. We all keep things to ourselves, and we're necessarily thinking more than we're saying. Only crazy people say everything they're thinking.

"Wait," he said to her. "Are you sure your boss is actually tracking us?"

"He read me our latitude and longitude, down to minutes and seconds."

"Okay, and you swear you didn't install the tracker?"

"Yes. I didn't know it was there until this morning, when it became the only explanation for what Eamon knew. In fact, I was counting on it *not* being there, on me being unfindable *because* I was on your boat."

He had no idea what to believe from her, had no intention of believing any of it, but that much did add up. Maybe.

"What I have to do is make one calculation," he said, "based on the idea that what you say is true. And then I have to do a second calculation in case the opposite is true, and then a third based on it being half true."

"In other words, it's like every interaction everybody has with everybody every day of their lives."

And then it dawned on him. Dmitry. Dmitry had put the tracker on his boat, it been there all these years—the boat had come from Dmitry, it was the easiest thing in the world for him to tag it. The Assassin worked for Eamon, Eamon worked for Dmitry. No, no—too much of a coincidence. It couldn't be.

"The last time I spent time with a sociopath he said the same thing to me," Frank said instead of any of that. "He was very much like you, in fact. He's the one I mentioned who drugged me. Who killed people. Or, as he liked to say, he had people like you kill people for him."

"I think now you are being cruel," she said. She seemed truly hurt, but he doubted that was possible. Dmitry, the sociopath he knew best, was, as far he could tell, immune from anything like self-doubt or emotional distress. And unlike the numerous sociopaths in political life, from Hitler and Mussolini through the more recent ones, Dmitry wasn't prone to anger, never got into a rage. He had only two emotional states—self-satisfaction and mild amusement—and he usually enjoyed them at the same time.

Frank had never seen him feel "hurt." Dmitry would sometimes claim to be hurt by something Frank had said or done, but it was always playacting in the service of mocking him, and he could never stay in character very long before laughing about it.

"Right now, for instance," Frank said. "Are you actually feeling hurt, or are you pretending to be hurt?"

"Isn't it the same thing?"

"No, it isn't," he said, but he hesitated—hadn't he once said something like that to Dmitry? Or had Dmitry said it to him? He had been reading William James that year, and James made you think of how performative emotional display often is. He really couldn't remember. But he repeated, "No, it isn't."

"Hm," she said, looking at him, and again he had the uncanny feeling that she was mind-reading in real time.

"Are you sure you couldn't tell Eamon, before he kills you, that you told me nothing?" Frank said, partly in jest, realizing, as he did, that he had already made the decision to do whatever she wanted. Otherwise he wouldn't be joking about it.

"Eamon would then do the calculus you outlined," she said. "And for him a 3 percent chance that I was lying would be enough for him to kill you. So, no, you are fucked. And I am sorry, I actually am sorry. Since you distrust me showing any emotion, I will say it with my poker face. I am sorry."

For some reason, he believed that.

"Is Eamon's boss named Dmitry?"

"I do not know his name."

"Dmitry Heald?"

"I will admit he is on my list of possibles. Why?"

Why would Dmitry be tracing him now, these years later? It made no sense. "A hunch."

"Okay. . . ."

"Okay." He had to admit she was right that they had no choice—if she wasn't lying about all of it—and that they had to do what this Eamon wanted. Frank knew every inch of his boat, and if there was tracker aboard, it had to be, as she said, baked in the fiberglass. Could it be in the keel? Inside the mast? The mast was hollow, after all, but it couldn't be checked without taking it down, something that could only be done in a shipyard.

"I assume you have the coordinates you want me to sail to," he said. "And come to think of it, I assume you were ready to sail there yourself if I was recalcitrant and you needed to kill me."

"*Recalcitrant.* You read too much and talk to people too little. -7.445286, 71.309462."

He punched them into his system and jibed, letting the boom all the way out and heading back on the same course he followed to come up. He ran downwind and hoisted his spinnaker. It would be a long, hot day. Maybe his last. He unrolled his sunshade and relaxed, as best he could with a killer on board, ready for a long few days.

When he first learned to sail, he had hated sailing downwind. The sails are placed in what is called "wing on wing," with the mainsail at ninety degrees on one side of the boat and the jib ninety degrees on the other, the bow pointed in the same direction as the wind. The sailboat is at its absolute calmest, staying flat abeam, with no lean at all, and everything goes silent as the ship catches up with the wind and hums along as quietly as it ever does. It can start planing and hit hull speed—the fastest any boat can go is called its hull speed—and stay there. It always felt anticlimactic. He loved, instead, a tight tack in a stiff wind, when the boat is keeled as far over as it can go, the wind rushing through the vacuum created by the mainsail and jib in tight formation, everything taut, every fiber of the ship vibrating and alive. When the boat is at full speed on a tack, going as close against the wind as the physics will allow, it is pure excitement.

But at hull speed going downwind, wing on wing, with a big spinnaker bellied out in front, you might be going just as fast, but you feel like you are standing still—going the same speed as the wind, you don't feel any. Only your wake lets you know you are moving at a clip. In the cockpit without a breeze, the hot sun can become heartless. But in the mess he was in, in the evening with the midday sun abated, the sea in long gentle rolls, going downwind was just fine. He didn't need any more excitement.

"I want to know what happens next," he said, when she came up from her room and once again threw her phone and SIM card overboard. How many phones did she travel with?

"Eamon's client has an installation on a small island. That installation has been invaded and captured, and our job is to find out where things stand now."

"These are what, pirates? Who invades an island? An army? What good are we against an army?"

"I like the *we*," she said, and he maybe blushed. "Who invades an island? Darkwater. You know who this is?"

"Yes, the paramilitary contractor."

"Exactly. So you haven't been a complete monk."

Do monks read the news? He really didn't know. "And why do they want the island?" he asked.

"Do we care? They are competition now. Eamon's client wants to become the biggest military contractor in the world. To become the new Darkwater. Bigger than Darkwater. Bigger than Wagner. Darkwater, of course, does not want this. So Darkwater tries to destroy the client's new base."

"Base?"

"Yes. Eamon's client is building a military base, or I suppose you'd say, a paramilitary base."

Frank thought of Darkwater as the devil's spawn—they ran black sites for the CIA, did all sorts of heinous things in Iraq and elsewhere, shooting civilians, corrupting local officials, wreaking havoc, and in general doing the US military's dirty work. They corrupted American politics, too, securing billions of dollars in contracts by spending millions of dollars on campaign contributions. Wagner and its nutty leader Yevgeny Prigozhin were in the news for war crimes everywhere from Ukraine to Syria to Mali to the Central African Republic until Putin had him killed. Who would think to go into this field? Another evil entity. Deeply evil. Profoundly evil. Dmitry.

"Darkwater is the devil incarnate," he said, not so much to her as to the air.

She brushed this off. Not an idea that interested her, maybe, or else she could think of worse people. Maybe Eamon's boss, for instance.

"The island in question is not really an island, but a man-made structure on piers set into the reef. They have built a tidal energy generation station on the island—or in the water off the island—and it was about to go online. This was big news in green energy. But it was a cover to build a military staging base for the other part of their business."

"Green energy . . ." Case closed. Eamon's boss was Dmitry.

"My client doesn't know if the attack was a coincidence, or if they wanted to disrupt the announcement of the tidal project. In any case, Eamon wants us to go to this island, this man-made island, and see who is there, and then, based on what I tell him, he will tell me what he wants me to do. If I don't do it, he will get someone else."

He scoffed—the defense of every evildoer ever.

"He *will*. And he will get that person, or another person, to kill us. Do you know how easy this would be? He can take us out with a drone whenever he wants."

Maybe, yes. Most likely. "Is it GreenCon? Is that the energy company?" That was the name of Yuli's company, and he could almost hear Dmitry saying it, relishing the *Con* part.

"I don't know. But when I search around to see who is doing big green energy infrastructure, then yes, GreenCon is a good guess." It was run by Yuli Heald, she explained, exactly the kind of person who will build a tidal electricity installation in the Chagos, because she liked to be in the news. There are a few other international players, but none that were likely to get in bed with the US military, and nobody could build there without them giving the okay. "Besides, Dmitry Heald, the husband, he is not so squeaky clean, right? So the list just got smaller and now, yes, my money is on them. Plus, from things he says, I think Eamon spent time in Asia, or is there even now. So, it's a good bet that he was hired by GreenCon—so, yes, my money is on GreenCon for this job."

"You know Dmitry Heald."

"No. And you do? That's why you asked about him?"

"Dmitry Heald is the client?" he asked again.

"Maybe. Now, probably."

"I'm telling you he is. He put the tracker on my boat. What does he want?"

"He is tracking us," she said, not in agreement, just trying it on. "If he is my Eamon's boss, then yes. What do these people want? In the grand scheme of things? I don't know. World domination? Or maybe he wants as much money and power as he can stockpile, like the rest of them. What makes you think he placed the tracker?"

"Trust me," Frank said. "He did."

"You need to tell me everything."

"You first," he said.

XXXIII
Alain

HE SPENT HIS time exploring the site, and found, on the northern end of the construction, a tunnel down to the energy generation station. An underwater set of hallways had windows three feet high by ten feet long every twenty feet or so, looking out onto a vast field of what looked like a giant's eggbeaters, forty-foot-high helix-shaped blades, hundreds of them, on complex mounts tied to each other and to the reef, with thick posts on the ends running down to the ocean floor or underwater ridge the reef was on. A monitor station every hundred yards or so along the hallways had a visual map of all the turbines in its section, with digital readouts of each one's status, gauges for its energy production, meters for speed and other performance data, and an eight by twelve window for analog monitoring. The display screens included feeds from cameras at several angles. He tried to see if any of the cameras could have caught Skye coming in for her recon mission. He guessed not, since they hadn't noticed the turbines during their approach. They had come in on the other end of the reef.

It was a massive installation, and they must have had a much larger crew come in to build all of it. Maybe they were in an interim period—after the turbine crew had done their work and before the military installation crew had arrived.

The middle platform looked to be the most solidly dug into the reef, and it held a large crane and other heavy construction equipment. It was all late-model stuff that looked like it had been new when they built the tide farm, and the crane could deliver to any of the platforms. As military bases went, it wasn't that large, but for a private military base, a paramilitary base? How big were such things? He had no idea. This installation could dock a sizable navy, and it could be built up several more levels. Maybe, for PR purposes, they had done photo shoots of the place as it was, with the green building crew, making it look like a reasonable size for an energy platform, and would build it up for military purposes later, when they could keep the press and other prying eyes out. It was far from its final size, shape, and personnel—that's why the crane, cement mixers, and the like were still there.

Maybe, then, if Skye was out for good, he would be able to switch teams. If GreenCon came in force, maybe he could, as Skye had just offered the Darkwater workers on their way to Diego Garcia, change his uniform and play for the other side.

If not, maybe he could get back to Diego Garcia, and they would help him get out and go back to his lonely island, serve out his time, and go home.

Home. If he had one.

As the sun got low, he boiled water, made his freeze-dried fettucine alfredo, and relaxed on the deck. In the east, he saw something moving and went to get his binoculars. It was a sailboat. Large, a yacht, coming downwind with a big blue spinnaker catching the evening wind as the air cooled from its midday highs. What the fuck is this? he thought. Tourists?

He should have been monitoring the surrounding waters, of course, with the instrument array in the first building, but he had become so inured to nothing happening in his last post that he had gotten lazy. He took a belated look at the radar at various distances, and this was the only thing on the water within range. He checked the skies and there were no aircraft, and checked the sonar: no submarine, either. Just this odd tourist ketch wandering toward him. He had been prepared for a number of scenarios, but this one? WTF.

XXXIV
Mónica

FRANK BALTIMORE'S LONG-LOST love was Eamon's client, or his wife, that is. As one of the English teachers Eamon hired taught her to say, *oh for crying out loud!* Part of her felt an odd jealousy, but the rest of her thought that there was something usable there, that knowing gave her a new edge. She wasn't sure how to use it yet, but she knew it was potential leverage.

She checked in with Eamon as they neared the target, and he told her that some of the Darkwater personnel had been wounded in action and were back at Diego Garcia, but that there may be a skeleton force on the platform, and that she should go in and secure it. In his voice she could hear that, for the first time since she had been working with him, Eamon was out of his depth. You don't secure anything out in this ocean. You can take it away from someone, but then you are easy pickings yourself—anyone with a slightly bigger gun can take it away from you. But she said nothing. She just said *yes sir, yes sir,* knowing that it was driving him crazy. *Jajajajaja,* she said to everything. She was a dick sometimes, too, she knew.

Late in the afternoon they approached the platform. She saw it on the radar before it became visible, and then, with the help of Frank's binoculars, she could see how it was laid out. The satellite photos gave the footprint, but weren't very good at depth, and now she could see the various partially-completed levels and the stairways leading from each to each. She saw nobody about, but of course that didn't mean anything.

After a fifteen-minute meditation in her stateroom, she felt cool and ready. She put together two bags, one that looked like an innocuous beach bag with a SIG Sauer MCX and a 9mm, and one with some heavier guns to grab if things got ugly. She brought them both up and convinced Frank to lower the dinghy and tow it behind. She would use it for the final approach, and they might need it for a quick getaway.

"Do you know how to use an AK-47?"

"No, and I don't want to," he said.

"Let's hope you never have to do anything with it, except maybe show it to someone. But come down into the cabin so I can show you, at least, how to hold it—whoever is on the island is for sure watching us."

He followed her down. She went into her room and got another gun, showed where the safety was, how to hold it, and how to replace a cartridge if he ran out.

"Don't pull the trigger, give it a little pulse. It will be harder for you to shoot a single round than to fire off ten. Try to slow it down as much as possible. Remember that it's powerful, with a powerful kick. Be ready for a bruised shoulder and sore hands." He looked distressed, so she added some words of reassurance. "Chances are you won't need to use it. You might, though, want to show someone you have it to keep them from coming at you. The rest is just worst-case preparedness. No worries. Just, if trouble comes, hold it tight, point and pulse."

She explained that she planned on acting like a tourist and talking to whoever was there, get the lay of the land, and come back on the ship. Chances were it would all be smooth.

"They won't be any the wiser when I'm done," she said, and gave him a smile that was a first-class imitation of a nice, real person.

She was back in the game, and she realized that she had already missed it.

She had Frank pull *God Sees* up a hundred yards short of the pier, and she pulled the boat up and hopped in. She drove it toward the dock, waving to the guy waiting for her. If he was alone, that was stupid. If there were snipers trained on her, it was smart. She always assumed smart.

She threw him a line and he held it, but didn't pull the boat up to the dock.

"Can I help you?" he asked. He was calm, wary, intelligent. He was unafraid to look her in the eye, and unafraid to look her over, check the boat, look back to Frank on the bigger boat, and straight at her again. He looked maybe African, maybe Indian, maybe Malagasy.

"Hi! We're going to moor overnight in this beautiful lagoon," she said. "Anything we should worry about? We'll be gone in the morning."

"I think you would be much better off to keep heading south with the autopilot on," he said. "It looked like you were headed south, anyway, and if so, there is nothing in your way for hundreds and hundreds of miles. And no weather coming. It will be much safer for you."

There was a bit of French accent to his English, and the boat had drifted up to the dock, so she could see now that he was definitely Malagasy. "I know it's silly," she said. "But I never get used to autopilot. I keep thinking, 'What if a tanker or a container ship is off track, and we ram into it in the middle of the night?'"

"Your autopilot will give you a warning, of course."

"I know it's supposed to, but I don't know," frowny face, "I just don't trust it!" She said this all doing her best airhead.

"Well, I'm sorry, we're expecting a number of large ships here shortly—this is a construction site—and they will be coming right up to the dock to unload people and supplies, and anywhere you could moor here would be in the way and dangerous for you. So, I'll have to say no, it's really not possible today. Besides, it will be quite noisy. No place to try to sleep. Sorry!"

"Too bad! What are you building here, by the way?"

"It's going to be a tourist hotel."

"How exciting!" she said, putting one foot on the dock as if ready to get out of the boat, and letting him see a lot of leg as she did. "Can you give me a tour?"

"No, no, no, no, and I'm afraid I'm going to have to ask you to stay in your boat, ma'am. We have very strict instructions from our insurance company. Like I said, it's a construction site."

"Such a shame!" she said, without putting her leg down. "Are you the manager of the hotel?"

"No, ma'am, I'm part of the security detail," he said, and lifted his shirt to show a handgun in a holster. "And, please, stay in your boat. Your husband looks somewhat alarmed. He's glued to his binoculars, and he ran below deck when I showed my gun."

The *part of the security detail* was a nice touch, but it meant he was alone. And you didn't have to be a pro to figure out Frank was new to the game. He would need a few lessons if he was going to be real help to anyone.

"Have a safe trip, ma'am," the man said, throwing her line back to her and putting his hand on his gun. She had a choice of a shootout now, which would be a disaster in the unlikely event that there were others on the island, and maybe even if there weren't. It was hard to see her getting the better of him without killing him. He was built like an athlete, and he by now had a sense that she was not who she said she was. Besides, if she was right and he was alone and she neutralized him, it would be the end of information. In any case, she couldn't get anything more from him right now.

"Of course," she said, and gave him her high wattage smile accompanied by a glance at his athletic physique to see if that had any impact. It did, but not enough. She climbed back into the boat, and before she was even seated, he had kicked the boat softly away from the dock. He had either good training or good instincts. At any rate, it was not going to be that easy.

She waved cheerily and started the engine, turning toward Frank and her next decision.

XXXV
Skye

YOU KNOW IT going in, that you can get hit, but it always comes as a complete surprise, and you always feel like it's your fault, that if you had moved better, shot faster, shot better, you would still be whole. You feel like a loser. Other people came out of the shit fine, but you, you and Ralf, you didn't roll right, you didn't roll fast enough. You bought the bullet with your own ineptitude.

The mission was not a total disaster, but it was at best only a partial success. GreenCon was for the moment stymied, and the Darkwater brass were dividing up the spoils on paper. But one Darkwater contractor was dead, one team leader wounded, and the intelligence value of the GreenCon employees was limited—they all knew their jobs and not much more. They divulged the codes to run the generating station, though, which was worth real money. A very qualified success.

She had convinced the Chief to let her head back, bringing J.T. and plenty of bandage changes and antibiotics for herself. There had been zero indications of a response, but they knew one was coming. They'd have to wait and see. The Chief told her to bring whatever technical staff she needed to get the turbines up and running. They would send another team to reset the substations. According to their prisoners, all of whom were being offered contracts to turn in their GreenCon badges and work for Darkwater instead, everything was in turnkey shape. They all agreed bringing those guys back to work on the platform was iffy—no way of knowing if there was some residual loyalty—but worth the risk given their training. She added three off-the-books guys J.T. suggested to keep an eye on them. The Chief gave her two small but efficient drones, armed with machine guns and small missiles, and agreed to pilot them from his station if they were needed. He also gave her two MANPADS, shoulder-held surface-to-air missile launchers. They provisioned up and motored back, towing a barge loaded with the drones and SAMs.

The ride out was starting to feel like a commute. She lathered on the sunscreen and kept her hat low. She had internalized the route of the five-hour trip, the engine on a high whine, the bow slapping against the waves, knowing bodily when they were halfway, when they were getting close. She spent the time going over protocols and possibilities with the other guys.

And then they arrived. When they landed, Alain took her on a tour of the generating station. The ex-GreenCon techs came along and explained how everything worked as they went through.

"Glad to see you on your feet so fast," he said to Skye.

"Me too," she said, and felt like he was, against all odds, an old friend. Hm. Strange. She had felt the same thing about Jean Claude on the ship. She liked it. She'd always been confused by the bathetic, starry-eyed girls at college, always more concerned with what they were feeling about this person or that person, consumed by what this person or that person was feeling about them. There were such better ways to spend your time. But now, she was starting to get it. Feeling close to people was nice.

She had the two tech guys review everything and report when they were ready to fire up. They went down the hallways checking out the equipment piece by piece.

"Back at Diego, they don't know what we should expect," she said to Alain, when they were alone.

"And you?" he asked. "What do you expect?"

"Fireworks. This is a big deal, and we stole it. People with this kind of pull, and with this much sunk in it—they won't walk away. They'll come back hard."

"We had a visitor," he said, and filled her in on the suspicious yacht and its suspicious Spanish sexpot envoy.

"Okay," she said. "That doesn't fit any picture I had." And it didn't. Perhaps it was a coincidence, and the Spanish woman was on a pleasure yacht wandering around the Indian Ocean. Except, as she knew, there was no such thing as coincidence.

"The tell," he said, thinking, "was that when I showed her the gun, she didn't react. I could see her *compute,* instead of react. She was totally cool. She is definitely in the game."

"Listen to you!" she said. "In the game!"

"Yeah, a lot of TV."

"So, we have to assume she was reconnaissance."

"Yeah. And when I told her I was *part* of the security detail, I could see she didn't buy it. She knew I was here alone. But she turned around, left, and the boat sailed off. I kept an eye on it from the top platform until it was gone. It's gone."

"They would calculate where your horizon was—I'm sure they won't be far. I'll call for a flyover, but if they keep their boat blacked out, a night flight won't find them. It will have to be in the morning."

"Didn't you bring drones?"

"Yeah, but I don't want to take the chance of losing one. I should get reinforcements in right away. How many do you think were on the boat?"

"Honestly? Just her and one guy, nutty as that sounds, unless others stayed below deck—but I don't think so. The woman was a pro, but the guy was an amateur, and nobody was minding him. The boat was top-line, all sorts of electronics on the masts."

"Let's hope they don't have a Stinger or RPG on there. But in any case, I need to game this out. What would they do if they thought you were alone? What are their assumptions and what are their moves? Where are their reinforcements? And not least, who are they?"

"Christ!" Alain said. "You don't know who they are?"

She squinted into the sun. "We can assume it's GreenCon," she said, "but there's a chance it's some kind of scavenger. There's a rumor GreenCon has a pair of female assassins that work together."

"The other one on the boat was a dude, for sure, and from what I saw, not trained. He did nothing to disguise the fact that he was watching me and ran around like a crazy person when I showed the gun."

"I'm calling in," she said. "Let's get troops and heavy gear. Whatever that was, it wasn't the end of it. I feel like an idiot coming this light, now that I'm here—I was just in a hurry to get back."

"And good to have you back, boss," he said.

"Good," she said, and meant it. "But we're in for some bad times. Bad, bad times."

XXXVI
Frank

WHEN HE SAW the guy flash a piece at her, Frank ran down to get the AK-47. Then he thought, what am I going to do with this? I can't shoot that guy from here. I don't even know if the bullets go that far. Do you point higher than the target when it's far away? The bullets fall a bit as they go, right? Should I head in to help her out? Or stay put? If she was shot and killed, he would need to get the fuck out as fast as he could. He ran back up top to see what was happening. She was fine, driving back toward him, in one piece. He was glad. Gladder, in fact, than he would have guessed.

"Head us due south at top motor speed," she said when she came aboard. "Keep the sails furled, though, we want to keep as thin a profile as possible. When we get five miles out, turn west."

She pulled a phone out of one pocket and a SIM card out of the other, put the SIM in and texted a message. Then she sat, watching the platform recede.

"You're not going to throw the phone away?" he asked.

"Not until that text gets an answer," she said.

When the text came, she visibly relaxed.

"And?" he asked. He turned to the west and slowed down to a crawl.

"It's all good. We can relax for a few hours."

"And what does that mean?" She didn't answer right away, and he waited. But then he added, *"Yo, te espero."*

"Sorry. I'm used to working alone" she said, as if that was the end of it. But then she looked back at him, readjusted herself. "Okay," she said. "We wait here until morning. In the morning, people from the company are coming on a ship, and they're bringing press—camera crews, boom mikes, lights, everything. This was already in the works, to open the facility and make the international news programs with it. So Darkwater will have to retreat or be on the news as, what did you call them before? Pirates? Yes, pirates. We win this round, no question."

"Then why do we have to wait here? Can't we go now, get the bug removed, and make our mistake?"

"Make our mistake?" she said, truly puzzled.

"Huh, that was weird. I meant to say *make our escape*."

"Calling Dr. Freud."

"Oy, yeah, okay. I'll admit I'm worried about everything."

"Good. It will keep you alert. We wait here, for now, because in the morning, we will go in first, an hour before the GreenCon ship, to give the Darkwater people some time to think through how they want to handle being on the evening news."

The sun set.

"Do we keep running or drift?"

"Yes, you're right, we can drift," she said. "I'm going to go meditate. I have to get myself centered."

He stayed outside, and an hour or so later climbed into his hammock to sleep—it was always better there than below deck when he was anxious. The sea was calm, a faint taste of salt on his lips, the slightest of breezes, and in a minute he was out cold.

He woke at first light. When he opened his eyes, she was already on deck, with two coffees poured.

"Good lord, my dreams," he said.

"Don't tell me," she said. "They will either be boring or bad for our relationship, or both. But hop up. We need to head in, now."

Our relationship. Huh. By the time he had gone down to the bathroom and come back, she had raised the sails and was on a close reach, the sails perfect, the motor giving an added assist, heading back toward the platform.

"We're in a hurry, I guess," he said.

"Yes, the press will be only a half hour or so behind us, according to Eamon, and this is a Darkwater guy we're dealing with—or guys if they've already reinforced, which they probably have. They will need to run their new plan up the flagpole before they act."

"Up the ladder?"

"Flagpole, ladder. It's corporate."

Two hours later, they approached the platform, and Frank saw the guy from yesterday, now with a woman. He told The Assassin and handed her the binoculars. She watched, hidden behind the hammock.

"The woman has taken cover, now," she said. "And I count two snipers, anyway. They've used the time well. There are two boats, one that seems to have major equipment covered with a tarp. Unless there are boats on the other side of the island that means eight soldiers."

She outlined the plan to him: they'd pull right up to the big pier, she'd hop out and explain the facts to them, and then see what developed. Soon after they arrived, the big boat full of press would be visible.

"That should make sure the Darkwater people have good manners," she said. "If they have removed all GreenCon's tech people, which I think they have, they'll have to fill in and pretend to be part of the GreenCon team, or else GreenCon will have to explain that Darkwater came in and took their staff away. That will be kind of fun to see, to watch them scramble and playact."

By the time they arrived, armed men still lay in sniper positions on either end of the largest platform, up two stories from the dock, in perfect spots to keep their colleagues covered from anything that might be thrown at them. The woman was nowhere to be seen. The guy from the other day was waiting on the dock.

"Well, well," he said. "We didn't expect to see you back so soon. Or at all!" he was light, joshing them, confidant, much more relaxed than the day before. "No need to come any closer."

Frank threw it in reverse and brought it to a stop a dozen feet away.

"The situation is fundamentally altered," The Assassin told the man on the dock. "I'm coming ashore to explain to you and whoever is in the position of authority here what has to happen next."

He ignored her and turned to Frank. "Who else is on the boat?"

Frank looked to her before answering, which was almost the right thing to do, and she answered for him.

"Nobody but the two of us."

He smiled at her, perfunctory. "Pull closer."

Frank maneuvered in, praying they wouldn't riddle his ship with bullets and scuttle it. The reddish-haired woman came out of hiding, armed, and the Malagasy guy hopped onto the boat and went below deck. He popped his head up and said all was clear, but came out carrying the two bags of guns.

"Go ahead and dock," he said to Frank. Frank threw lines onto the dock and hopped up and tied it off.

"Please," the woman said. "Come with me."

The Assassin joined Frank on the dock, and the two snipers, or two other armed men, materialized. They came up and told Frank and The Assassin to spread their arms.

"We are unarmed," The Assassin said. One of the men shook his head and went about frisking them anyway. He took her small handgun from her leg holster and put it in his belt. No judgment.

"Okay," the woman said. "Who do I have the honor of addressing."

The Assassin answered, with a smile, "I could give you a name . . ." They both laughed.

"You can call me Skye," the woman said.

"Okay," she said, not bothering to reciprocate. "Here is the deal,

Skye. A boat, a mega yacht, will appear, in a few minutes, coming in from the north. You've probably already seen it on your radar. It carries principals of GreenCon as well as their press managers, along with a passel of international media—print, radio, and TV. There will be, as I understand it, four camera crews, from BBC, Al Jazeera, ITV, and CNN, some live-streaming websites, and some papers and radio. They are here for an announcement of the launch of this electric generating station, and then they will give the media a tour of the facility."

She let this sink in for a minute.

"I see," Skye said.

"Good, I was hoping I didn't need to explain. You will want to discuss with your employer, I am sure, but first, can you tell me how many GreenCon employees are still here, and what shape they are in? How we move forward will depend on that information."

"All of the former GreenCon employees have been offered new positions with our company, which they have elected to pursue. They are all now employed in another location. Here we have a total of eight people, more on the way."

"In that case," she said, "we think the smart thing for Darkwater's exposure would be—"

"I didn't say Darkwater," Skye said.

"I know you didn't. The best thing for Darkwater's exposure would be for your team here to assist us in this press event, posing as GreenCon employees. I'll need their names and areas of expertise in order to reassign them. I'll let you discuss with your superiors. Five minutes will be enough, yes?"

Skye nodded and went into one of the rooms.

Her Number Two—the athletic guy from the day before—spied the big ship appearing and talked into his shoulder.

Skye came back out.

"Here are your employees for the day," Skye said, handing over a list.

“I’d lose some of the armament,” The Assassin told her. “This is a commercial enterprise, not a military one. If you can assemble your people, I will give them each their assignment. And you can put my guns back on my ship. Frank, you’ll need to move to the smaller dock to make room for this big pig of a boat coming in.”

XXXVII
Alain

THE BOAT LOOKED like Jeff Bezos's yacht or Putin's—a long, tall, sleek, up-to-the-minute international superstar, a football field's length, with the gleaming glamor of a *Yachting* magazine cover shot. The crew waiting to help dock it, all dressed in a uniform of white shirt, navy slacks, and white sneakers, outnumbered everyone on the platform, with several of those crewmen poised to jump down to the second pier to tie it in. Alain and the rest of the Darkwater people all stood there feeling foolish, as if an evil magician's wand had turned them from international spies and warriors into bellboys and parking attendants. The Spanish woman had explained to him that he was to act as the head of security for GreenCon, assigned to this facility to ensure that nothing interfered with its supply of electricity to the surrounding islands and nations. She asked him to repeat that, and he did.

"Excellent," said the Spanish woman. "Don't deviate from that script. As I told the others, it doesn't matter how many times you say the same thing. This is the press. They expect you to repeat yourself as each of them asks you the same question. If you are asked what kind of threats you are prepared to meet, you say, 'We foresee none, but we are ready for any.' If they ask, 'Any like what?' you repeat, 'Anything, but we foresee none.' If they push, smile, say 'Thank you,' and walk away."

The yacht expertly approached the dock, and once it was secure, a ramp was extended. The press piled out, set up their cameras and sound stations, placed their portable transmitter dishes out on the pier, ready to send footage to their networks. The Spanish woman was hanging in the back of the crowd, with her inept sidekick, scanning the platform and keeping track of everyone. He couldn't figure out the guy she called Frank's role—he seemed even more fidgety; maybe he was IT? Alain guessed the Spanish woman was more than just a messenger.

Down a second gangplank the yacht's crew had set up, a tall man in his forties emerged, with a bit of a smirk on his face, carrying himself like someone of importance. He was followed by a female assistant and a bodyguard. They were met with a phalanx of microphones and the clicking and flashing of dozens of hefty cameras. A TV crew was setting up to talk to Alain—that is, to talk to the head of GreenCon's security at the location—and he was running his few lines through his head. But when the boss man showed up on the walkway, they left him behind, saying they would catch him later.

Alain clocked Mr. Big give the Spanish woman a slight nod before he began talking to the press, and he noticed that the inept sidekick had vanished.

He looked over his left shoulder to see Skye standing behind him, watching. "Who is this guy?" he asked her.

"He's Dmitry Heald, a partner, with his wife, in GreenCon, and one of the richest men in the world."

"Measured by the size of his yacht, I would think yeah."

"We want to welcome you all," Dmitry Heald was saying in a British accent to the cameras, as if there was a great crowd behind them. "To this momentous day. It is the day that the Indian Ocean islands, from the Maldives to the Seychelles, and from the British Indian Ocean Territory to Mauritius, the Comoros, and La Réunion, become energy independent, and 100 percent green, if they want to be."

Alain leaned in toward Skye. "Who is he selling what?" he asked.

"He wants everyone to be independent from every energy supplier except him," she said quietly so only he could hear. "And he wants the press to think this is only about energy, when it is really about military contracting. The biggest buyer for the tidal farm energy is the US base. He thinks of that as his lever to oust Darkwater from the region."

"If you will follow Cindy here, GreenCon's head of communications," Dmitry was saying, as Cindy waved. "She can show you the turbine field and the control centers that monitor it and transfer the energy to thousands of islands, many as much as a thousand miles away, many of which have never had reliable energy before."

The press throng followed the brightly smiling Cindy into the tunnels.

Alain watched them leave until Skye punched him in the arm.

"Look at that Chinese guy!" she said.

A Chinese man in his thirties was in the press scrum.

"What about him?"

"He was on the expedition boat. How did he get here?"

"You sure it's him?"

"Are you kidding?"

"No, I'm serious—you sure this isn't a 'they all look alike' situation?"

"Have you ever been to Shanghai? Beijing? Hong Kong? Taipei? Xi'an? Xining? Harbin? Tianjin? Shenzhen?"

He was shaking his head no to each.

"Well I've been to all of them, so shut the fuck up. This dude was on the ship, pretending to be a scientist."

"Okay, tell me what you want me to do."

"I'm going to follow him down and see who he talks to, while you shadow Dmitry Heald—" She paused, as if grasping that he didn't have any training in this kind of operation. "Don't let him know you're on him. If he challenges you, or his security guys challenge you, say you are a big fan of GreenCon, and interested in a job with them. They will say you should email the HR director and leave you behind, or at worst shunt you off to someone else on their team. At that point you can ask for a business card, so you can get in touch, but that you need to get back to your post. Got it?"

He assured her he did and headed off to execute his first tail. He was right, he should have been sent to spy school, but he'd watched enough thrillers to know how to tail someone and stay inconspicuous. He scrutinized Dmitry Heald glad-hand with the journalists. If you were stupid, he concluded, you would think Dmitry was charming. He was not stupid, but he couldn't decide whether the guy was a garden variety con man or a bona fide beast. Watching him in action, he was leaning toward the latter.

XXXVIII
Frank

WHAT ARE THE chances, Frank thought, of Dmitry showing up here? By some freak accident, he had once again become mixed up in Dmitry's orbit, and despite the warning from Kennedy, he never expected to actually run into him. Even when he saw him get off the yacht, he thought he could avoid actually meeting him. He slipped away and hid out in the comms room. Then it occurred to him that he might need to skedaddle from there, too, if it turned out to be on the tour for the press corps. It came to him with a start that the room he was in, and all the equipment in it, was owned by Dmitry, or if not him, by his wife.

Frank stepped outside. Everyone had gone into the tunnels to look at the turbines, except for two security men near Dmitry's yacht, and he decided that the only place for him to be safe, and stay out of the way, was on his own ship. He crossed the slab to the *God Sees,* looking puny now compared to the conspicuous space-age monstrosity on the next pier. He ducked into the cockpit, and from there straight into the cabin.

Sitting there, lounging at the dining table, was, of course, Dmitry. Adrenaline shot through Frank's system.

"Come, come, Franky, you can't be *that* surprised!" Dmitry looked quizzically at Frank and then laughed. "Okay! Maybe you can be. Your capacity for ingenuousness thrives unabated, I see!"

"Well, I knew it was your company we were dealing with, but

yeah, I guess I am surprised." He had dreaded the possibility of their paths crossing, but now that it had happened, after the first shock, he felt oddly calm. "You had kind of turned into a figment of my imagination. In a way, I no longer really thought you existed."

"Well, Franky," Dmitry said. "I most definitely do! And I find myself in a predicament now, as I'm sure you can appreciate."

He appreciated nothing but wasn't about to say it.

"You put the tracker on the boat way back then, in Taiwan. Why?"

"Yes—well, not me of course—but yes, we put a GPS tracker on your yacht, because at first, well, we needed to know you wouldn't do something very stupid. And then, over the years, I suppose I never stopped thinking of it as my money, and thus my yacht. Same with your dinghy. Dinghy! Funny word. Do you know the origin?"

Frank didn't take that bait, either—Dmitry used little verbal meanderings about word origins to keep his auditors off balance, dousing them with useless information. He was a master of noise.

"And surely, Franky, you know that I had no choice, right? What if you were to get yourself to Gallup, New Mexico, say, on your famous Route 66, and take it into your head to run for public office, and the FBI do a background check and one thing leads to another—if you were going to start blabbing, I'd need to take you out, wouldn't I? I mean, practically speaking."

"Practically speaking, a tracker on my boat would not track me to Gallup, New Mexico."

"Funny. But Franky, you are quite a predictable person, you must know that. Why do you think I'm sitting here waiting for you? I could have had your trail followed from wherever you had parked the boat. You do bugger all to cover your steps, you have been using the same password for fifteen years—adding a couple letters when people started requiring eight letters, and an exclamation point to the beginning when they started requiring symbols as well. I've been tempted to empty your accounts, in fact, except that the banks chase that stuff down so thoroughly, and you've remained so agreeably quiet I didn't want to rile you up, stoke up the sacred rage." All of this without disturbing the smirk. "Still, I do, I don't mind saying, make a point of siphoning two points or so off your brokerage accounts every year, just for *auld lang syne*."

How he hated the man. He would change all his passwords now and change them again tomorrow. What did this hooligan want? He decided to ask him.

"What do you want?"

"Ah, at last, we come to the nub. You have come to know my Nikita."

"Nikita. Is that her name?"

"Who knows, Franky? In her line of work everything is a lie. The Shining, people call her, but I call her Nikita."

"And everything in your life is a lie, too." He paused, but he had to know. "She's Spanish—why Nikita?"

"Have you never seen the film, *La Femme Nikita*? No of course not, you don't sully yourself with such things, do you, resolutely lodged in the empyrean with your little collection of literati. Has it ever occurred to you, Franky, that your obsession with literature is just overcompensation for your humble origins? But no mind. The film was my inspiration, but she's turned out a bit more like that Sandra Oh show which of course you've never seen either, and I hadn't seen when we set her up. And since you asked, no, it is decidedly not *all lies* in my line of work."

"I didn't ask. I just said it, straight out. It wasn't a question, it was a fact."

"Ah, yes, but haven't you ever noticed how people often say something not because they are sure of it, but because they think it might be true, and they want some confirmation? They will produce a declarative sentence, but it is actually in an interrogative mood. It's like a hypothesis, and so the question comes along with it—'God is dead,' we say out loud, and we ask, silently, 'Is he?' We can say, 'You're an asshole,' and then sit back and let the other person answer the implied question. But lies? Yes and no. I rely on people's confidence. I rely on their investment. They require a great deal of truth in that bargain. Most things I say are lies, yes, but the true things are just as important." Frank had to concede this. "And if you're being honest," he went on, "you'd have to admit that in your old line of work, you used a lot of convenient lies, too. 'Yes, we can have the roof on by Thursday,' you would say, thinking maybe, if everything goes perfectly and we have a little luck, it *could* happen by Thursday or Friday. But let us not wax philosophical, shall we? I'm in a practical mood. I don't know how much you know about our friend Nikita, but she cut off her stepfather's dick—*and balls!*—and stuffed them in his mouth *while he was still alive!* I *mean!* You *have* to respect that kind of decisiveness. That level of follow-through. She's a visionary! I read about her in the paper and sent my associate—you remember your small Irish friend? From Tokyo?"

"Eamon."

"Yes, Eamon is one of the names he has been known to use, although—well, never mind, let's call him, yes, Eamon, and I'll remind him never to use it again! Eamon went to Zaragoza, Salamanca, or whatever dusty town she was locked up in, straightened out her legal situation, and brought her along, maximizing her human potential like Rex Harrison did for Audrey Hepburn. Anyway, here is my predicament—"

Frank had hardly been listening. He was lost in the past, feeling a mix of shame, nostalgia, and panic, reliving the time he had rushed to Asia to "save" Yuli, Dmitry's wife, who didn't need saving and who he had only met once, although that one time was long enough to find himself entranced, ensorcelled, or whatever it was. The bank building where Dmitry worked had exploded, killing dozens of people, with Dmitry assumed to be among the victims. Frank flew to Yuli's aid and, well, she had known all along that Dmitry was not dead, that he was just fine, that he was probably behind the blast. She knew her husband had been up to his neck in corrupt rackets of all sorts, abetting the worst kind of global criminality. Probably knew what a deluded sot he, Frank, was being...

"I regret everything," Frank said, mostly to himself.

"Ah, but *do* you, my boy? I'm not at all sure you do. You have taken to the high life quite nicely, compared to the poor boy who hated the rich with 'the smoldering hatred of the peasant'—wasn't that it?"

And Frank had, when everything was revealed, taken millions of dollars—stolen them wouldn't be correct, since they were being laundered and stashed in accounts in Frank's name, accounts Frank didn't know Dmitry had set up. As he thought about it, he realized how convoluted and implausible it all sounded.

"Close enough," he said. And in fact he didn't regret *everything*. He might never have understood his own idiocy, or his own misogyny, if it hadn't been for Dmitry. He might still be—what did "Nikita" call it?—a moony little boy, trying to be a player in his pathetic way, but thinking he was a sensitive guy because he wasn't as bad as this person in front of him. "Maybe you're right," he said.

"Hard-won knowledge, eh, Franky? I am so glad to have been a catalyst for your education, even if, in your New England, moralistic, Dimmesdale-like way, you've got it all wrong still. But on to more pressing matters."

"Not just a catalyst, Exhibit A."

"Ah, Franky, you may have learned many things, but not, it seems, how unattractive resentment is. As I was saying—"

"I'm sorry, sir—" One of the communications director's assistants had poked her head in the cabin.

"Yes?"

"Lauren would like you to answer a few follow-ups from the press."

"I will regale them fulsomely once we are back on the boat."

"Ship," Frank said, absentminded, thinking about how, again, just as he had been those years ago with Dmitry and Yuli, he was enmeshed in some cheesy plot.

"Ah, ever the pedant! I was using 'boat' as an endearing diminutive."

The assistant started to say, "She thought it might be better to talk to them here—" but she trailed off looking at Dmitry's stony face, became inaudible, bowed, and backed out of the room.

"Have you ever inspired fear in another human being, Franky? It is quite delightful. I'd call it the fear of God, but that would be immodest. As I was saying—"

"You are willing to besmirch all of green energy to do what, make a few more bucks?"

"To 'besmirch' it? You should be proud of me, Franky, I'm an environmental justice warrior! We're making tidal energy fiscally respectable. We're making it *Wall Street Journal* respectable! And it isn't yet truly profitable, you know, compared to fossil fuel—I'm fudging the numbers, with the paramilitary base picking up the slack. Ah, but that's enough high finance, then, because here she is!"

Dmitry stood up, but did not move toward The Assassin, who had arrived in the hatch.

"Nikita!" he said, with his obnoxious big grin. "We finally meet!"

They kept their current distance like cats meeting for the first time. The air felt bristly, and Frank imagined them both with their fur up, ears twitching. But as he looked at them, he saw that neither of them betrayed a single outward sign of discomfort, save that maintained distance.

"Sir."

"So formal! Although I do appreciate the deployment of tactical servility. I was regaling Franky here with tales of your derring-do!" He went on, calmly continuing his unbroken series of wry observations, all of them perfectly balanced between affability and threat, between hyperbole and insult.

"Sir," she said again, with the same lack of affect.

"Ah! But, come now!" he said, sitting back down. "I have eavesdropped on a conversation or two of yours, my dear Nikita, and so I know this laconic delivery is out of character. And I should tell you that I recognize the syndrome—Baltimoritis, I call it—our friend here somehow manages to engender a protective response in women, and although scientists have yet to isolate the precise etiology of the disease, I have always assumed it to be based in a notion, which he encourages subliminally, that he did not receive 'good enough mothering', stimulating a desire to make up for that deficit. *Anywho,* I'm sure you can both see that this further complicates our arrangements."

"We have no arrangements," Frank said.

"I am going to have to disagree with you there, Franky, my boy. We have all sorts of arrangements. We—you and I—have an ongoing arrangement that I leave that money of mine in your hands"—Frank was not about to get in a pissing match about whose money it was—"and Nikita, you and I have understandings and arrangements as well."

"I believe our last arrangement is concluded," she said. "I discussed it with our friend, and let him know the situation is in control and in your hands."

"So! You do speak! You can come in and sit down, you know. I am not going to kill you and you are not going to kill me with the international press floating around the island, so let's relax, shall we?"

"*Jajajajaja,*" she said. "We will not kill each other right now." But she didn't move.

"All things considered," Dmitry said, "I think things went quite smoothly here. The Darkwater folks are doing a good job pretending to be GreenCon employees, and the press all found a story or two, all of which redound to our credit, and our new folks will arrive shortly to recommence building, *et cetera, et cetera, et cetera*. I'm afraid, though, Franky, I must ask you to take your *ship* and leave, if for no other reason than your dock space here will be needed for the construction materials coming in. And Nikita, I will ask you to accompany me to my yacht, where I have had a magnificent stateroom made ready for you. We have so much to talk about!"

To Frank's chagrin, she nodded to this suggestion and withdrew.

"I'm so sorry, Franky," he said having seen Frank follow her out with his eyes. "If you had asked, I would have told you that professional assassins are not the most loyal and trustworthy people in the world, and one shouldn't pin one's hopes on them. But I'm sure you'll be fine. You've recovered from losing the love of your life so many times. I'm sure you can do it once more."

"Don't you have enough money by now?" Frank asked, and it was a real question. He was disturbed, but he was curious.

"Come, Franky, do you really think money is the sole motive to pains and hazard, deception and devilry, in this world? How much money did the devil make by gulling Eve?"

"Then what?"

"Ah, Franky. You know quite well that the perversity of the human heart knows no bounds." He stood up and looked deeply bored. "Try not to cross my path again, will you, old man?"

With that he walked out and stepped onto the dock. Frank got up and watched from the hatch. Nikita was waiting for Dmitry, and the two of them made their way, side by side, security guys following, to his gaudy behemoth.

I have no one to blame but myself, Frank thought. Nobody, nobody but me.

XXXIX
Skye

THE CHINESE GUY did a perfect, quiet job of blending into the press corps, and when the tour was over, they all either headed back to the two hundred million dollar yacht (Skye looked it up while she was waiting) or worked putting their cameras, cables, boom mikes, and other gear away. She lost track of him then for a minute, and after scanning the platforms, decided to skip onto the yacht with the stragglers to find him there. She stashed her handgun in the comms room to get through the metal detector on the yacht's ramp, and headed in.

Once aboard she saw why the journalists were in such a hurry to get back. The Vegas-like chandeliered ballroom was scattered with instantly replenished buffets of sushi, finger sandwiches, a dozen classic tapas, hot and cold mezas, seafood cocktails of every persuasion, and waitstaff walking through with trays of wine, champagne, Aperol spritzers, and martinis. It was a floating party, and they had missed it during their half hour of work. The Chinese guy was nowhere to be seen, and she corralled one somewhat tipsy bro she recognized as a camera operator and asked him if there had been any Chinese media. He was having trouble focusing, and when he did it was on her chest. But then he said no, just American and European, plus *Al Jazeera*. Unless some of the print people were from a Chinese rag—he didn't really pay any attention to them, since it wasn't his *thing*. She left him trying to figure out how to say something interesting.

There were several low-slung seating areas, two bars in the center of the room and a fountain, and she needed to walk around until she found sight lines to the whole room. She walked as fast as she could without attracting attention and poked her head down a few hallways on either end. She saw Dmitry enter along with the Spanish advance person that had sailed in with the civilian. She still couldn't figure out his part in this. When Dmitry walked in, the press bowed and scraped around him as he breezed through the room and out the other side. She wandered to the large windows along the pier and saw Alain at the bottom of the ramp, trying to talk his way onto the boat. It worked, and a minute later he was in the room.

"I lost the Chinese guy," she told him.

"Careless of you."

"Yes. Did you see him?" Alain shook his head no. "If he's on the boat he's hiding, which means he saw that I spotted him. If he's off the boat he's up to no good. We can't do anything else here, let's head back."

"Dmitry went on the sailboat," Alain said.

This was a new wrinkle, maybe. "And?"

"He was on the boat for a few minutes, then the civilian joined him. They were below deck for ten minutes and then the Spanish woman came and got him."

As they headed out of the room, the ship's horn sounded an all-aboard warning. They gave one last scan of the journalists enjoying their early happy hour, and then headed down to the dock. As soon as they stepped off the ramp, two of the crew freed the bow and stern lines, went back on board, and pushed the button that retracted the ramp. Almost immediately, the ship began pulling away. The sun was close to the horizon, and they saw Frank standing on the deck of his boat, watching the ship depart.

"I don't like how quiet it is," she said, and she could hear a bit of panic in her own voice. She looked at Alain, who was, she saw, keeping his cool better than she was keeping hers. She found herself grateful. "I don't like it all."

She ran to the comms room, Alain on her heels, and it was empty. She opened the cabinet where she had left her gun, and it was gone.

"Something is very wrong here," she said.

They ran down to the turbine tunnels, all quiet and empty, but in the first room, Alain heard something and stopped to listen.

An engine had started outside. They looked at each other.

"The sailboat?" Alain asked. "Shouldn't we debrief the sailor, Frank, and see what he talked to Dmitry about?"

"Absolutely," Skye said. "You go and see if you can stop him. But something is very wrong here." Alain ran out and she kept going into the tunnels. Around the first corner she saw two bodies. One of the tech guys and J.R., both with bullet holes in their foreheads. It crushed her. She pulled open the cabinet where they had stashed guns, and they were there, and her handgun, too. But all of them had been emptied of ordnance—there wasn't a single bullet in any of them—and each had a small but necessary central part removed, rendering them useless. She ran farther in and found J.T. and the other techs, also prone, and she checked their pulses. All stone dead. Again, there were drawers where they had stashed weapons. Again, bullets and parts had been removed—bolts, firing pins—she assumed dumped in the water somewhere. The Chinese assassin had moved fast and had shot J.T. and J.R. first, got the tech guys to point out the weapons, and shot them next. All with silencers, all while she was looking for him on the fucking yacht.

J.R. dead. J.T. dead. On her watch. Her friends were dead, her colleagues dead, gruesomely dead, holes in their fucking heads. Maybe it wasn't entirely her fault, but it was more her fault than anyone else's. It was her command. And why? She had the sickening realization that it was a message. Her people had been murdered to send a motherfucking message. Was there a chance the killer was still on the island? She ran back out and Alain was on the dock, looking through the binoculars. Frank had come up to join him.

"Look at this," Alain said, and pointed to the receding yacht. He handed her the binoculars. The Chinese guy had taken their two boats, driving one and towing the other, and they watched as he sped toward Dmitry's mega yacht. They could do nothing. Frank's sailboat, even with more wind than there was, could never catch him. The murderer turned and stabbed the boat behind him, the one with the two drones, and it sank quickly. He pulled next to the yacht and a crew member lowered a ladder. The killer grabbed it and slashed the second boat. He climbed up the ladder as the boat sank.

"That man killed my friends and killed my coworkers," Skye said as she stared at the receding ship. "I am going to hunt him down and kill him. I am."

Frank's mouth hung open and Alain was shaken. "Killed? All of them?" he asked, although he knew.

"All of them," she said. "J.T., J.R., Eddy, Bill, E.N." They had trouble looking at each other. "I need to call Darkwater. We need a recovery boat."

"I'll call it in," Alain said. "I've got this." He pulled out his phone and walked off the boat onto the pier and back toward the tunnel.

Frank was a civilian, and he was, like any normal person, having trouble processing the horrible, basic facts.

"All five of those guys are dead?" he asked her. "Are you sure?" And then off her silence, "Why? Who?"

She turned to Frank and said, with as much kindness as she could muster: "Yes, I am sure. And their murderer is the guy we just watched scuttle our boats." She had been at a loss, but now she saw that she had to pull it together. She needed to tell Frank what to do. "I'm afraid, Frank," she said, "we are going to need your help."

XL
Mónica

HOW VERY STRANGE, she thought, sitting in her oversized stateroom on the mega yacht, running over what had just happened. How strange it had been to see those two sitting in Frank's sailboat—the brutal and scary employer she had never met and the hard-to-define wanderer she had developed an inexplicable attachment to. And how very strange to be, a few minutes later, in this super-luxury stateroom, a swanky prisoner, having been disarmed by his security people.

She had two tasks: foiling the surveillance systems in her stateroom and scaring up some weapons. Dmitry understood those would be her goals, so the first thing he did was send two crew members down to bring her up to the dining room for dinner. She didn't mind, because she was starving, and observing him close up could only help. She knew that he had to be a little torn. She was the best at what she did, a star performer he could be proud of as a businessman and as a power broker, a great weapon in his arsenal, and an amusing one. He had complimented her, as they walked to the yacht, on several stylish kills in recent months, including the CFO in Madagascar. On the other hand, Eamon must have told him that she was flaking out, maybe a problem, maybe at the end of her usefulness, maybe a liability. Any normal employer would be torn.

But he was so unperturbable, so unflappable, amused, even, by the state of affairs, that she wondered if he had either not heard Eamon's concerns, discounted them, or already decided to kill her and was amusing himself with her in the meantime. She decided it was prudent to assume the last.

The dining room was outfitted like a set-designer's vision of an elite men's club in London circa 1912, all dark wood paneling and brass fixtures, and overstaffed even if some of the waiters, butlers, and sommeliers, or whatever they were supposed to be, were just bodyguards posing as servants. It made her think he was born poor—he had built a simulacrum of an aristocratic setting, a Downton Abbey on the high seas, aping a lifestyle nobody actually lived.

"Have you ever considered," she asked him when she sat down at the table and accepted a glass of champagne, although he had sparkling water instead, "the possibility of a normal life?"

"And leave show business?" he said.

"Yes."

"No," he said, with an understated shrug.

"Did you ever consider becoming a dentist?"

"Once, after watching *Marathon Man*." A total of four waiters brought them an appetizer covered in silver cloches, and executed some baroque choreography that again, struck her as a comic exaggeration of fine dining service. Maybe it was. She didn't pay much attention to the food, watching him as she chewed. He, in full aplomb, with his devilish grin, said, "But please, make your point."

"I'm serious," she said. "I think we basically understand each other, don't we? We are people who do not live by any rules but our own, who are incapable of squeamishness. We don't care about anything except whatever it might be that we happen to care about at a particular moment. Is this sounding familiar or foreign?"

"Everything foreign is familiar to me, so . . ."

"*Jijijijijiji*," she said. "You won't talk seriously, okay. We don't talk seriously." She poured oil on a small plate, added salt and pepper, and swirled a piece of bread in it. "But you disappoint me."

"I am mortified."

"*Jajajajaja*. I have entertain you, okay." Time for some bad grammar. "Your turn now. You entertain." She chewed the bread, making a point of having a mouth full so he would talk.

"Why don't you want to work for me anymore?"

"Do I work for you?"

"Who doesn't want to talk seriously?"

"What do you want, finally?" A quick change of subject always worked for her.

"Ah, the world's oldest question!" He said, with his goofy grin. The waiters repeated their dumb show with the covered plates, this time uncovering a filet mignon in the middle of a circle of demiglace. That's what she needed, a little red meat. She took a bite.

"Really?" she asked. "You want sex? I don't think so."

"Why not?" He kept his amused mien, always ready to enjoy what life had to offer. She concentrated on eating her meat and took her time answering.

"Because you are rapist. I won't let you rape me, and I guarantee you wouldn't enjoy if you tried."

"Fair enough," he said with a slight laugh, like he was a customer at a comedy club, waiting for the next joke.

"I'm going to bed." She stood up.

"Okay," he said. "But one last thing—"

"Yes?"

"I want you to kill Frank Baltimore."

"Okay," she said. "Then why drag me away from him?"

"Oh, don't worry. He will come looking for you. He has a knight in shining armor complex. And you know that he fucked my wife?"

"How would I know that?"

"Figure of speech. I want you to kill him in a way that I, as the contractor *and* as the cuckold, will appreciate."

"I love a narrative through-line."

He smiled. She had no idea what it signified. She smiled back, but she was afraid any fool could have read her smile as the worried sneer that it was.

XLI
Alain

ALAIN WALKED BACK into the tunnel. At the first station he saw J.R. and Eddy, with blood in pools around them, bullet holes in their heads. He felt a wave of nausea, and tasted silver. How? How did their killer get them to stand still long enough to shoot them both in the middle of the forehead? Or was he that fast? His stomach clenched, and he bent over to puke, but managed not to and went on. He went down a flight of stairs, past a bank of monitors, and found J.T., Bill, and E.N., all, too, with the signature forehead shot. He thought about checking for pulses, and that sent him over the edge. He turned and threw up across the hallway. He turned back to the bodies and saw there was nothing to check. They couldn't be more dead. He tried to phone the base at Diego Garcia, but had no reception.

He headed back up the stairs and outside, and tried the phone again. Five dead, he reported when he got the watch commander. All shot in the forehead. He recounted, as best he could, the sequence of events. He told them their boats had been taken and then scuttled, the drones at the bottom of the ocean. They would need a recovery team as soon as possible, since they had no land in which to bury the men, no refrigeration, and no transportation.

The watch commander put him on hold, and when he came back, he explained in a matter-of-fact tone that a recovery team would not be coming, that Darkwater would deny any knowledge of the events there. Alain stood in the spot, unable to speak. Five people he had been working with an hour earlier were lying, twisted, in their own blood, already fetid, already stiff, and they were to be left there? Abandoned? "Really?" he asked, and got no answer. "Are you fucking kidding me?" he said, and the call clicked dead.

He walked back toward Frank's boat. Skye was sitting with Frank and looked up at him. He could see that she was worn out by the day, crumpled by the deaths, still weak from her own wounds. He felt a wave of tenderness toward her. He was trying to figure out how to tell her that they were being abandoned when she read it in his face and waved her hand, as if to say *don't bother saying it, I know those bastards, and I don't want to hear it.*

She looked around at where they were, and came to the same conclusion he had. There was no place to bury a body. It was all concrete and coral. The only possibilities were to find a real island with unused soil or burial at sea. Given how little land there was in the surrounding miles, and the lack of refrigeration, burial at sea was the only option.

"Frank," Skye said. "I am so sorry you have gotten tangled up in this—you're just a civilian, right?—but we are going to need your assistance." She waited for him to catch up with her: he was in shock and his brain was moving slowly. "We have five dead comrades, and given the circumstances, many of which are classified"—Alain was impressed that she could, even as she was written off by her employer, invoke their authority—"we need to give them a dignified and solemn burial at sea."

Frank blinked at this for a moment.

"Our first grim task," she said, and she included Alain in this, "is to prepare the bodies and bring them out. We will understand, Frank, if this is too difficult for you." She looked at him with tenderness and concern in her eyes. It was as if returning to her role as leader had given her new strength. That is how she could work her magic, even in distress. She gained strength and vigor by making things happen.

"I can help," Frank said.

"We so very much appreciate that," she said. "These were friends as well as colleagues, and it is a shattering tragedy. We so appreciate your courage at this moment."

She sounded like a flowery press release, and Alain wondered if this was gilding the lily a bit, but no, Frank took it to heart and looked, somehow, more courageous.

"We have so little to work with," Skye said, as if to both of them, but really to Frank. "We need to wrap the bodies."

Frank thought for a moment, and then said, "I have my spare sails."

"That is perfect," Skye said, and she got him to bring the sails, rope, and scissors to the dock. Then the three of them went back into the tunnels to dress their dead.

XLII
Frank

FRANK HAD NEVER had to deal with a dead body before. Human beings everywhere, stretching back generation after generation to the beginnings of time, he knew, had had to learn how to handle dead bodies, but in our sterile age, we can get through an entire life without ever putting our hands on one, leaving it all to professionals, undertakers, and mechanics of the dead. He, Skye, and Alain, thrown together by circumstance, seemed to be learning it at the same time. They worked for a military contractor, but seeing the depth of their grief, he thought perhaps they were new to it, too. They cut the sails as needed, pulled each of the bodies away from the sticky blotches of blood, folded their arms over their chests, and wrapped them tight in sailcloth, tied off with his extra lines. They found a metal cart near one of the work sites and he and Alain lifted each of the bodies onto it, wheeled them down to the dock, and lashed them, one by one, to the front deck of *God Sees*.

As the sun set, they headed to sea, leaving the bloody scene behind them. Two hours out, they stopped and lowered the sails to give each of their former friends and colleagues a makeshift funeral. Skye had marked each of the wrapped bodies so they knew who was who, and as they lifted the first body, Eddy's, to the rail, Skye said a brief homily, a few words about him, some general words about resting in peace, and a few other borrowed scraps of mourning language. Then she asked for a moment of silence, which was easy as she was the only one talking, said a last sentence or two, and then they let the body fall over the side. Eddy's body floated for a distressingly long time, though, bouncing against the side of the sailboat, a small fold of his wrapping coming undone, blood seeping through the sailcloth, generally destroying whatever dignity had been built by Skye's improvised ceremony. After that she asked Frank to start the engine and put them on a slow course, so that they could move gradually but firmly away from each body after they dropped it, and wouldn't have to watch, up close anyway, its too-slow swallowing by the waves.

As he paid attention to each of the men during the minute of silence, Frank wondered at the human need for sacrament, at how absurdly effective ritual was. He hadn't known any of these men, had only interacted with them after they were dead, and Skye was uncharacteristically ineloquent, which Frank chalked up to a state of shock and anguish. But he nevertheless felt genuinely moved by each mini-ceremony, and felt in communion not just with each of the men, but with the ancient, eternal grief of all people confronted by death. He felt the weight and inevitability of mortality.

They finished lowering the last man, named J.T., into the sea, and had one more long moment of silence, sitting in the growing dark. None of them, it seemed, had any desire to move, and none of them, either, seemed ready to do whatever it was that needed to be done next. They sat where they were. The engine on a low idle pushed them slowly across the ocean surface as the night fell over them.

XLIII
Skye

THE FUNERALS WERE not enough, they didn't even come close to giving her peace. It was her fault those men were dead. Her fault, and hers alone. She had argued to have them detailed here. She had been tailing their murderer and had lost him. She fell down on the job. And they died.

The journalists had boarded the mega yacht in the Maldives, and it was taking them back there. That was where she could pick up the Chinese guy's trail. She had to find him. Nothing else would let her face what she had done.

They sat in the dark for a while, all stewing in their private grief. But it was time, she decided, to get started.

"Frank."

"Yes?"

"Would you mind taking us to the Maldives?"

"I could do that. Why there?"

"I assume that is where Dmitry is, along with the man who killed my friends—the man who he ordered to kill my friends."

"Yes," Frank said. "I can very much do that."

And that was when she realized what she needed to do. She needed to kill Dmitry Heald.

"I will be forever in your debt," she said.

"That isn't necessary," he said.

Alain came out of his fugue state to say just one word.

"Okay."

"Okay?" she said.

"Yeah, okay."

She was flooded with gratitude. He was the only one she had left, except for maybe this Frank guy, who she still found confusing. And she was grateful that Alain stuck with her despite what was clearly her colossal failure as team leader. She felt terrible about having dragged him into it all. She had ruined his life, too. Instead of making amends for the colonial past she had written a new chapter of it. He had been sitting on his island, unhappy, sure, pissed off, but not in the middle of a paramilitary turf war, not with his livelihood, his identity, his future ripped away. She didn't want to be too dramatic about it, because when she met him, his future was no great shakes and he hated his present, and so she hadn't needed to work very hard to turn him—he was already three-quarters turned. But those few short days earlier, he hadn't been at risk of being murdered. He wasn't a man without a country. He wasn't adrift with a man and woman he didn't know, all his marbles in a game he didn't quite know how to play.

She needed to make it right for many reasons, but one of them was because she needed to make it right for him.

XLIV
Mónica

ALL SHE NEEDED to do, Dmitry had told her, was wait for Frank to dock in Malé. His Darkwater friends would figure out that the Maldives was where the *reconquistadors* had come from and gone back to. She thought, maybe, yes, Frank would come follow her there. But Frank was weird, so who knew. She stayed in her room as much as she could—it was a beautiful suite, deluxe, a bedroom, sitting room, and superb bathroom, a balcony over the sea, all in shades of white and linen. She gave a different excuse every time Dmitry sent word that he wanted her to join him for a meal. She was seasick, she said the first time. She had a town council meeting, she said the second. She was getting a massage, she said the third.

It became a game. He would send a card that said, "Lunch?" and she would send it back saying, "I have the flu." The messenger would come back with tea, honey, and Theraflu, with a card that said, "Late lunch?" She would tell the messenger to explain she was out with a friend. He would send back a note saying he would send a cab, and her friend should join them, just give him the address. She claimed she would send the friend in the cab to meet him, but she couldn't join them, she had a Zoom call with her mother. He said he would love to meet her mother. She said she had to cut the call short so she could testify before Congress. That one, she recognized too late, might be too close to the bone—don't get legalistic with an outlaw.

Finally, she answered the knock at her door and instead of the boy in white shirt, navy slacks, white sneakers, and a message tray, it was Dmitry himself.

"If I didn't know better," he said. "I would think you were avoiding me."

"*Jajajajajaja*," she said. "Of course I am avoiding you. I would like to continue to live, and I'm not sure you have the same goal for me."

"Well, of course I want you to live!" he said with the maddening grin. He walked into her room and sat in one of the plush armchairs facing her balcony. "I told you. I want you to murder Frank Baltimore, and I want you to do it in a deliciously ghoulish way, fitting his crimes. I want artistic perfection! For this, you must be alive!"

"And then?"

"Oh, then! Yes. Perhaps the next time we have dinner would be a good time to discuss the rest of your future. If the town council and Congress can spare you, that is. Or, if you prefer, after this one, quite personal, for me, assignment, we can agree that you return to our old ways, reporting to He Who Used to Be Called Eamon, but who henceforth we will call Liam."

"I worry that I have pissed Liam off one too many times."

"Oh, my dear, Liam's anger is, as Franky says, completely performative. You must know that! He has no feelings whatsoever. It is why he is so good at what he does."

"You think I am too emotional."

"My goodness, my dear! I don't really know you, do I? I only, before the last days, knew you through your work. So, to me, you are simply an artist. Artists we do not judge on the same scales we use for other people. Artists can be whoever they need to be."

"So that's a yes."

He laughed at that. "Maybe it is! But not to worry." He stood, quickly, turned, headed to the door, and left, throwing a "Ta-ta!" over his shoulder.

He was, as she was sure he hoped to be, an infuriating man. He had miraculously provided her with a full wardrobe, without a missing piece. She had never had a man buy her a single thing that she actually wanted to wear. Of the hundreds of gifts that had come her way, she had not kept a single piece of clothing, not a single piece of jewelry. But Dmitry's stuff was all, or almost all of it, very, very good, almost all things she could well have bought herself. And it all fit. Did the metal detector on the yacht's entry ramp have body imaging software that could be used by a tailor, could it calculate ring size? In any case, it was not only tasteful, it felt tailored. Maybe Eamon—that is, Liam—had long ago rummaged through her closets and made a note of everything. In any case, impressive. And it was a timely reminder how difficult it would be to get a jump on the guy.

That was part of the message.

In every way, so far, he had been ahead of her. It was completely aggravating. She was determined to change that, and soon.

XLV
Alain

HE COULD SEE that Skye had changed. She was as determined as ever, as decisive moment by moment, but something was lost. They talked out what had happened, and he tried to convince her that of course it wasn't her fault—it was the fault of the killer, and the guy who had hired the killer. It didn't really help, he could see, and as he spent time with it, and with her, he understood that the real problem wasn't just losing her friends—although that was hard on her, of course. The debacle was a major derailment of her career. Darkwater had been her only client for so long that she didn't have any network to fall back on. And she had a rep in the business as Darkwater's premier fixer. If she went out looking for new work, people would know Darkwater had dumped her, and that gossip, she was convinced, would be the end of her. Her only hope, she told him, was making it right somehow. And the thing that left her wan and depleted was the fact that she hadn't figured out how in god's name she was going to do that.

And it wasn't lost on him that he no longer had a job at Darkwater either. She reassured him that the company had a vested interest in not going back on their agreements, that the family support would always be there, because it was guaranteed by the company, and they had a solid reputation for honoring their commitments. They knew he could be gone in a flash, and that she could, but the deal was the deal. Angela and Raissa would continue to get their checks. He wanted to say okay, what about the fact that you and I are out of work? Darkwater was leaving them high and dry—how was that living up to their word? Was that loyalty? But he thought it would be cruel, given her anguish about being dumped. Besides, she had told him they were contractors, not employees, that they were freelance. That there was no pension plan.

This dude Frank he couldn't quite figure out. He was pretty chill and down to earth, despite his occasional hippy-dippy Buddhist talk and his tendency to quote from famous authors. He was doing them a major solid—if it weren't for him, they'd be stuck on that platform with a stack of corpses waiting for the GreenCon goons to come back. He was helping them without griping, and gratis. He seemed to really care about them and their well-being, despite having just met, and despite, in a way, being enemies, maybe—the last person he had helped and been chill with was Miss Bikini Legs, and she was playing for the other team. Frank said he knew nothing about her and GreenCon, and maybe that was true. If he did know who she was, and what he was dealing with, as he said, he might not have stuck his neck out so far. And that, in a nutshell, was the conundrum, wasn't it? Was he oblivious? Or was he a selfless bodhisattva? Or something else? Was he a double agent reporting on their every move? Or a babe in these dark woods? Was he some kind of evil genius or an unwitting but generous dope?

As unlikely as it seemed, he *could* be an evil genius, which would mean he was working for Dmitry. He had been holed up with him and the Spanish woman before they got back on the mega yacht, just before the Chinese guy went on his killing spree. Alain hadn't been able to get close enough to hear what they were saying, but it was suspicious. As he watched Frank go about his business, though, he decided no, nobody was that good an actor. He couldn't be playing on Dmitry's team and fake all that empathy.

He was curious about the Buddhist thing and asked. Frank said that the Buddha had taught that all suffering was the result of desire, and all Alain could say to that was *Amen, brother.* Frank looked at him funny, and then said, *cherchez la femme*? Alain had to nod to that, saying maybe, but it didn't matter, they found him anyway. Frank gave a mild laugh at that and then said, "Yes, I know what you mean."

"But," he added, "after a long time thinking women were somehow my problem, I had to conclude that I was *their* problem."

"Amen to that, too, brother," Alain said, and he kind of meant it. Frank told him about the Four Noble Truths, the Eightfold Path, and it all sounded right to him. If you stop desire, you stop suffering. If you did the right thing, thought the right way, had compassion, everything was that much better. He knew this was true.

They were getting close to Malé. If Skye was right, they would once again be in the shit and would know soon enough where Mr. Baltimore stood, whose interests he had in his Buddhist heart. He assumed Frank would find it very difficult, in the rockets' red glare, to maintain his Zen disinterestedness, if that's what it was—it is very difficult to be neutral in a firefight. On the other hand, isn't Frank right that it is all based on illusion? Alain had only very recently become a person who shot and killed people. Wouldn't it be nice to stop being that kind of person? To stop thinking like this? To get free of this fear and hope and anger and longing? Wouldn't he and everybody else be better if he stopped? If he and everybody else got off the wheel of karma?

He glanced at Skye and knew he was now talking a bunch of borrowed crap to himself. He knew very well that whatever options a white man with a yacht had, there was no way out for him. Not right now, anyway. Maybe not ever.

XLVI
Frank

AS THEY SAILED north toward the Maldives, he had trouble thinking about anything except the five dead men he had helped wrap in sailcloth and bury at sea. One morning he watched himself have the following thoughts: *death makes you think*. Then: d*eath makes you consider your own mortality*. Then: *there is nothing like death to make you think about mortality*. Almost every thought and feeling he had had, for days, had been trite, syllogistic, and pointless, and maybe, just maybe, equally profound and revelatory.

The winds were steady and kept him on an easy reach, a stable ride that left little work to do. He sat at the wheel, watching his instruments, not because he needed to, but because it gave him a sense of purpose, and a way to focus his wandering mind. The roiling spiral of shock and grief, like water eternally going down a drain—he knew he would need to ride it out, that this, too, would pass, some day. He had been through it all before, not least when everything blew up with Dmitry and Yuli those years ago, and he was sent spiraling across the oceans of the world.

As he watched Skye try to figure out her next move, he was convinced more than ever that the Buddhist path he had been on, no matter how amateurish, inchoate, and inexpert he was, had been exactly right for him—talking to Alain about it, too, had felt helpful. Skye was in mourning for her friends, but she was also despondent because she couldn't think of how to regain her position. She wanted her old career back. It was understandable, her great shame, and natural that she should blame herself for everything going so horribly wrong. But it had been a destructive, filthy, horrible career. She should be glad to be out of it. She should be trying to put it behind her.

Easy for him to say, of course. Perhaps he could hire her and Alain as crew on the boat, so they wouldn't have to worry about jobs—he could pay them whatever they were making before. That would have the added benefit of removing two killers from the roster of killers, taking two people trained to violence out of the violence game. He could help them and contribute a modicum of improvement to the world. All that aside, though, he felt for her, felt her agony. The desire for redemption is by definition a desire, and therefore as the Buddha said, the root of all suffering, but as desires go, isn't redemption a good one?

As he clipped through the small waves licking at his hull, he let himself feel the peace of knowing that his ship was trimmed perfectly. The weather was a gift, with that warm Indian Ocean breeze he had learned to love, and he would be able, for the next few hours anyway, to enjoy the peace the sea affords its acolytes. And in that moment of peace, he saw how foolish he was to lecture Alain and pity Skye's discomfort. After all, what he really should be thinking, he upbraided himself, was *physician, heal thyself!* He had been thinking about The Assassin at all hours, wondering where she was, what she was doing, whether any of the things they talked about, any of the feelings she expressed, her desire to leave her lethal profession, her desire for a better life—wondering if any of that were true, or whether it was all dissembling, all simulation, all a way of marking time until she was back cavorting with Mr. Big—with *Dmitry!*—on his grotesque mega yacht. What had he expected? Was he a dupe? What had he wanted? He'd been telling himself he was staying clean, steering clear of all the old, ludicrous longing for love, keeping out of the muddy swamp of desire. But given how he was feeling now that she was gone, he had to admit he hadn't been as successful at self-denial as he had thought, as he had pretended, to an audience of himself alone, to be. He had been falling, slowly but surely, into the same old, old, old illusory trap yet again.

"We'll be pulling into port in a couple hours," Skye said, startling him out of his daft reverie. "We need to make a plan."

They looked at the GPS. The south island was built over to within an inch of its life, with at most a block of a green park here and there, and otherwise hardly a tree or blade of grass to be found. The north island had the international airport and was also overbuilt or under construction. There were shipping ports, ferry terminals, breakwaters sheltering boat harbors, a fishing harbor, and piers for oversized ships in between. There were a half dozen places Dmitry's ship could be docked, and another half dozen where they could be tied up for the night.

"I'm wondering," Skye said. "When we arrive in Malé, do you register with a harbormaster, or with immigration?"

"Usually one or the other, yes, why?"

"It might help if we don't announce ourselves. Every extra step we can stay ahead of them will help."

"I can put off the harbormaster, tell him I'll do the paperwork later, and stall him along for, I don't know, twenty-four hours?"

She thanked him. Then he realized that it was beside the point.

"Oh, fuck, I'm sorry," he said. "I should have mentioned this earlier, but in all the madness I spaced it out."

He explained what he had learned from The Assassin about Dmitry and the tracker. It meant that in all likelihood, Dmitry would know exactly where they were as soon as they got there.

Skye did her calculations. "Our two options," she said. "We can find that tracker and attach it to another boat in less time than it takes his goons to get to whatever harbor we use, and sail out of there before they arrive. Or we could park and wait for them to show up and deal with them on our terms, but I don't think we have the firepower."

They decided on a harbor that was out of the way and too small for Dmitry's yacht to use, but big enough that they could find a suitable boat to use as a decoy, since whatever happened, they would want to escape undetected at some point. Skye called her own fixer in Malé, a guy who could scan the boat and bring them the other equipment they needed. He agreed to be waiting for them at the dock. Frank had been there before and knew the dockmaster.

"How can we not know where Dmitry's boat is?" Alain asked. "I thought that, like in the Jason Bourne movies, your satellites could send real-time close-ups of anyone in the world."

"Yeah, can't you get your friends at Darkwater to send you their location?" Frank asked.

"I'm not sure I have any friends at Darkwater at this point. And besides, why do you think we bombed so many weddings by accident in Iraq and Afghanistan? It ain't all it's cracked up to be."

Frank had a sense that Skye wasn't going to share everything with him. She might be telling Alain more, but if so, Alain kept it to himself. Perhaps it was cowardice that made Frank ask as few questions as he did. Maybe she was there to murder his former friend, and maybe Frank didn't want to think about that, maybe he was too deeply conflicted to think straight, or maybe he knew she was there for murder and didn't want to face the fact that he was an accessory. How he wanted things to end up he just couldn't say.

Not that it mattered much. There were a lot of bridges to cross before he would have to answer any serious questions, a long time before he would have to worry about anything except how to stay alive day to day.

XLVII
Mónica

THEY HAD ARRIVED in Malé forty-eight hours earlier, and Mónica had yet to leave her stateroom except for that first meal with Dmitry. She tried to work through each of the possible scenarios. Frank shows up versus Frank never shows up. If the former, who knows. If the latter, who knows. Maybe she finds someone else with a boat, someone whose boat doesn't have a tracker installed by Dmitry's thugs. Or maybe she goes straight to Malé's international airport. All she needed to do was get on a flight and improvise from there. She could do it above board, go see Dmitry, shrug and say, okay, goodbye, have Liam get in touch if you need anything, then go to the airport and fly on another passport. Or she could walk out without the exit interview, call Liam from the airport and tell him to let her know if he locates Frank and she'll take care of the situation.

If Frank shows up, does he have the sense to neutralize the trackers right away? Even if so, giving him a little time might be necessary. Does he have the sense to stay hidden? Maybe, maybe not. If he does, do they still have a chance of escaping? Maybe, maybe not.

What about killing Dmitry? Was that the answer? The last time she was at dinner, she noticed that his security detail, always waiting at the door to his private dining room, included a Chinese thug that she understood at a glance was both a killer and someone who had her résumé in his head. The other guys would be tough, too, since why would he have second-rate people in those positions, given that he knew enough to hire her and the Chinese hitman? If she killed him in the room, though, would it be like *The Wizard of Oz,* when the Wicked Witch of the West dies, and the guards all rejoice? Or would they, to protect their professional prospects, go ahead and kill The Assassin for damage control? She suspected the latter. It's what she would do.

In other words, killing Dmitry would require a general bloodbath. For that to happen, she needed accomplices, so teaming up with Frank and whoever else she could rustle up would be smart.

Was there a way out otherwise? Could she disappear without any help? Or by turning the head of a man or two on Dmitry's staff?

And then, of course, there was always the option of killing Frank, as Dmitry wanted. Would that give her any protection? Wouldn't Dmitry have her killed next, preferably on the island here, where she could be fingered for killing Frank? Dmitry's happy-ever-after scenarios, his idea that they could return to the past, to the status quo ante, had the distinct ring of total bullshit.

Her only good option was to get out of there, get away from Dmitry and Liam for good. The only way she could do that was to go dark on them long enough to escape. And the only way to do *that* was to set off on the mission to kill Frank. There was no other way to leave the boat without layers of escort—security men watching her, and other security men watching them. She had to assume there would be some of that, in any case.

Getting away with murder requires darkness. They would need to let her disappear long enough to do her thing. Whether or not she would have to actually kill Frank was still an open question. Maybe she would, maybe she wouldn't. She hoped not. But she needed to convince people she was on her way to do it. She had to start there.

XLVIII
Skye

"**AND I NEED** to borrow some money," Skye said to Frank as they got close to Malé.

"How much?"

"Fifty thousand if you have it."

He looked her in the eye, and she gave him her most sincere and humble gaze. She wanted to say look, I am tired, I can't work up the energy to bamboozle you, trick you, torture you, or any of the other dozen options I have. Just give it to me, the gaze said, you know you want to.

He went below deck again and came out with a paper bag that had five half-inch bundles of hundred-dollar bills, each with a wrapper that said $10,000.

"I won't use it all unless I need to," she said. "But we need weapons and ammunition, the scan and replace work, pay for the local fixers, then maybe other things."

Frank went back to his wheel and instruments to guide them into port, and she went into the cabin to talk to Alain, who looked up at her from the charts he was studying.

"I want the Chinese guy, first and foremost," she said. "He's the guy whose forehead shots were a big 'fuck you' to me. So he goes first."

"You're the boss," Alain said, and it didn't sound ironic or peevish, she thought, so good. He was still on board. She felt a quick pang at the idea of his loyalty to her.

"We leave Frank on the boat. He's not good at staying hidden, and he isn't ready for any more action yet, I don't think."

"Roger."

They were in this thing together, however oddly and unhappily it had worked out so far. They were approaching the harbor, the island outlined against the twilight like an amateur painting—too simple, too perfect, too blue. Frank was lowering the sails, the winches whirring, the water flattening as they entered the lagoon.

"Don't we put him at risk?" Alain asked. "Leaving him exposed like that?"

"They had every chance to get rid of him at the platform and didn't. That says to me they don't want to, for whatever reason."

"They could have offed us if they wanted to, too."

"No, not really. Dmitry and friends were below deck with Frank and could have left him there with a knife in his face. We were in view of the press to the very end. Once they know we followed them here, which they likely already do, we are their number one targets. But Frank, who knows?"

"Got it."

"One thing that might help is that even if they know Frank is here, they might not jump to the conclusion that we are with him. They wouldn't be in quite as much hurry to descend if he was alone. But we can't count on that. The minute we tie off, we get right to work. We arm up and figure out where we wait for them." She looked at the GPS. "I'm thinking me here and you there," she said, pointing to the edges of their harbor, "but we won't know until we see the place. Once we're set up, the rest is jazz, we improvise."

"Got it."

They pulled into a small harbor, sheltered by a breakwater on each side. Unfortunately, they were the biggest boat in the place, which meant they stuck out a little. But it also meant there were unlikely to be any rich folk around, the people Dmitry and the international press might bounce into at the Raffles or the St. Regis. They pulled into the slip Frank had arranged and tied off. Frank made the electric, water, and sewage hookups and then went to talk to the harbormaster, bringing a lot of cash to insure his discretion.

Skye's guy, Yameen, was waiting with a case full of weapons, night vision, and comms gear. He said he hadn't been able to ask very wide, that he only had time to talk to his suppliers, and none of them knew where Dmitry's yacht had docked. He got right to work scanning for the trackers. She had narrowed down the probable docking spots for Dmitry's yacht to three, and figured it would take them between twenty and forty minutes to get to this harbor from any of those spots.

She and Alain sorted through the gear Yameen brought, putting together bags of guns and supplies for every contingency. They scoped the harbor and picked out where they would set up sniper nests, one on each side of the harbor with clear shots to Frank's boat. They put their gear in those spots and then walked, at a good pace. Alain stayed right with her, not fast enough to arouse suspicion, into the town and down the esplanade, full of souvenir stores and fried fish joints. She pulled him into a shop to buy them both hats, straw for him, cotton for her, both with wide brims to help them look like tourists, but dark for night work. They went back out and ordered a paper roll of fried fish, standing at an outdoor table scanning the neighborhood. They couldn't see anybody who acted like a lookout. Nobody looked like a local hood that could have called and alerted Dmitry. They walked to the far corner of the esplanade and scanned it until it felt all clear, too.

A cabbie said yes, when they asked, he knew where the mega yacht was, and he named the spot forty minutes away by water. They paid him two hundred dollars to wait for them right where he was and walked on. They found a second cabbie and asked him. He asked them to wait while he called a friend, and then gave them the same answer. They gave him two hundred to wait for them too. They had forty minutes if the goons came by sea—thirty-five now—and half that if they came by car.

She had let both cabbies see a big wad of bills, so they had visions of a continuous parade of hundred-dollar bills coming their way. They would be waiting all day and night. Good to have them in reserve.

"We need to watch the harbor for now, and see what develops," she said to Alain. "Like I say, he could have left Frank dead on his boat if he had wanted to, could have had the Chinese guy add one more notch and take care of it after the press was out to sea, but he didn't. If they guess we are with Frank—which I think I would have gamed out if I were them—they will be coming after him in order to come after us. We can't know. So tonight, we lay in wait. If they come, they come. If they don't, we go after them." She looked over at Alain and saw that he was attentive and alert. They were a team. "For now," she started to say, they'd wait and watch, but he gave his efficient nod, and she left it unsaid.

XLIX
Frank

YAMEEN AND HIS helper Ahmed gave Skye and Alain bags of gear as soon as they arrived, and they jumped all over his boat, having been told they had minutes, not hours, to find the trackers. Within five minutes they found two. The main one was fiberglassed into the radar dome housing, and they found another boat with the same model radar, a fairly common 19-inch Furuno 4kw, and after Frank checked with the harbormaster to be sure the owner of the other boat wasn't around, they swapped the two out. There was always the chance the owner of that boat would notice that his radar unit looked newer than he remembered, but probably not—it was way up his mast. The second tracker was in the outboard housing of Frank's lifeboat, and they removed it, placing it in the other boat's outboard cover. Skye had paid Yameen already, but Frank gave him a ten-thousand-dollar bonus as loyalty money, and an extra ten thousand dollars to the harbormaster for looking the other way.

He thought about the many ports he had stopped in over the years, how excited he always was to go ashore, have a meal, have some human contact, see a new town, buy some new foodstuffs, and take in the smells, sounds, and salutations of an unfamiliar spot on the audacious globe. Even now, he took in the beauty of this small harbor, the stalwart masts of the other ships and boats, the serene fisherman mending their nets in the shade of the harbormaster's house, the fresh smell of fish. But he had no desire to head into the town. He had had enough of humankind for the moment.

His boat was free and clear. If Skye and Alain were out committing murder, the smart move would be for him to take off right away and let them face the consequences. It would leave them high and dry, though, and he couldn't see himself doing that. Instead, he threw a towel over the boat's name and set about filling up his petrol tanks, loading up with fresh water, food, and supplies from the harbormaster's store, and looking for his next stop, which he decided would be Chennai, only a thousand miles away. In a city of seven million people, it would be easy to hide, especially in the poorer sections. The people were friendly and helpful, and he could stay lost there for as long as he needed. Skye and Alain could, too, if they wanted.

They might have a better idea, of course, but he doubted it. He could always drop them in Colombo on the way, or anywhere along the Indian coast. Maybe, just maybe, he could get out of this without any more people ending up dead, and without Dmitry on his tail.

Maybe, though, this was the way all people got sucked into crime, into violence. They made a compromise for the moment—I can condone *x* if I can avoid *y*. I will help criminal *a* because he is less horrible than criminal *b*. I will put up with *y* because I do not deserve to die from *z*. Or in this case, I will allow *z* to die so that *z* does not kill me. He wasn't about to change anything right now, he knew, so all his speculations were academic at best, or delusional. He was going to regret it all. Whatever else he knew or didn't know right then, he knew he was going to regret it all.

L
Alain

HE AND SKYE put on their Kevlar, and carefully slid into sniper positions well above the water. Now there was nothing to do but wait. The gulls were still squawking and swirling around a bit, but they were getting ready to call it a night. The breeze was a couple knots, enough to stay cool, not enough to confuse them by throwing sound around. He could see Frank on the boat, swabbing the decks, putting up supplies, glancing around, and generally acting nervous. And he should be nervous. It hadn't hit Alain right away, but they were, it turned out, using Frank as bait.

He asked Skye quietly, whispering into his earbud, whether they should warn him, have him keep his head down at least. She wasn't visible, but he got a glimpse of her rifle barrel trained down at the harbor.

"I think he's safer not knowing," Skye said.

"How's that?"

"Look at him. You see how agitated he is? Imagine if we made him even more nervous? He'd be flailing his arms in the air and make himself a bigger target. I've been on a concentrated program of trying to make him feel safe."

"How's that been working?"

"Ha, yeah," she said. "But, okay. Say we tell him the danger he is in right now, and he runs—takes off in his boat and we never see him again. He's safe, but we're fucked."

"You're okay with that?" he asked. "Risking his life for our advantage?"

"Every risk ends up being to someone's advantage. And everything's a risk, Alain, you know this."

He did. He still didn't feel right about it.

"Frank knows it too," she said. And he thought true, but cold. Real cold.

They lay in their posts and waited for the inevitable. Despite being as close as they were now, and as in sync as they seemed to be, Skye remained a mystery to him. Was the anti-colonialist, social justice warrior stuff just spouted for his benefit, or was it real? If it was real conviction, how could she square that with this life?

"You think this job is making you hard?" he asked her.

"Maybe not hard enough," she said.

"What? Because why?"

"I'm too easy on people," she said. "Too easy on myself. What am I doing? Why am I helping Darkwater, and through them the US or other governments? They're all up to no good."

"They are the last gasp of settler colonialism," he said.

"Exactly," she said. "Although last gasp is pretty optimistic."

"Fuckers," he said. Okay, so maybe she was reading his mind a bit. Or maybe she was just, like all of us, doing her best.

The gulls had settled down for the night, but a few dark birds flew by and squawked or trilled. A small surf hit the seawall. Metal stays jingled against the masts of the sailboats in the harbor, and the noise of the city and a trace of its lights spilled over the hill.

They waited.

LI
Frank

FRANK PUTTERED AROUND stashing his new supplies, kept an eye on the comings and goings on the dock, and made himself an omelet as the day wound down. He got nervous when Skye and Alain didn't reappear, but reasoned that they might have had to wait until dark to do what they needed to do. He noticed that even in his private thoughts he was using euphemisms: *do what they needed to do*. How had he become so callous? He tried telling himself that murdering a murderer was not as bad as murdering anyone else, but he knew that was nitpicking. He knew that *what they needed to do* might include murdering his murderous ex-friend too. Could he live with that? He spent the last hours of the day going down a shame spiral, while justifying himself to an invisible audience that grew more and more skeptical.

He had found himself deep in a world of violence he had only known before theoretically. He knew there were wars everywhere, had always been, violent crime everywhere, domestic violence, political violence, police violence, fistfights, stabbings, shootings—it happened all the time, but before this it never happened to him. The closest he had come to it was the violence Dmitry had perpetrated years ago, but he had only read about that in the news, too, a small story in the daily deluge of international terror. Now, he was not only in the middle of the blood and guts and brutality of the world of killers he had magically avoided. He was, in fact financing it. He needed to get away, and soon, and then he needed to think, recover, and try to understand what claim such knowledge made upon him.

As he waited in the dark, he realized that he was a sitting duck. The trackers were only a few boats away, so if Dmitry found the decoy boat, they'd see it wasn't his, figure it out, and it wouldn't take them long to find him. He turned the cabin lights off. He grabbed a flashlight and a book—though he had no illusions that he'd be able to read—and slipped over his gunwale, on the side of his boat facing away from the street, onto the dock. Staying low, he belly-crawled down the dock a few slips to a smaller boat. He slid under the tarp and pushed the front of it up slightly by sticking a coil of rope under one edge, giving himself a sliver of a lookout.

Alain was a good kid. He reminded Frank of a Guatemalan immigrant who worked for him briefly in California, a guy who had joined the army because it was the best job around for someone with questionable immigration status. He was a sweet guy, very smart and capable, but there was a deep hurt there, a deep sadness. Frank never found what had happened to him—he wouldn't talk about it—but he had been in Afghanistan, and had done or seen things that had marked him forever. Alain was in a different state now, not PTSD—he was living in traumatic stress, there was no "post" about it. But Frank imagined Alain carried an additional burden: the legionnaire, like the immigrant soldier, suffers from the violence just like any soldier, but with the added kick that they did it for a country that hates them, or for a country where half the people hate them. Alain made no secret of the bad blood between him and the French. Bad blood. It was all bad blood.

Skye was something else again. She was, in her odd way, an idealist, a peculiar woke kid in a paramilitary's Kevlar. She talked like someone who had gone to a fancy liberal arts college and could tell you what the neoliberal, ideological state apparatus, crypto-capitalist, settler-colonialist, extractive, corporate, militarized surveillance state had wrought, and how she was ardently opposed to it all, even while working for the quintessential institution of that system. She would be the first to tell you what was wrong about white saviorism, but she had decided she was going to save Alain, nonetheless. She believed in non-state participatory democracy and nonviolent social action while carrying a gun for a corrupt private army. It wasn't just a front, or self-deception, exactly. She cared for the men who died, for Alain—it was all real, all true. She had ideals. She only embodied some of them and was riven with contradictions. So are all of us, he reminded himself. It occurred to him that she was out there somewhere, watching. That she was using him for bait. Hm.

His hideaway smelled of stale canvas and moldy rope. He tried, without rocking the boat or making any other visible movements, to raise the edges of the cover here and there and let some air circulate. And then he waited.

LII
Mónica

IT WAS TIME. The sun was setting, and Dmitry sent a messenger with a card with nothing on it except a set of coordinates: latitude and longitude. She checked them on her phone, and it was for a small harbor on the other side of the island. So Frank had arrived after all. Why not let the Chinese hitman kill him? she wondered. Because the Chinese thug's job was to follow her and kill her as soon as she dispatched Frank. She recognized the sociopathic logic of it. She had been disloyal, so he would make her kill something she loved—wait, *what? loved?*—before he killed her. He wanted her to die with the taste of loss and defeat in her mouth.

Why was she thinking this way? She didn't *love* Frank! That would be stupid and out of character. But Dmitry knew something was up, that something about her relationship—*relationship!*—with Frank was odd. She knew exactly what her thinking about Frank would elicit in Dmitry: he would need, like a junkie needs junk, to make them both suffer in any way he could devise. *¡Mosca!*

So. What to do. They would need a new boat—again! *they!*—unless they could somehow get rid of the trackers. She didn't see how that could be done quick enough to keep them alive, proof of which was that she had the coordinates in her phone. So a new boat. And sink Frank's boat with a body on it? That would at least buy time, even if Dmitry followed up with the morgue and found out the body wasn't Frank. Or her. The ideal situation would be to use the Chinese thug as the body on the boat, of course, and she liked the idea of bullets going through him and then through the bottom of the hull. Frank wouldn't like that she sunk his boat, but from the way he talked, he could buy another one with cash he had lying around. Or she'd buy him one. What? *Wowowowowowow!* She was out of her mind. She must have come down with something, she thought, with some illness.

Maybe this is how trauma worked. All her life she had heard about trauma, and the prison doctors and the lawyers, one by one, told her that she had it, so maybe she did. It would explain why, everywhere she went, she saw people retreating into each other's arms, spending every minute of their whole lives together, like mindless swans. Everybody was abused—you can see that on the TV every day—and so they all, to keep themselves from falling apart, fell in love with whoever was around. Maybe she was succumbing too. *I'm in PTSD recovery with you!* people should say, not *in love*.

When the Chinese thug showed up in the security detail at the dining room, it meant Dmitry wanted her to see him, wanted him in her head. Only a civilian could mistake that guy for anything but a killer. Not only did Dmitry assign this psycho to her case, he marched her by him to try to freak her out. Well, she was un-freak-out-able. The Chinese thug helped her, in fact—helped her focus. Her first task was to get rid of him, and then, with him gone, see who else needed to go before she retired from this fucked-up life.

She had the equipment Dmitry had supplied laid out. She put on her bathing suit and a vest, some street clothes on top of it, packed a waterproof bag with her guns and supplies, a mask and snorkel, and a pair of fins. Then she waited.

A new message came from Dmitry precisely at midnight.

"What on earth are you waiting for?" the card asked.

She took the pen on the tray and wrote, "Well, if you must know, I'm waiting for 3:00 a.m. I know his sleep patterns. Try to get some sleep yourself." She sent the messenger on his way, grabbed her go bag, stayed a few feet behind him as he walked down the hallway, caught the staff door before it closed—it otherwise required a key card to open—gave him a head start, then headed into the bowels of the ship, down the warren of staff hallways and staircases, and out to the docking deck on the stern. She was ready for the two guards she knew to be there, and using her 9mm with a long silencer put bullets in their heads before they could stop smiling at her. They slumped into the shadows, and she checked each of them. Yes, they were dead.

She took off her clothes and vest, put them with the guns in her waterproof bag, put on her fins and mask and slipped into the water. She swam until she got to a pier ladder hundreds of yards away. She saw nobody, climbed out, shed the water gear and bathing suit, put her clothes on, grabbed her weapon bag and left the rest behind a trash can. She struck out for Frank's harbor. She decided that a slight jog it wouldn't take much longer than a cab, and the exercise would clear her mind, anyway. Lord knows, she said to herself, her mind wasn't clear.

LIII
Skye

SKYE PINGED ALAIN.

"It's midnight. I don't think they're coming."

"I was starting to think the same thing."

They stood up and walked toward each other, turning around and scanning their surroundings as they did, Skye with night-vision goggles on.

"Look at that," she whispered, pointing toward a big black SUV parked up the hill from the harbor.

"Dmitry's guys," he said.

"There's no other reason for a fancy vehicle up here at this time of night. I didn't hear it come up, and it's not putting off any heat—no idea how long it's been there, but it looks to be empty."

"Wait, watch," he said. "Right?"

"Right. Back to positions. When the shooting starts, you pick them off left to right, I'll go right to left."

They slunk back. Their shooting strategy required the goons to walk onto the dock and approach Frank's boat, or, more likely, the boat with the trackers now installed. What were they waiting for? A signal? Some other development? Something wasn't right.

Skye got back on the walkie-talkie. "Scan the hill behind us," she said. "Maybe they're there." They both stood up and scanned the hillside with their rifle scopes.

Then Skye felt a bullet enter her leg. Shot with a silencer. She made her best guess about where the bullet had come from and started wildly spraying automatic rifle fire with one hand and popped off rounds from her handgun with the other. She could hear Alain responding in kind, and sporadic fire back from Dmitry's men. They didn't want to betray their position by consistent fire, but yes, they were above them. They must have been watching when she and Alain got up. They were as open as the targets at a firing range. She rolled away from her perch and saw that she had been hit more than once.

Then the shooting from the hill slowed and stopped. Maybe she or Alain had hit someone? More than one? Alain made his way over to her, still firing, sprayed up and down and sideways, blindly and erratically, to keep them back and down. She thought again what a great choice she had made choosing and training him. He dragged her under the cover of an overhanging concrete roof slab. It was all quiet again, no shooting and no sound of anyone moving. They must have hit one or more of them. Either that or the bad guys were repositioning themselves for another attack and managing to do it silently.

Alain took a quick look at Skye's wounds. She was bleeding from her left thigh and right arm. He was bleeding, too, but his own was just a graze. He felt the hole in his sleeve and the wound, and it stung, but was harmless. Skye's were substantial. and he tied a tourniquet at the top of her thigh and another at the top of her arm.

"We hit them," she said.

"Or," Alain said as he tightened the tourniquets, "that's what they want us to think."

"Always that chance," she said, but she was engulfed in pain. At least one of the bullets must have hit bone. "Motherfuckers knew where we were. Ambushed us."

"I'm going to go get Frank to help me carry you down and doctor you up. Shoot anything that moves. You can do that? Can stay awake?"

"Yeah, I'm good," she said, and she kind of meant it.

"Great," he said. "Don't worry. Sit tight. I'll be right back. I'll ping you as I get close."

She grabbed his arm.

"Go in sideways," she said. "They'll be looking for you straight on."

"Sideways," he said.

"Sideways and sideways," she said, and clenched her eyes in pain.

LIV
Frank

HE HEARD GUNSHOTS. Single shots and some kind of machine gun fire—or are they even called machine guns anymore? Anyway, automatic weapons fire. And it was close. He had a momentary hope that it might be fireworks, but think about it, numbskull, he said to himself. Dmitry is in town with a known assassin, you have been ferrying two paramilitary soldiers looking for revenge around the Indian Ocean, and they are loose in the city. Do the math. It was gunfire.

And among the combatants were people that worked for Dmitry. That meant they were fighting outside his boat because he was there. Was it her, The Assassin? He really didn't want to believe that, didn't want to believe she would come to kill him. But would she?

Of course she would! She had gone off with Dmitry, and wasn't that proof enough of how untrustworthy she was, how insincere all that talk of getting out of the game had been? He had thought he was helping defend the victims, Skye and Alain, but *he* was the prey, and he was putting them in danger. That would explain why the harbor was under attack. Dmitry wouldn't know Skye or Alain were there, just that he was.

Maybe, of course, Skye and Alain had tried something that exposed them, and then had been followed on their way back and hadn't quite made it. Maybe, just maybe, he held out hope for a moment, it had nothing to do with him—what did he know about gang violence in the Maldives? He would wait it out in this other boat and see who showed up. At least here in this little skiff he might be safe. If Skye and Alain showed up and the shooting stopped, he could hop out of his hiding place and they could sail away. If it was anyone or anything else, well, he had no choice but to play it by ear.

LV
Mónica

WHAT THE FUCK? A black SUV was parked a block above the harbor. She approached and saw that it was empty. Dmitry had sent his people ahead of her, the bastard. If she was on the mission she was supposed to be on, he could only fuck it up by sending whatever thugs these were, and of course he knew that. He didn't care. He wanted her dead and gone and wanted her to be humiliated in the process. *¡Coño!*

And then, as she walked toward the harbor, she heard automatic weapons fire, at most a block or two away. It sounded like four or five shooters, one group up the road to the left, the others closer to the harbor.

Then it stopped as soon as it had started.

The only possible explanation was that the Darkwater people had come with Frank—Frank had no guns, and more than one person was firing from each side—and that they and Dmitry's thugs had exchanged some rounds. For now, one of the two sides had neutralized the other. The Chinese thug, it was safest for her to assume, had come out on top.

Would he assume she was in cahoots with the Darkwater people? Would he decide to get preemptive with Frank? Who had lost who in the fight? She had to assume, again to be safe, that Mr. Thug and his goons were fine and back on plan, whatever that was. In any case, her 3:00 a.m. ploy had not fooled anyone, and they had the jump on her. She needed, before anything else, to figure out who was still in the game.

She went back to the SUV, cracked the driver's window with her elbow, and grabbed a sweatshirt someone had left behind. She pushed the sleeve down into the gas tank and let it soak. She pulled out the ignition wires, sparked the car to life, then pulled the sweatshirt out, put the other sleeve into the tank to soak, and lit the sleeve hanging out with her lighter. She put the vehicle in neutral and pushed it down the street toward the harbor. It would take about two minutes for the sweatshirt flame to reach the gas tank. She waited until the vehicle ran into a stone wall with a small crash.

She heard voices in the dark, which was good. It meant Mr. Thug and his friends were still outside the harbor, and that they were processing what they were looking at. She made her way around the block, put her weapon, vest, and sneakers in the waterproof bag, strapped it on her back, and slipped into the water around the corner. It would be a tough swim with her bag over her shoulder, but she could get there in four minutes, max. Halfway there she heard the explosion of the car. If the gunplay earlier hadn't brought the cops, this would, without a doubt. The arrival of cops, with their cherries flashing through the night, would scramble the game, and at this point that could only help her. She hoped.

LVI
Alain

WHO THE HELL had done that? Alain wondered as he scrambled down the hill. Why would Dmitry's goons blow up their own SUV? The cops would show now, for sure, if the gunfire hadn't already assured that, and why would Dmitry's gang want that? Maybe so the police would catch Skye and him bloody, wounded, and armed? He had even less time than he thought. He scaled a fence and made his way over the roof of the harbormaster's office and down onto the dock, staying low and scooting from shadow to shadow and then from boat to boat. When he got close, he saw that all the lights were off on the *God Sees,* and Frank was not in the cockpit and not in his hammock. That was ominous.

He heard someone make a *psst* from behind him, and he jumped around.

"It's me," Frank whispered from under the tarp. Alain climbed aboard and got under the tarp too.

"Skye's hit," Alain told him. "We need to get her out of there before cops start crawling all over this place."

"What the hell's going on? We're ready to go, the trackers are out, installed on another boat," Frank said. "How bad is she?"

"Hard to tell. We need a tarp to carry her."

"My sunshade will work. Is it safe to go to my boat?"

"I really don't know. I'll get it."

Frank looked down at Alain's automatic weapon and said, "I'll go. You cover me." It sounded absurd coming from Frank, like he was role-playing, like it was paintball, but he was right, it was a better division of labor. He knew how the shade was attached. He didn't know how to use a gun.

They crawled out from under the tarp and Frank moved fast, took the shade down and came back. Nothing else moved. They left by the back way, retracing Alain's steps, and climbed back up to where Skye was. They heard sirens approaching as they lifted her onto the tarp.

"You hanging in there?" he asked her.

"Barely," she said.

"We'll get you on the boat, it's clean now, Frank will take us out to sea, and I'll doctor you up," he said as they carried her back the same path, all unmolested. It wasn't easy getting her over the wall, and it jostled her enough that she passed out from the pain, but they managed to get back to the dock. From the dark behind the boathouse, they saw a man standing on the dock next to Frank's boat. They laid Skye on the deck and Alain motioned Frank to lay low. Then he leaned against a post to steady himself and looked at the man through his scope. He could see an AK-47 in the man's hands and he aimed quick and put a bullet through the man's forehead. The intruder was a big man, and he slumped and sat awkwardly on the dock, still holding the gun. Alain darted a dozen feet closer and crouched behind two large boats. Everything was quiet. Nothing had made a sound except his single rifle shot, loud enough that nobody could have missed it. But nobody else showed.

He went back and he and Frank lifted Skye again as police lights arrived in the street and ricocheted off the masts. They carried Skye in the sling across the dock.

"I killed a guy out in the open and nobody reacted," Alain said in a half-whisper to Frank. "He might have been the last of them."

They brought Skye onto the boat, and laid her on the cockpit.

"Let's get her in the cabin," Frank said to Alain. "Then you untie us, I'll turn on the running lights and engine, and we'll get out of here."

They lifted Skye into the cabin and flipped on the light. Sitting at the dining room table was a very large Chinese man, looking oddly unperturbed.

LVII
Mónica

MÓNICA STAYED LOW in the water and held on to the side of a small sailboat as someone fired a rifle, and the man holding an AK-47 slumped down on the dock next to Frank's boat. She recognized the dead man. One of Dmitry's. That meant someone—Frank or a Darkwater person—was still alive. The shooter was not Frank, taking the man down with a single shot like that.

Why would one of Dmitry's guys be standing by the boat? Did he have Frank locked up below? Was Frank dead? She was having trouble figuring out the players *and* the game. Then she heard a ruckus and slid farther into the shadows. Two men, carrying something heavy in a tarp, were coming down the dock. As they got back to the boat, she could see that one was Frank, and yes, the other, the shooter she assumed, was the Darkwater security guy from the platform in the Chagos. She made her way closer, as they were very involved with their package and were not paying much attention to anything around them. They brought the package into the cabin and switched on the lights.

She swam over to a fishing boat straight behind Frank's, and pulled herself up and in. She found a rain slicker and a bandana, put the slicker on over her wet clothes to make her outline less recognizable, and wrapped the bandana around her head to hide her hair. She climbed onto the roof of the boat's cabin. The police action surrounding the exploding van had attracted some neighbors living on their boats and some people who had pulled over and got out of their cars. If anyone saw her in her slicker and dirty headgear, she would look like just another eccentric harbor denizen trying to get a look at it all. There was a lot of noise and hullabaloo on the street, and a quiet murmur of spectators talking to each other in the harbor.

She could also see into Frank's cabin. The package was an injured woman, probably the one from Darkwater—her face was hidden by a balaclava, but, yes, she had the head of curls. She was wet with blood and appeared to be unconscious. They had lifted her into the cabin and switched on the light. Frank was grabbing things from his first aid kit. Alain pulled off the injured woman's balaclava. They cut off her pants leg and her sleeve and ministrated to her, one working on her leg, one on her arm. They kept glancing to one side. She moved to see why, and there, sitting calmly watching them work, was her own Chinese nemesis.

LVIII
Frank

ALAIN KNEW WHO the Chinese guy was, Frank saw, or at least knew he was bad news. But of course neither of them could say anything. The guy had hard, ugly energy, and it could not possibly be a good thing that he was on the boat. Frank followed Alain's lead and ignored him while they worked on stopping Skye's loss of blood and getting any bullets out of her flesh that they could. He hung a bag of saline from the light fixture and stabbed a vein. He screwed a vial of antibiotics into the drip line and made sure it was all flowing. She hadn't regained consciousness, but she was getting fluids, was breathing okay, and seemed stabilized.

He looked up at the weird guest and the man stared back at Frank in a way that was pure challenge. Frank was not about to take the dare. He noticed that the police lights had stopped whirring, and the commotion that had followed the explosion had died down. He stuck his head out to see what was happening and saw The Assassin in a bizarre outfit on the roof of a fishing boat. She held her finger up to her lips, and it didn't take him long to realize that if the choice was her or the Chinese psychopath sitting in his kitchen, he was with her.

He pulled his head back in and decided that providing her with a little cover might be smart.

"We need a doctor," he said, to both Alain and the Chinese man.

"Agreed," said Alain. "I'll go get one." He looked up see the psycho's reaction, but the man was already standing, out from behind the table, and ready to strike, having moved to the doorway incredibly quickly and noiselessly for such a large guy. He stood there and his body language was clear: nobody was going anywhere.

"She is going to die," Frank said.

The Chinese man made a poof sound, like a French person rejecting a corked wine.

Someone else stepped on the boat. The Chinese man stood aside to let the new person in, and Frank thought, oh great, The Assassin's working *with* him.

But it wasn't her, of course, it was Dmitry.

LIX
Alain

"**WELL, WELL," DMITRY** said. "The gang is nearly all here."

"She needs a doctor," Frank said.

"I've called for one," Dmitry said. "Although it seems he will be too late for my colleague out on the dock." He said this with his usual smirk, as if it was vaguely amusing to him. "The doctor would be here already, but I seem to be short one car," again, close to a chuckle. "That looks to me to be the work of our Spanish friend—why isn't she here? She's an integral part of the proceedings!"

Nobody said anything to that, so, never at a loss for words, Dmitry went on.

"Now that I've sent the police on their way, the traffic should have thinned out too. I convinced them this was a small domestic disturbance and that I would straighten it all out in moments. That and a few euros and they were on their way." He turned to Alain. "And you, my Malagasy friend. What do you do for Darkwater, exactly?"

"I don't work for Darkwater. I work for Skye. She contracts with them."

"Yes. And how is that working out for you?"

"It pays the bills," he said.

"Well, it did! Your boss here may not make it—I hate to be rough about it, but—what will you do if she is not able to employ you?"

Alain ignored the question. "Is your doctor coming?"

"Excellent! I like the refusal to act cowed, and yes, the doctor is coming. But I ask about your job because I happen to have a few open positions after tonight, including that of our dead friend on the dock. I will pay you what you are getting now plus 20 percent."

"Doing what?"

"Security work. That's what you have been doing, yes? I understand you know how to hold an island against all invaders."

This knocked him off balance—he had been operating under the assumption that Dmitry had no idea who he was.

"If you know that," he said, trying to regain his feet, "then you know it is not true."

Dmitry laughed. "Yes, I do! And speaking of what we know and what we don't, you also know that Darkwater—and just because Skye here was technically off the books, we don't let that fool us, do we?—she worked for Darkwater, exclusively, her entire career. They paid her through a shell company, that's all, like we all do. I pay Mr. Wei here through a shell company—" Mr. Wei bowed slightly. "Anywho, as I was saying, Darkwater, and again I assume you know this, has been on the side of the colonialists and the neocolonialists every step of the way. They are handmaidens to the French, to the Americans, and in general to the worst of the worst—and they are racist to their core. Any country that needs their services is, by the admission of hiring them, up to no good and an enemy to its own people."

"Okay," Alain said.

"No, my friend, it is not okay. We, on the other hand are an Asian company, owned by an Asian woman." Dmitry paused and looked at Frank. "Frank, be a dear and get me a beer, will you?"

Frank didn't move, except to continue working on Skye's wounds. Eventually he said, quietly: "You are hiding a military installation behind a green energy project."

"Yes, a brilliant touch, right?"

The Chinese man waited a beat, then went to the refrigerator, pulled out a beer and handed it to Dmitry, who thanked him, saying, "*Xièxiè*. Mr. Alain, would you like one?"

"*Bù, xièxiè*," Alain said.

"Ah, and you speak Chinese!"

"I worked with tourists. I know how to say a dozen things in a dozen languages. I don't speak Chinese."

"Well, there is some disagreement about whether I do or do not, too! I say I do, my wife says I do not. Speaking of my wife, we are a very male group here, aren't we, save our unconscious friend? The missing member of our party, our lovely assassin *de Hispania*, I assume will not appear until this ship, the ominously named *God Sees Everything*, is a tad less crowded. Franky, you are still an atheist, aren't you?"

"You must know by now it's impossible to have an honest conversation when your hired killer is hovering, don't you?"

"I get your point Franky, although I feel obliged to point out that having, as you say, a hired killer in the room is more often than not a wonderful goad to honesty. You would be surprised how many liars become truth-tellers with a gun to their head. Nonetheless, as I was saying, the boat is too crowded, so Mr. Wei, I will ask you to now leave, and I will be leaving soon as well." He held up a finger. "Mr. Alain, have you decided to accept my offer?"

"I have," he said. "I'm in."

Frank's head snapped around.

"I'm sorry, Frank, I have mouths to feed." Alain shrugged. "I need the money."

"*Attaboy*!" Dmitry said. "Mr. Wei will show you to our car. But first, why don't you two drop our dead man on the dock into the water?"

Mr. Wei waited for Alain to exit—Alain didn't look back, didn't want to see Frank's dumb shock—and then walked out himself. The two of them picked up the dead man's limbs, pulled him to the edge, gave him a push, and let him slide into the water.

LX
Frank

"**IS THERE REALLY** a doctor coming?" Frank asked when they were alone.

Dmitry stood up, walked over to Skye, felt her pulse, put his ear to her chest for five seconds, and stood back up.

"Yes," he said. "I have been planning to make her the same offer that I made your Alain. Of course, she is in significantly worse shape than she was yesterday, and therefore she isn't quite as valuable as she was, but hey! We can make a deal. I have found that soldiers of fortune are true to their appellation and are in it for the fortune. A 10 percent raise often works, a 20 percent raise always works. I'm thinking, given her current state, a 3 percent raise would reel her in. But—ah, Franky, lovely to see your moral dudgeon all afume again!"

"Afume?"

"Is that yet another contribution of mine to the language? You're welcome! But where oh where is your girlfriend?"

Right as he said it, she stood in the hatchway, an automatic weapon slung over her shoulder, her finger on the trigger guard, looking ridiculous in the big slicker and bandana.

"My darling," Dmitry said. "You have taken your sweet time!"

She stepped aside, twirled, and shot Mr. Wei in the throat just as he appeared behind her. He fell forward, dropping his gun and clutching at his throat, blood squirting as he writhed. He somehow managed to maintain his sociopathic emotional blankness as he careened up to the hatchway and fell through.

For Frank, time slowed down and his vision tunneled—all he could see was Mr. Wei's writhing body and stony face. He was so focused that he didn't even notice, at first, that Wei had fallen on Skye's torso. When he realized it, he shoved the huge man aside to protect his charge. He checked her pulse and her breathing, and had no idea what else was happening around him. Perhaps The Assassin was there, perhaps not. Perhaps Dmitry and The Assassin had said something, perhaps not. He checked Skye's IV and pulse again, and she seemed stable. He looked over and Mr. Wei had stopped moving, stopped breathing.

"Mr. Alain," Dmitry said out into the darkness. "I assume you are there. Now would be a good time to start earning your salary."

There was no response from the night. But then Alain stood at the hatchway. He had a large automatic weapon in one hand and a pistol in the other. He had that one pointed at The Assassin, and he motioned her toward the hatchway.

"Well, better late than never, and now, now, now, *mi guapa* Nikita," Dmitry said, walking up to the door. "Speaking of earning your salary, I'm not sure you've been doing such a bang-up job. *Bang-up job* is an Americanism that means—"

"I'm familiar," she said. She kept her distance.

They stared at each other, she, like him, a master of the slight smirk. Frank could only see Dmitry's back, but he knew the smirk would be there, too. In his debilitated state, he could only look from one to the other and back again.

"Nikita—" Dmitry started.

"Don't call me that," she said. "That was a bullshit movie."

"That movie made your life. You'd still be in prison if I hadn't seen it."

"You know that weaponized femininity is redundant, don't you?"

"Perhaps I should call you Villanelle?"

"Pah! More bullshit. You think I'm a sociopath? No. I'm just trained to kill. Anyone can be."

"I have the distinct impression that our tastes in cinema are not in alignment. But to the matter at hand. You know that you are tactically at a deficit. My soldier has an automatic weapon, and of course I am armed. And you see our poor friend Frank here is reduced to a somewhat moronic state. He's a bit of a stranger to gunplay, I'm afraid, and none too quick in the recovery department. He will be of no use to you for quite some time, nor will she," he said raising his chin toward Skye. "But before we go any further, I am curious as to why you decided to blow up one of my SUVs. From whom were you distracting what?"

"Dmitry," she said. "Have you considered the possibility that instead of attempting to enrage me, your time would be better spent retreating to your yacht to fight another day?"

"Ah, yes, the lovebirds would like to sail into the sunset. Perhaps. Perhaps." He reached into his pocket, and she reflexively raised her handgun so that it pointed to his face. Alain stayed with his gun trained on her.

Dmitry made a big show of having a gun in his pocket, and it maybe was a gun, but certainly looked like a finger.

"Do you want to make a bet?" he asked her, but before he finished, a shot hit her. "That this is not my finger?" She flew back as the gun, silencer on, fired three times fast. She tumbled backwards over the transom with a splash. Dmitry was smiling, Frank saw as he ran after her, slipping on the blood on the cockpit floor, smashing his head into the captain's wheel, and then everything went dark.

LXI
Alain

ALAIN CAME IN, put down his guns, and went to Frank, checked his pulse and breathing. He then walked past Dmitry and checked on Skye.

"The doctor is coming, my new friend," Dmitry said. "I see that you are concerned about them, but Franky has just beaned his noggin. He'll come to in a minute or two, and the doctor will load her up with some new blood." Alain checked Frank's pulse anyway. "We will leave Franky here to receive him, and he will have no problem paying for any treatment the good doctor might order. I will have the doctor report to me as well." Frank, did, in fact, start to stir, but didn't open his eyes. "I find myself otherwise oddly content, feeling that this is a better ending for our story than having him ritually murdered, after all. Alive, losing it all again. Good. At any rate, we're off!" Dmitry said, his hand still in his pocket. He turned to Alain. "We're off?"

"Yes," Alain said. "I'm ready." He stood, picked up his gun, walked out, stepped back onto the dock. As he passed him, he could see Frank trying to get up, looking around as if trying to remember where he was; he glanced at but ignored Dmitry, who stopped to watch him, and went back to check on Skye and tried to feel a pulse. Kneeling, he put his head on her heart. He stood and went back out to the cockpit as Dmitry was stepping onto the dock.

"I don't believe you called a doctor," Frank said, and Dmitry stopped, turned to face him. Alain stopped on the dock.

"Franky, it does my heart good to hear you speak," Dmitry said. "I was afraid you were permanently deranged."

"Don't worry about calling one now," Frank said, ignoring the comment. "She is dead."

Dmitry shrugged. "Love and war," he said, and stepped onto the dock. Alain stood fuming. Dmitry sighed and again without taking the gun out of his pocket, he fired four quick shots, throwing Alain backwards into the water, where, weighed down by his guns, he sank like an anchor.

LXII
Frank

SO MUCH DEATH. He had come to and walked to the doorway just as Dmitry killed Alain, and he fell to the floor and wept as Dmitry walked away.

He didn't know how long he sat there—fifteen minutes? a half hour?—until he came to his senses and thought about the mess he was in. There would be police at some point, probably soon. A woman whose last name he didn't know was lying in a pool of her own blood in his kitchen. An enormous Chinese gunman lay dead a few feet away. The blood of how many others were spattered on the cockpit? He had to get out of there, he had to clean everything up, he had to leave, he had to pull himself together.

He pulled the Chinese assassin into the cockpit, but he was too heavy to lift, he would have to rig something up with pulleys when he got out to sea. He used the hose on the dock to do a quick rinse of the boat deck, and started the engine.

With a start he heard his name, hushed, urgent. He peered over the side of his ship and saw Alain, finger to his lips, hanging onto one of his bumpers.

"Drive out of the harbor," he whispered.

Frank was still too stunned to think, but he untied the boat from the dock, gave the engine some gas, and drove out of the harbor and into the open sea, where he cut the throttle as Alain was pulling himself up onto the deck.

"Keep going," Alain said, as he fell to the floor.

Frank wasn't sure where to take them, but once he cleared the port buoys, he set the ship on full throttle and automatic pilot heading northeast. That was smart, he decided. They wouldn't hit anything for days, and later he, or they, could figure something out. They'd be close to Colombo, where he knew people.

"I saw you get shot," Frank said, going over to see how damaged Alain was. "I saw you sink."

"Yeah, all those guns," he said and started taking off his Kevlar vest. Under it was a second Kevlar. After peeling that away, he gingerly pulled off his shirt and his chest had four nasty purple bruises, but no blood. Frank brought him a new set of clothes and went back into the cabin and sat next to Skye. When Alain walked in, she opened her eyes.

"You're alive!" Alain shouted.

"Yes," Frank said. "I just thought it would be good if Dmitry thought she was dead. She needs blood. I have a bag of type O negative for myself, but I don't know her type."

"She'll have dog tags," Alain said.

Skye smiled slightly as Alain opened her shirt, then passed out again.

"O negative," he said, reading the dog tag.

Frank added the blood bag to her IV.

"We'll continue under motor," Frank said. "We want her to stay as flat and as steady as possible. I'm thinking Chennai."

"Ay, Captain."

Beyond that, they didn't speak. The boat beat against the current for an hour or more, every fifteen minutes or so one or the other checked on Skye, and the rest of the time they just sat, not looking at each other or anything except whatever demons their consciousness was chasing. Then, without speaking they both got up and started dragging the Chinese guy aft. He was heavy, he was big, and he was slick with blood, but they got him over the gunwale and into the ocean.

They spent the next hours using what was left of the second set of sails to soak up as much of the blood as they could. Then they started scooping buckets of sea water and swabbing down the decks. They took turns checking on Skye.

"About Mónica," Alain said finally.

"Who?"

"Mónica, Dmitry's assassin," he said, his head cocked as if to ask if Frank had lost it.

"I never knew her name." They both sat with that for a beat. "I must have loved her."

"I know," Alain answered him, even though he doubted he'd be heard. Frank was lost in a catatonic world of grief. "We have a saying in Madagascar," he added. "'Don't be so in love that you can't tell when rain is coming.'"

They looked at each other, and Frank felt Alain's compassion.

"I had a conversation with her," Frank said. "It was only days ago!" He paused, then went on. "She told me about watching *Nikita*, the film about a female assassin pulled out of prison, and said that she hated it, but liked the fact that for once, the 'bad' woman didn't have to die at the end. I said I knew what she meant, that always in fiction, the women that had broken the rules—Anna Karenina, Edna Pontellier, Lily Bart—had to die. But here we are, in the middle of another tragic story, and it has the same hideous ending. She had almost avoided it. But no. She had chosen—maybe there was a bit of coercion, but not much—a violent profession, and had died by the sword she wielded. Anna, Edna, Lily—they weren't killers. This was a different story. She was different. Still—"

He was babbling and had lost the thread. He walked outside. The sun was shining like nothing had happened.

Alain followed him out, squinted.

"She told me, our last night together," Frank said, still on a kind of verbal automatic pilot, "that anyone could be a killer, that it was stupid of us to think otherwise. Always, we're surprised when the Tutsi's friend and next-door neighbor, a Hutu, takes his machete and cuts him up. But it happens every day. Hundreds a day in peacetime, thousands a day during a war, and there is always a war. We like to think only extreme circumstances make people into murderers. But once you do it, she said, it's no different than hunting. The most popular movies are the ones with the highest body counts, the most popular games are called 'first-person shooter games,' and again the highest body count is the goal. People spend more money on those games now, she said, than they spend on movies."

"Everyone knows that Frank," Alain said.

"Okay, yeah, okay. But the point is that we can all kill people, people have always killed people, it's who we are, not *homo sapiens* but *homo homicida*."

"She was a smart person," Alain said.

"She wasn't a bad person."

"Well, I mean . . . ."

"In a way."

Alain looked up at him.

"What?" Frank asked.

"I don't want to give you false hope, but she told me, when we were outside," he said, "that I should put on a second vest, take it from the dead man, and she put on a second one, too, under that crazy MacIntosh. It saved my life. There's always a chance it saved hers, too."

It took a minute for Frank to process this.

"If she had lived," he said, without hope, "she would have been hanging onto a bumper, too."

"Maybe not," Alain said. "She said to tell you that there is a new tracker on your boat, and if you never want to see her again, you should have it removed. It's in the engine compartment."

Again, Frank was slow to take this in. He didn't know what to say, and he said nothing.

LXIII
Frank

HE MUST HAVE slept because he woke up.

He was lying across the deck as the sun rose in front of them. He saw Alain wake up a few feet away. The shambles, the bedlam of the previous night played in his mind, and he tried his best to shake it off and figure out what needed to be done. They replaced Skye's blood bag and antibiotic vial. She looked better, sleeping, not fretful anymore, coming back to life.

"I've texted a guy I know in Colombo," Frank said. "And he's going to have a doctor meet us in the harbor there. We should land in twenty-four hours." Alain nodded. "But I think we should then go on to Chennai. I know it better. I can get us a house and great care there. If the doctor says we can go another day or two, I think that would be best. Are you okay with Chennai?"

Alain took a minute. He had told Frank the night before that he had fantasies of revenge, but that he had no idea who he would revenge himself against. Dmitry, presumably. He was also worried about his income, and Frank offered him, for the interim, the job of first mate. He accepted.

The next evening, as they approached Sri Lanka, the city of Colombo was turning on its lights, and Frank turned to Alain.

"It occurs to me I have no idea where in the world I should go once Skye has recuperated. Where we should go, I guess. What do you think?"

"I don't want to sound ungrateful, since you've given me a job, but I need to go home."

Alain said he had realized, during the night, trying to answer exactly that question, what he had to do. He had a new identity, the one Darkwater had given him. And that new person wasn't AWOL. That new person was honorably discharged from the Legion.

"I need to be a father to my children," he said, "whether or not my wife will have me. The new me is going to be a good father. I'll go back to guiding tourists. I'll start over."

"You're like the reverse Martin Guerre."

"Martin?"

Frank told him, maybe getting some of the details wrong, that Martin Guerre was a Basque peasant in the 16th or so century, and like people did back then, he got married at fourteen and had a son, got into trouble with the law—thievery of some kind—and skipped town, leaving the wife and child behind. Eight or ten years later, a man showed up and said, *hi, everyone, remember me? I'm Martin Guerre.* He moved in with Mrs. Guerre and the now teenage son, inherited Guerre's father's money when he died, and lived a good life.

But then some travelers came by and said, *hey, that isn't Martin. Guerre, that's some bum named Joey who owes everybody money, and the real Martin Guerre was in a Spanish king's army and lost a leg, but he's still alive in Spain.* The imposter was put on trial and the real Martin Guerre showed up. His wife had to say, *whoops, okay, I guess this guy with one leg is my husband, not the guy on trial.* The imposter was hanged in front of the house where he had lived as Martin Guerre.

"How," Alain asked, "is it possible that the wife didn't know which man was her husband?"

"Yeah, well, that is part of why people love the story—it's a bit scandalous. But I think she was happy to have a new partner, maybe liked him better than her husband. And besides, it wasn't easy to be a widow then."

"Or, in Madagascar, now."

"You could court your wife, and even get married to her, as your new self, and if, as you say, she'll have you, she, and everyone else who cared, could swear you were the new person, not the old husband, just like they all vouched for the fake Martin Guerre. It's kind of a cake-and-eat-it-too situation—you could do what disgraced people over the world sorely want to do, start over as if the disgrace had happened to someone else, and get your old life back."

"Yeah," Alain said. "Martin Guerre or not, that's what I want. We'll see."

"Your new identity did a stint doing security for Darkwater, right, after his time in the Legion?"

"That's right," he said. "I could start my own security company."

"Exactly what I was thinking. Is there a market?"

"Yeah, there are rich people. There are rich foreigners. I could be a tour guide that was also a bodyguard."

Even as he told Alain it was a great idea, a security company run by a local with experience in the Legion and with Darkwater, Frank felt an additional loss. He would drop Alain back in Madagascar, and Skye wherever she was going to chase her dream, whatever that would be when she woke to it. He was living his own dream—his only dream had always been to sail the world, and here he was. He hadn't developed a new one. His reach no longer exceeded his grasp, so maybe it didn't still count as a dream.

Would he ever feel safe, feel secure again? In these last many days, he had decided to reenter the world of human intercourse only to find himself in a maelstrom of unending violence—maybe that was ironic or maybe just the way of the world, as The Assassin had said, and he'd been in denial. Had he been crawling around like Swee'Pea in the Popeye cartoons, oblivious to the danger everywhere, all his life? Had there always been assassins and corporate militias spraying gunfire across the globe while he dallied in some benighted, unaware cocoon? Was his momentary flirtation with the idea that The Assassin might renounce her profession equally naïve? Theoretically, he was comfortable with the idea that, as the Buddha said, the world is illusion. But the bullets were terminally real. The Assassin had been exquisitely real. And now she was, in all probability, dead at the bottom of a lagoon.

He was lost, again.

LXIV
Alain

STANDING IN THE airport in Chennai, Alain wondered about the choice he was making. His old life seemed so long ago.

Frank had rented a luxurious townhouse in Chennai, with rooms for all of them and round-the-clock nurses for Skye. She was stable, and improving, and Alain could see that it gave Frank a sense of purpose and usefulness, helped keep him from succumbing to grief and regret, to care for her. They had hauled the *God Sees* out of the water for fresh paint and maintenance, and to replace the sails and canvas they had used in their macabre chores at sea. Everything was being taken care of. He wasn't needed anymore.

The only ticket home was a crazy forty-eight-hour trip that took him from Chennai to Abu Dhabi, and from there to the heart of the enemy in Paris, to Istanbul, Mauritius, and one of France's last colonial outposts in Réunion, to his former and future home in Antananarivo. He'd be sleeping in airport chairs and economy seats if Frank hadn't sprung for airport hotels and business class flights. Frank had more faith in his ability to make a life back home than he did. But he'd almost convinced himself he could do it. Almost.

Frank set up a business account for him, with the capital to start his security firm, explaining that it cost him nothing, he had more money than he could ever spend. If Alain ever decided he needed to pay it back, he could, Frank said, but there would be no point. Pay it forward someday, he said, to someone else.

The idea to combine tourism and security made sense. That very year, an enourmously rich and powerful tourist had been murdered in what had always been one of the safest destinations in the country, down in the baobab trees. *Why take chances?* the pitch would go. Frank had agreed. He suggested: *Let a man trained by the French Foreign Legion and the world's largest military contractor protect you and yours as you tour the world's largest island and see its untold wonders.*

Alain pointed out that it was not the world's largest island—Greenland, New Guinea, and Borneo were all larger. Frank said that Alain should hire a marketing company if he wasn't prepared to lie for himself. He said he learned that from Dmitry—advertising is a form of deception. But like all deception, it works because it's true enough and it answers people's desires.

Frank also argued that, with any luck, Alain could help people who needed his help. A lot of different people would be interested in his services, and once he had a rep and word of mouth got around, he could pick and choose his clients: some tourists, some local people who needed a private investigator, a fixer. He could offer security to people who both needed it and deserved it. And he could skip the CFOs of evil corporations, let them face their own consequences without his help.

A pretty picture. But Alain wasn't ready to think only about the future, even though he was heading home. He had watched people die, and some of them had died because he had shot them. Part of him would remain sullied by their deaths forever. Part of him, too, had been redeemed by the lives he helped save. He wished, more than anything, that the ratio of living to dead had been much, much higher. He wished, too, that he had never screwed things up so severely at home that it had sent him out to seek his fortune in the wide, violent world. Part of him would forever be sullied by that, too. His only restoration was waiting for him to effect, waiting for him to make good, with some luck, some work, some grace, and some more work, day by day.

He was Martin Guerre. He was the anti-Martin Guerre. He was ready to perform his final imposture, and with a little help, make all the reparations he had the wit and will to make. *Mivovo ny alika rehefa matahotra—the dog barks when he is afraid,* the old people say. He would keep his own counsel, hold his head up, and make things as right as they could be.

Frank had said he, too, was determined to make amends. He didn't know how, but he hoped that it was possible, for both of them. For either of them.

Around Alain, the airport buzzed and jangled, anxious people everywhere, late for flights, waiting for flights, waiting for what came next.

They were calling his flight. He was going home.

LXV
Frank

IT WAS A gruesome scorecard. Mónica, his Assassin, dead. Skye was laid up for months, several operations to go before she was whole. So many of her colleagues dead. Alain's colleagues, Dmitry's goons, dead. The man who should have died, Dmitry, had walked away.

Skye seemed to be unburdened by such worries. She agreed with him when he condemned it all, the whole military-capitalist complex, but he could see that she was still in the game. She was furious. She would have her revenge. She would get her place back. And although he had much higher hopes for Alain, Frank had to admit that the man was, like him, broken in a way that might never be fixed.

A week in, he heard Skye talking on the phone. She was making plans.

"You aren't well enough to leave yet, according to the doctor."

"I know," she said. "I'm just lining things up for later."

"Lining up?"

She looked at him with an angry seriousness. Everyone always said, she told him, that coming near death changes you, that you are never the same, and she indeed felt that yes, she was forever transformed. She was a new person.

"Before this, I was basically a child. I saw death around me, but somehow it never occurred to me that I might die. Now I know I will, and, as a result, I am fully adult. I see that my death is coming. I have seen it coming and I see it coming."

He agreed with her. Facing death changed you. He just wasn't sure how, not entirely sure what it meant.

"I suspect that the answer is kindness," he said, not sure where that came from.

She scoffed.

"You're kidding, right?"

He shook his head no. Her eyes were on fire.

"You think kindness fixes Dmitry? You think kindness is the appropriate response to that psychopathic Chinese henchman of his? No. I have put aside childish things. Evil kills unless you kill it."

He looked at this young woman and wondered if anything he could say would be of any help to her in any way.

"What will you do?" he asked.

"I'll tell you what I won't do," she said. "I won't let that asshole ruin my life, and in fact I won't let any asshole ruin my life. No more Ms. Nice Guy. I'm going to show these fuckers who's the big bad wolf. It's me, dammit."

She was huffing, and red in the face, and then she plopped back on her pillow. "But not quite yet," she added, and closed her eyes.

He checked her IV bags and they were fine. She had immediately conked out. Or she wanted him to think she had. He went back to the living room, and then out the front door.

He walked into Chennai as the sun was setting. As always, in the back alleys, people of all ages milled around and came and went, and, as always, he marveled at how so many people could manage to inhabit the same space with so little drama and tension. The smell of dosai browning on griddles mixed with the light odor of too many people in too small a wet space and the wind coming off the water. He was, as the only Euro-type around, an object of mild amusement, but he had been in the neighborhood long enough now that he knew a number of people. He went to the cart where Gaurik made podi dosai, and the owner-operator greeted him with the same friendly surprise as always. The sun was gone, and it wasn't exactly cool, but it was distinctly cooler on Frank's side of the griddle. Gaurik, as always in a loose, less than clean sleeveless T-shirt, was sweating over the blazing charcoal cookers, as always. The dosai, as always, crunchy, sweet, savory, and hot, hot, hot, steam-cleaned his sinuses, seared his mouth, and made him start to sweat, cooling his skin. The little kids ran by making faces at him—they had learned that they could make him make faces in return, and it had become their little game, wrinkling noses, wiggling ears, and sticking out tongues sideways. Their parents were, as parents are at best, inordinately proud of them. As always, he felt treated like a guest, like a favored uncle, like a human being.

And yet he knew, even as he romanticized this scene, that too many of them would die before their time, also the result of too many people in too small a wet space. And he knew that some percentage of these kids would grow into the bad guys of the future. Some tiny percentage would kill someone. A much, much tinier percentage would do it for a living, become the assassins and Dmitrys of tomorrow. This, he supposed, was what he found so relaxing about these crowded streets—seeing the vast humanity and the tininess of that percentage, the sense that most of us, most of the time, were good, and good to each other. An extraordinary amount of kindness made up the average day, and that was what he hoped Skye might understand: we just need a little more, that's all, a little more kindness, a tiny percentage more.

He worried about Alain, how he would manage. He worried about Skye, in her new angry phase. He worried, too, that he might be done with this part of his life, that his dream might be over, that he might be waking up.

We'll just have to see what happens, he said to himself.

As always, people walked by, and the food stands kept the air sweet and spicy, while he took in the burble of conversation, sprinkled with light laughter and the squeals of children, the Doppler curve of tuk tuks, scooters, and cars going by, bugs bouncing off the street lamps, families being families, young people being young people, old people being old.

I have no idea, he said to himself, as the last deep blue backlit the horizon.

Yes, we'll just have to see, he said to himself.

We will just have to see.

BIOGRAPHICAL NOTE

TOM LUTZ is the award-winning author of *Doing Nothing: A History of Loafers, Loungers, Slackers, and Bums* and over a dozen other books, including fiction, travel narrative, and cultural history. His work has been translated into twelve languages and featured in *The New York Times, Los Angeles Times, Chicago Tribune, The New Republic,* and many more. Lutz is the founding editor of *The Los Angeles Review of Books,* producing numerous literary pieces, books, films, and podcasts. A former Distinguished Professor and Chair of Creative Writing at UC Riverside, he splits his time between Los Angeles and southern France.